ST A

DOCTOR WHO – THE NEW ADVENTURES

Also available:

THE NEW

DOCTOR WHO

ADVENTURES

ST ANTHONY'S
FIRE

Mark Gatiss

First published in Great Britain in 1994 by
Doctor Who Books
an imprint of Virgin Publishing Ltd
332 Ladbroke Grove
London W10 5AH

Cover illustration by Paul Campbell

ISBN 0 426 20423 9

Phototypeset by Intype, London
Printed and bound in Great Britain by Cox & Wyman Ltd,
Reading, Berks

Grateful thanks to all my friends and family for their love and support, particularly:

Simon
Lou, Sara, Matty and Sandy (up the Gunners)
Ian
Gary
and Roger (for particular unhealthiness)

For William,
Love, laughs and two peaches in a bag

'We worship saints for fear, lest they be displeased and angry with us or hurt us. Who dare deny Saint Anthony a fleece of wool for fear of his terrible fire, or lest he send a pox among our sheep?'

William Tyndale

Prologue

By the end of the night Neerid knew she would be dead. Her whole body shaking, she sank down on the grass, breath coming in rasping hiccoughs. Exhaustion flooded through her like anaesthesia, seeping into every bone, every aching sinew; forcing her heavy head down towards the pasture. Neerid's eyes clamped shut and there was a brief period of luxurious, cool darkness. She listened for the sounds of the world around her.

There was nothing. No wind. No voices. Not even the mournful cries of the *beshet* which normally wheeled and flocked in the winter sky. Nothing. She kept her eyes shut and ran both her hands down her body, feeling the wet sheen of her skin as though for the first time.

Almost over.

There was a deep, startling rumble from the far horizon. Neerid's yellow eyes flicked open and she cocked her head to one side. Above, the sky was darkening, thickening.

She leapt to her feet and took off across the pastureland, long toes digging deep into the ground. Something seemed to rush at her and she stumbled, knees ploughing into the soil. She gasped, winded, and struggled for breath, willing air into her screaming lungs. Sniffing the air, Neerid's small, warty face wrinkled in disgust.

It was coming.

She could smell it.

The thunderous boom came again, rolling into one long, disquieting peal. Ahead, the forest stirred as though

1

unnerved, spindly branches tearing at the air like the hands of ebony skeletons.

Neerid bolted towards the only shelter she knew, clutching the spool in her sweat-soaked hands for dear life.

So little time.

All at once, Feeson was in front of her, waving his hands frantically and casting anxious glances at the darkening air. He was bellowing something but Neerid couldn't make it out. Behind him, the polygon shone dully, like a fragment of storm-cloud ripped from the sky. Feeson was already half-way inside.

'Quickly! Run, Neerid! Run! Run!' Spit flew from between his teeth.

Neerid scrambled across the pasture, her long arms scuffing at the earth as she struggled to maintain her pace. One glance over her shoulder at the sickly, liverish sky confirmed her worst fears.

She choked back a tide of overwhelming panic. Blood roared in her ears.

She didn't want to die. Above all things. But Feeson said it was inevitable. And Feeson was never wrong.

The small man flapped his hands in agitation and grabbed Neerid by the scruff of the neck. She stumbled over the threshold into the polygon and fell back against the padded walls. Feeson took the spool from her hand and rammed it into the black console by his feet.

'I'd all but given up,' he said, his voice little more than a tiny, tight whisper.

Neerid nodded wearily, her head dragging itself down onto her shuddering chest. She held out her hand and watched it tremble. There were tiny half-moons of blood on her palms where her nails had dug in. It would all have been for nothing if she'd dropped the spool.

Three low chimes sounded from the black console and Feeson nodded slowly.

'It's done,' he said simply, holding out a hand for Neerid. She looked up at him and saw tears brimming in his sun-yellow eyes. The feel of his rough hand in hers was almost unbearably reassuring.

Feeson pulled Neerid to her feet and wrapped his long, thin arms around her. The room began to shake violently.

'Well?' said Neerid.

Feeson smiled a small sad smile and together they stepped out of the polygon.

When they were dead, when the last of Neerid and Feeson's glutinous blood had disappeared into the inconceivable darkness, the polygon slid silently below the ground, gently excavating a pit for itself and its secrets.

1

Planet of Death

Not for the first time, Grek thought it a very bad place to
have a war.

The north-eastern jungles of Betrushia extended endlessly in a curious splayed pattern; isthmuses of dense
vegetation broken by swollen rivers, like the imprint of
monstrous hands on the planet's surface. There were crescent-shaped encampments by the dozen on each finger of
land, hollowed from the mud and reinforced with wood
and steel.

Every few days a squadron of Grek's men would make
a futile attempt to cut back the encroaching jungle in
order to limit its inexorable advance. But the mass of
deep, dark, leathery foliage spread like bacteria over the
straight lines of civilization, sticky seed pods and mosses
choking every effort at clearance.

Worst of all, though, in Grek's considered and very
weary opinion, the jungles were wet. Relentlessly, unmer-
cifully, unbearably wet.

Rain seeped into the wide, thick fronds of vegetation
which littered the ground; permeating the drenched
jungle, causing clouds of steam to drift in ghostly displays
from the tree-tops to a floor deep in rain-pocked shadow.

Few breezes stirred the landscape, but an occasional
garish flying mammal would squawk into the dank green
gloom, its cries merging with the constant background
ticking of beetles.

Grek looked around, narrowing his eyes in an effort to

focus on the rain-blurred landscape. He turned, rubbed his snout and suddenly realized he was lost.

Pulling at the ragged hem of his uniform, Grek sighed heavily. Beneath the fabric his scales itched and little rivulets of moisture were insinuating themselves into the bony grooves which ran parallel to his spine. Cold rain splashed off his head, dripping from the impressive crest which rose in a wide line from his nostrils to his bulbous temples. Grek sank beneath a tree and let his eyes lose focus. His black tunic rumpled as he pulled his booted legs under his chin.

Distantly, the constant crackling of gunfire formed a strange backbeat, as though life had been set to particularly discordant music.

There was a splash right by him and Grek was immediately alert, springing to his feet and ripping his well-oiled gun from a shoulder-holster. He tensed then, seeing who it was, relaxed.

'Oh, it's you.'

'Sir!' The younger soldier clicked his heels but the soft, wet jungle floor rendered the sound distinctly unimpressive.

'What is it now, Priss?' sighed Grek, sinking back to the ground. 'I told Liso that he was in command. So bother him. God knows he's been desperate to be in charge for long enough.' He looked up at his eager subordinate, narrow blue eyes scarcely blinking. 'Bother *him*.'

'With respect, sir . . .' Priss's voice trembled slightly. 'Portrone Liso is unavailable. I was told to report to you for further instructions.'

Grek almost laughed, recognizing a buck when it had been passed to him. Once, he reflected sadly, Priss's enthusiasm would have been commendable. Now it almost made him sick.

'Further instructions, eh lad?' He looked the smaller man up and down, resenting the starched stiffness of his breeches and tunic, the elegantly polished scales of his crest.

5

'I could tell you to go off into there.' He waved a claw at the impossibly deep jungle all around them. 'Assess situations, devise strategies, formulate manoeuvres . . .'

Priss's wide mouth formed into an excited smile, his tiny, pearl-grey teeth biting into his lower lip.

Grek slipped a claw under his own chin and let his heavy head slump.

'Prepare my bunk, soldier. I'm coming back.'

'Sir?'

Grek snorted. 'Oh, get out of my sight.'

Priss's whole frame shrank with disappointment. He turned swiftly on his heel, scarcely bothering to salute, and tramped back towards the dug-out. The thoughts buzzing inside his head were unpleasant, mutinous even, but increasingly difficult to ignore. Perhaps Portrone Liso was right after all.

Some time later, after a burst of mortar-fire had caused him to take shelter in a particularly damp shell-hole, Grek ploughed his way back to camp through the thick foliage.

Sheets of freezing rain pounded onto his head and he could feel pools of moisture forming around his clawed toes. He needed new boots but was far from sure whether the quartermaster's stores had any supplies left at all.

He strode on, disturbing the low clouds of steam which hung around the boles of the gigantic, spindly trees surrounding him. Reaching for the too-tight collar of his tunic, Grek almost jumped as a sentry stepped out in front of him. Hastily he smoothed down his uniform and made a frantic but vain attempt to disguise the salty stains blossoming all over the fabric.

Grek returned the sentry's efficient salute.

'Everything in order?'

The sentry was terribly young and no less eager than Priss. There was scarcely a trace of fatigue behind his wide blue eyes but there was a familiar sense of disappointment, almost contempt, about him as he set eyes on his commander.

6

'All in order, sir.'

Grek put his claws behind his back in what he hoped would appear to be a convincing military swagger.

'And yourself? How're . . . how're conditions? Morale?'

The sentry seemed nonplussed, embarrassed even. He looked away. The rain hissed in the uneasy silence.

Eventually clearing his throat, he replied, 'Never better, sir.'

'Good, good. You lads eager to get back home, I expect?'

The sentry's mouth puckered slightly, thin lips curling as though on the point of sneering. He averted his commander's gaze. Grek's claws tensed behind his back. A trickle of cold rain scuttled from his crest to his chin.

Damn you, man. Answer me.

At last the sentry's face settled into a fixed, expressionless mask.

'Oh yes, sir. There's nothing we're looking forward to more.'

Grek nodded slowly. 'Very good. Carry on.' He turned and walked away, feeling the sentry's gaze bore into his back.

The dug-out was visible now across the muddied field of cleared jungle. Grek stooped instinctively as the familiar sound of shell-fire erupted in the distance.

There were two entrances to the dug-out. The first, worn down into a muddy track by the constant traffic of soldiers, was at the far end of the field opposite the jungle perimeter. The second, a simple ladder-hole known as Number Seven, had been bored into the ground in the middle of the same field. Ladder-holes One to Six had, over the years, succumbed to the fickle, shifting mud and collapsed in on themselves.

Spools of viciously barbed wire cluttered the pathway and Grek had to manoeuvre between them and slide towards the ladder, churned-up soil caking his boots.

There was a brief burst of gunfire somewhere in the distance. Grek looked over his shoulder. When he turned back, Liso was emerging from the trench. Immediately, a tiny knot of fear and anger began to writhe in his stomach.

Liso's black uniform was pristine and his serrated crest swept in an unusual, graceful curve from his one good poison-bottle-blue eye. A handsome man, Grek had always thought, but dangerous.

'Good morning, sir,' said Liso as he swung himself off the ladder onto the surface. He saluted with a gloved claw and then allowed the gesture to fade into an abstract stroking of his empty socket.

Grek had seen the Cutch bullet which had destroyed Liso's eye, and had nursed him back to health through long months in the field infirmary. They had been good friends then and young Liso had admired Grek to the exclusion of all others. But that had been in the early days of the war when Grek had a reputation, a string of victories to his credit and the Pelaradator's star pinned to his chest.

Grek acknowledged Liso with a slight nod. The younger man rocked his jaw slightly, as though nervous, and again traced a line over the powder-burnt socket of his empty eye.

Grek looked at him thoughtfully. 'Found something to do with young Priss yet, Mister Liso?'

'I was informed, sir, that you had refused to give him further instructions.'

'Not exactly.'

'With respect, sir . . .'

Grek's claws were shaking behind his back. 'Look, Liso . . .' He shivered as a fresh curtain of rain pelted down from the jungle canopy. 'It's dangerous out there. Still. In spite of everything. And I'm not about to risk a good soldier's life on some pointless exercise just to keep him occupied.'

'But, sir, the war . . .'

'The war is over, Mister.'

Liso's handsome features twisted with anger. 'No, sir. It's not over. Not by a long way.'

8

'The Pelaradator is pushing for an armistice, Liso, and I agree with him. I just want to go home. Home to Porsim. With my skin and my men as intact as possible. Is that so terrible?'

Liso was pacing about, almost stamping the sodden ground in his anger. The rain sizzled around them, sending fresh clouds of steam into the hazy air.

'Sir, until we receive orders from Porsim . . .'

'Liso,' Grek cut in with a trace of irritation, 'it's over. Face it, son. Fifteen years of war. Over. It may not have worked out quite as we'd planned . . .'

Liso snorted. Grek ignored him.

'. . . or as we'd hoped, but surely it's better to have peace.'

'Peace!' spat Liso. 'A diplomat's peace is no peace at all! How can we trust the Cutch to keep their word? They're beneath our contempt, sir, surely you can see that? Surely you *know* that? The only victory lies in their total annihilation!'

Grek smiled slightly. 'You sound like Hovv.'

Liso's gaze hardened. 'At least he knew how to command.'

Grek's claw lashed out and cracked Liso across the face. The young man stepped back, genuinely shocked, for all his bravado.

Grek's features darkened, his voice dropping to a grave, dangerous whisper:

'I've been out in these jungles thirteen years, Mister Liso, and that's a lot longer than you. I've seen half my friends slaughtered in this bloody war, and God knows how many troops. The last thing I need is for a swaggering little prig like you to question my authority.'

Grek's breath seemed to seethe from between his clenched teeth. 'We're going to do as we're told. Mop up any Cutch resistance. Tie up loose ends. And then we're *all* going *home.*'

Distant shells crumped in the electric silence. Liso stood staight and still, his expression unreadable.

9

'That's if we have a home to go to, sir.'

He saluted stiffly, turned and descended the ladder into the dug-out.

The old man with the spiny grey crest paddled his claws over the polished blond wood of the desk, sheaves of stiff paper rustling under his nails. Some documents fell over the side onto the carpet. He cursed. It had to be here somewhere.

Pulling at one drawer, then another, he dug deep into the layers of ephemera which formed a sediment of bureaucracy within his desk. Finally, angrily, he wrenched out a whole drawer and hurled it across the room. It bounced off the window and shattered, disgorging its contents in a wide fan over the floor.

He felt his shoulders sink and rested his head miserably against the studded fabric of the chair.

The room was in darkness now. He stood up to reach for the gas jet but then checked himself, letting his arm fall to his side. All supplies had been requisitioned for the barricades. On his orders. Couldn't he even remember that?

He ran a claw over his wrinkled crest, feeling tiny beads of white sweat springing from his pores. Glancing out of the window at the vista below, the old man sobbed.

Porsim. The most beautiful city in the world. The place where he had been hatched, sired seven litters and risen from Local Menx to City Menx to the undreamt of heights of Pelaradator within twenty years.

In the days before his rank had excluded the possibility, he had loved to walk through the teeming streets, admiring the sandstone palaces and ancient wooden crescents. It had always been a wonderful, faintly magical place. Even the war had scarcely touched it and that had been dragging on – God – longer than he could remember. Fourteen? Fifteen years?

As Pelaradator, he was justifiably proud of his part in the peace negotiations; had been confident enough to boast that the conflict was almost over. In the back of his mind he had nursed a secret dread that everything was going too smoothly, that a price would have to be paid sooner or later. He could never have imagined it would be like this.

The Pelaradator's rheumy eyes looked out on a shattered, devastated city. The proud palaces and eight-hundred-year-old streets lay flattened as though by the fists of vengeful gods, crushed by forces he couldn't begin to comprehend. Fires bloomed everywhere and a vast pall of sickly black smoke hung over Porsim like the night-dark folds of the Reaper's cloak.

Perhaps it was true. Perhaps *they* had come back.

The infirmary was long and low. Its walls, built from concave wooden struts, groaned under the pressure of the wet mud behind them.

Huge, looming shadows danced about, thrown by the flaring of two dozen gas jets fixed precariously to the ceiling. The distant corners faded into stygian darkness, a suggestion of tattered uniform or the glint of a fevered eye the only indication that they were occupied.

Rising like an altar from a mass of bunks, mattresses and stretchers was a cast-iron operating table, its pocked surface mottled with dark stains. Injured and dying soldiers filled the room, their agonized moans booming around the cramped quarters, limbs outstretched in hopeless appeal.

Maconsa, standing at the operating table as though presiding over an infernal last supper, stepped back and hurled a scalpel into a porcelain dish by his side.

He was an elderly, well-built man, his lined face and crest grizzled with spiny white hair. White-coated orderlies shrank back as Maconsa gave a low grumble of exasperation. He pointed a claw at the scarcely breathing form stretched on the table before him.

'No, son, you're not getting out of it that easily.'

The soldier's chest already had a brace fixed into it, the

11

spliced rib-cage cranked partially open. Maconsa examined the soldier's pulse and dilated pupils. The lad was in a bad way, his breathing shallow.

A large brass machine by the side of the table was fixed to his throat via three heavy cords, curled into liver-coloured pigtails through much use. A drum of paper spun slowly round, the soldier's heart-rate registering as a thin, spiky line of black ink. All at once, the line sank to an ominous horizontal.

Maconsa cursed as the soldier began to thrash about on the table, his muscular arms scrabbling at the iron surface. Spasms wracked his open chest and his legs kicked out as panicking orderlies clustered around their chief.

'Damn!' barked Maconsa. 'He's arresting.'

The old man cranked the brace still further and the soldier's ribs opened like the petals of a fly-trap, steam billowing into the cold air. Maconsa plunged his claws into the chest cavity, his rubber-sheathed digits slipping around as though in wet clay. The arresting heart was suddenly exposed, its livid purple surface cut by slivers of shrapnel. Maconsa swore again as his claw caught a vein and a jet of blood streaked across his apron.

'Come on. Come on, lad!' he hissed between his tiny teeth. Carefully he lifted the heart a little way out of the soldier's chest, a membrane of fibrous tissue straining beneath, and began to massage it. White sweat coursed down his face, forming sticky rivulets in his beard.

The heart remained still despite Maconsa's efforts and he looked up desperately at the anxious faces of his orderlies. They could offer no advice, no support. Blood began to pool in the boy's chest cavity.

'Swab! Swab it for God's sake!'

One of the orderlies was shocked out of inaction and began to drain the blood from the gaping rib-cage with a pad of cloth.

Maconsa bent low over the table, claws gripping the fragile heart, just as a long, rasping, unquestionably final breath streamed from the soldier's clenched mouth. His

12

face seemed almost peaceful, its grey-green pallor untroubled by care or age. His blue eyes rolled upwards.

The surgeon gently let go of the heart and it slipped wetly back into place. He stepped down from the table and sank back onto a bench, immediately swallowed up by the shadows.

The orderlies were already fussing over the corpse, removing the brace and mopping up the blood which pooled like thick scarlet glue over the whole area.

'Lost another one, Maconsa?'

The old man looked up wearily, scarcely bothering to acknowledge the stranger's voice. Some of the orderlies were peering inquisitively over their shoulders into the gloom.

'Who's there?' barked Maconsa. 'Show yourself. I'm in no mood to play games.'

It was Grek's first officer, Ran, who stepped into the pool of light thrown by the gas jets, his flattened crest and tic-ridden face thrown into sharp, gargoyle-like relief.

Maconsa made his usual grumble. 'Yes, Ran, I've lost another one.'

' "For the Greater Glory",' said Ran.

' "For the Greater Glory of the Ismetch. My Country of My Soul." I know, I know . . .'

Ran strolled up the old surgeon, one claw resting on the hip of his breeches. 'Do I detect a note of dissent, Maconsa?'

Maconsa sat back against the dug-out walls and the boards groaned, streams of muddy water trickling down from the surface.

'You do, Mister Ran, you do.'

'Careful. I could have you shot.' Ran's twitching face almost cracked into a smile.

'I'd thank you for it.'

This time Ran did smile and laughed; a high, humour-less chuckle. 'Oh, come on, Maconsa. You positively thrive on all this! The pressure, all the odds against you . . .'

Maconsa turned bleary eyes onto the young officer. 'All this death?'

'Yes! Why not? After all, that's what we're here for. These lads didn't come here for a holiday, my friend, they came to lay down their lives for the Cause. "For the Greater Glory of the Ismetch. My country . . ."'

'We've done that bit.'

Ran smiled again. The muscles under his eyes twitched convulsively. 'What's the matter? We've won, Maconsa. Another week and we'll all be on our way home. Isn't that what you want?'

Maconsa stood up suddenly. 'Of course it's what I want!' He thrust his claws into the pockets of his apron and bit his lip angrily. 'It's just . . . well, this wasn't just another war, was it Ran? I've been in enough of those. This was different.' He tailed off, chin sinking onto his chest.

'Go on.'

Maconsa looked up, his blue eyes peering deep into the shadows. 'When I was drafted again I was so . . . relieved. Another few years in civilian practice and I'd have curled up and died through sheer boredom. It was good to be back at the Front. With people I understood.'

'And the Cause?'

Maconsa flicked a glance at Ran. 'I believed. I believed *absolutely* that the Cutch had to be utterly destroyed.'

Ran crossed his legs and leaned back against the strutted walls. 'Believed? Past tense?'

'As I said,' Maconsa sighed heavily, 'this wasn't just another war. This was the Cause. Everything the Pelaradators told us about the Cutch. About the menace they represented to our society, to our entire way of being. It all seemed so right. So obvious. Indisputable.'

He rubbed his face wearily, voice muffled by his sheathed claw. 'How many more of these children do I have to stitch back together before something good comes of it? I'm sick. I'm sick of it all.'

Ran let his gaze wander around the darkened room.

14

The orderlies were pulling the dead soldier off the table. His head cracked dully off the planked floor. It would only be a few minutes before the next screaming casualty was shunted into the infirmary.

'But as our esteemed commander is forever fond of telling us,' said Ran quietly, 'the war is over.'

Maconsa rounded on him. 'And this is what we've fought for? *Fifteen* years, Ran, *fifteen* years. We came out here to annihilate the Cutch. Now we're sitting down to breakfast with them!'

'That's politics, I'm afraid.'

Maconsa thumped the wall. A lozenge of mud seeped out of the boards in response. 'I did believe, you know. A surgeon, committed to nothing less than genocide.'

His voice became quieter, sadder, eventually descending to an inaudible grumble. 'But what right did we have, Ran? All those millions slaughtered. For what? It's all been so pointless. Disgraceful. I feel . . . unclean.'

Ran smiled, but his twitch made it seem more like a grimace. 'At least the Pelaradator has learned a different tune. There aren't many like Hovv left in government.'

'That old warhorse. Has he been found yet?'

'No.' Ran stood up, brushing the dust off his uniform with his gloves. 'Still missing. And the whole eighteenth brigade with him.'

Maconsa sucked in his scaly cheeks. 'Silly bastard's probably sulking because of the armistice.' He cocked his head slightly as another thought struck him. 'And Porsim?'

Ran shook his head, all his jauntiness deserting him. 'Nothing. In fact, no word from Arason or Tusamavad either.'

'What the hell's going on?'

Ran began to pick his way through the bloodied, sweat-soaked mattresses. 'Who knows, Maconsa?' He reached the entrance to the infirmary and looked back. 'But I'll tell you one thing.'

Maconsa looked up from his contemplation. 'Hmmm?'

'If there's nothing from Porsim soon, I'll be recommending that Grek ignores the possibility of an armistice and carries on with the war.'

'For the Greater Glory?'

'Well,' Ran began to fade into the shadows. 'For a few weeks at least.'

The Pelaradator had used his last day in office – for that was surely what this dark hour would prove to be – to send an appeal to the last of the military. If Tobess in the north and Grek, perhaps even old Hovv, in the east could bring their forces back to Porsim then it might not be too late.

But the transmitters were erratic at the best of times, he thought sadly, and there was no guarantee his plea would get through on time, if at all. Could it be true? Could it be *them?*

His gaze flicked to the shattered drawer and the detritus on the wood-tiled floor. All at once he saw what he had been searching for. In amongst the debris, something was glinting, and carefully the Pelaradator bent down to retrieve it.

It was a painting in a tiny oval frame, the beautifully detailed brushwork seeming to glow in the half-light. The picture showed his first litter and two of his surviving wives. He wanted to smile but his face felt tight with emotion. Instead he simply pressed the picture to his chest, feeling the frame snap as great, wracking sobs shuddered in his breast.

Save for the sound of his tears, the room was silent. The inferno in the city below raged soundlessly, unable to penetrate the thick plate glass of the office window. But then another sound crept into being, so faint at first that the Pelaradator thought he was imagining it.

It seemed to vibrate from some impossibly deep source, throbbing so that the old man's jaw shook, like time's own pendulum swinging beneath the earth.

He looked about quickly, his head jerking back and forth, chicken-like. The sound was getting louder. He could feel it thudding inside his head. He banged his fists against his temples, terrified.

The glass in the picture frame began to rattle. He glanced down at the shuddering floor and then, in a bolt of realization, at the ceiling.

The sound grew louder still, echoing the frantic hammering of his heart. The ceiling began to shudder.

In the next instant, the Pelaradator was blown off his feet, flying across the room to land in a crumpled heap by the remains of his desk drawer. He winced as a blast of intense heat slammed into his face, as though the door to an immense furnace had been thrown open. Something sharp and metallic was digging into his side and he glanced rapidly down.

The signalling device was his last point of contact with the outside world. The unwieldy conglomeration of valves, wires and keys was jammed into his ribs, having been blown off the wall. If he could get a message through ...

The Pelaradator felt the floor rise up and crack against his chin, a delayed, muffled roar pounding at his ears.

The ceiling heaved and shattered, releasing shafts of blinding white light into the room. He squealed as the windows blew out, fragments of glass ballooning outwards into the sky. The lights probed around the room like anxious ethereal fingers, searching, analysing, recording.

The Pelaradator scuttled towards the sanctuary of his desk, the precious picture frame rammed against his ribs, dragging the signalling box with him. He was aware of a sharp electric tang in the air and motes of dust which swarmed in the shafts of light, forming strange geometric patterns. His foot crunched on a sheet of shattered glass as he hauled himself closer into the shelter of the desk.

The sound began to encroach once more onto his terrified senses. The soft spines on his neck rose and he hugged himself, convulsed with terror. Something was sliding over the top of his exposed office – sleek, black, impossibly massive.

The Pelaradator blinked slowly like a child woken from

17

a deep sleep. The thing was hovering over the building, its sheer size causing the structure to groan and buckle. The floor began to shift beneath him, tiles and broken glass bursting into the air.

Out of the darkness, something began to form. The Pelaradator felt his lips trembling and an awful, gushing fear sweeping over him. Dazzled by the light and dust, he could nevertheless make out a change in the shape above him. The thing seemed to be blistering as though something inside were anxious to get out. Feeling his throat working up and down, the old man felt his way behind the desk, claws digging into the ruined floor-tiles.

His clothes stretched and ripped as the thing dragged at him. His claws scrabbled desperately at the floor and he looked over his shoulder, stricken, as the white light turned to a hot, glorious crimson, like looking down a tunnel of flame. The Pelaradator groped for the signalling box and keyed in his final message with the sudden clarity of mind of a condemned man. Someone had to know.

Then the tunnel of flame erupted outwards.

The throbbing sound continued for some time, agitating the vortex of dust and glass it had created, as though contemplating its actions.

Then the blistered darkness resealed and the room was silent. The black shape slid away like a leech detaching itself from an exhausted host and hovered low over the dead city.

The Pelaradator's children stared out from their water-colour world; innocent, painted eyes now spattered with the blood of their father.

2

Battle Fatigue

All things considered, reflected Bernice Summerfield, it had begun rather well.

Her researches into the decline and fall of the Shovoran dynasty had turned up some unusual data on the Tytheg, a humanoid race whom the Shovorans had subjugated through centuries of war and slavery. Interest in these long-dead people had thrown light on the planet Massatoris and its (mildly) famous colonies.

Even a twenty-fifth century adventurer of dubious scientific repute like Bernice had heard of the colonies of Massatoris, but it seemed that the always dependable TARDIS library and its erratic indexing system had not.

She had found a few references to Massatoris on several of the yellowing, spider-scrawl index cards but the space where Bernice deduced the relevant records should be housed had instead revealed a well-thumbed copy of *The Moonstone*, sixteen wax cylinders of indeterminate origin and a luminous hat box.

Bernice ran a hand through her short bob of dark hair and pulled a face, her puckish features crinkling in dismay. There was only one way to progress now and that was to find the Doctor.

Threading her way through the long, white corridors which led away from the library, Bernice passed Ace's room. The door was firmly closed. A small, grimacing wooden mask had been pinned up just above the handle like a warning to anyone thinking of entering.

For a moment, Bernice imagined Ace's face transposed onto that of the mask, like the ghost in the Old Earth story, her long hair projecting spectrally through to the other side of the door. The look of permanent disapproval the mask wore could have been modelled from life.

Bernice paused for a moment outside the plain white door and sucked her lower lip thoughtfully. Raising a hand to knock, she thought better of it and continued down the almost featureless corridor towards the console room.

Even before she reached it, Bernice was aware that something was different. The threshold of the door was wreathed in shadow, blurring the corridor roundels as though night were encroaching into their very structure. The reassuring background hum, always present in the huge chamber, was unaccountably low, scarcely impinging on her senses.

As she slipped through the doorway, she was shocked to discover the room in complete darkness. The air was cold to the point of frostiness and she half expected to find a carpet of mist creeping around her ankles.

There was no light coming from the console itself but she could make out the rising and falling of the time rotor, its glass column whispering up and down like the shallow breathing of a dying man.

Bernice felt her way inside. When she was sure of the roundels behind her back she took a deep breath which rasped painfully in her lungs.

'Doctor?'

There was no response. Only the steady rhythm of the console. She could make out shapes, looming hugely out of the darkness, but whether they were items of furniture or unknown hostiles she couldn't tell. Then, almost imperceptibly, a panel of dials and switches on one side of the console glowed into life.

The pale, ghostly light illuminated a hand and a suggestion of cuff.

'Doctor?' Bernice called again, a little louder.

20

'Hush.'

'What's going on?'

'*Hush.*'

The hand stretched out, beating a tattoo on the console. At once, a second panel flared into brightness.

Bernice could make out most of the crumpled three-piece linen suit which the Doctor had recently adopted but his face was still hidden.

'Now,' whispered the Doctor, his breath like a pistol-shot in the icy air. 'The moment of truth.'

There was a brief, frantic flurry of movement as the Doctor's hands danced over the console.

As Bernice watched, the room was drenched in light, the temperature rose and the background hum reached its familiar pitch once more. She felt immensely comforted.

The Doctor stepped back from the console like an exhausted conductor and beamed delightedly. 'Well, that's that. Three cheers and pats on backs all round, I think.'

He was a small man of indeterminate age, his brown hair rather long, his bushy brows and stern expression enlivened by a twinkling gaze. Bernice noticed that his neck was almost swallowed up by a black cravat and stiff Gladstone collar, the ends of which bent down whenever he smiled.

'What have you done?' said Bernice, crossing to the console and looking down worriedly as though expecting some drastic alteration.

'Just solved a little problem,' smiled the Doctor, stuffing his hands into his trouser pockets. 'A little problem . . . of chameleonic fluctuation.'

He rolled his eyes like a Victorian side-show owner.

'Chameleonic what?'

'It's a problem inherent in the long-term maintenance of one particular program on the exterior continua.'

'Sorry I asked.'

'No, no. It's quite simple.' The Doctor took one hand out of his pocket and tapped the console affectionately. A flat tablet had risen from the console and the Doctor

21

prodded the screen, scrolling down a detailed depiction of the TARDIS exterior.

'Police box, you see. Earth. Mid twentieth century. You know the drill,' he continued, waving his hands effusively. 'Anyway, after all these years in roughly the same form, the program deteriorates a little.'

Bernice fixed him with a worried frown. 'Deteriorates?'

'Things tend to ... drop off.'

Bernice raised an eyebrow. The Doctor harrumphed. 'Well, not so much drop off as disappear. Here today, gone yesterday as it were.'

'And that's chameleonic fluctuation?'

The Doctor nodded vigorously. 'Lost the whole stacked roof once. Took ages to come back. And there was a sort of badge on the door panel. If all's well, there should be again. Shall we go out and see?'

Bernice held up her hands. 'Hang on, Doctor. Before we examine the paint-job, I thought we might take a little trip.'

'Why not?' drawled the Doctor. 'Where would you like to go?'

He began to fuss around the console, reeling off sights of universal interest which Bernice could scarcely make out let alone understand. She put a hand on his shoulder in an effort to stop the flow but he seemed to look through her towards the interior door.

'Of course, we'd better consult Ace,' he said. 'She'll only get sulky if we plan something without her.'

The Doctor moved off, his head full of possibilities. Bernice cleared her throat. 'Ever heard of Massatoris?'

The Doctor stopped and turned, his brows frowning low over his eyes.

'Massatoris? Massatoris ... Nice place if I remember. Had some boots re-soled there once. Why?'

'And the Colonies? I've been doing some research into the Shovoran Empire. The Colonies have come up quite a few times. And I seem to have some vague recollection from when I was a kid. The eleventh colony was famous for something or other. I was wondering if we could take a look.'

The Doctor tapped his fingers against his teeth. 'The eleventh colony of Massatoris? No, I can't say it rings any bells. Have your tried the index file?'

He pointed to the console, his stiff shirt-cuff creeping over his hand. 'Look it up. Make a note of the co-ordinates and we'll have a shufty. Back in a tick.'

With that he was gone and Bernice crossed to the console. She blew air out of her cheeks noisily and began her work.

The Ismetch dug-out resembled a huge bomb crater. An area of jungle a quarter of a mile in diameter had been cleared for it, and a network of tunnels bored into the soft, peaty soil. These had been strengthened by innumerable wooden and iron struts, making the whole base resemble the inside of a barrel.

The half-moon shape of the trench faced the muddied, barbed-wire-strewn field and, beyond that, the dark immensity of the jungle. The trench was packed with exhausted soldiers, their rifles projecting over the lip of the ground like a flattened picket fence. Rain streaked down from the dismal grey sky, pelting off helmets and filling the excavation almost knee-high with filthy brown water.

Grek kept his head down as he emerged from the jungle and bolted towards the dug-out, dodging the bales of wire. He was down the ladder and wading through the water towards the entrance in seconds. Priss was waiting for him.

The young officer saluted but Grek ignored him and ran straight inside where it was quite dry and reasonably warm. He pulled off his tunic and scrambled about in search of a replacement. Moisture dripped from his warty hide.

Priss was hovering close by.

Grek turned to him sharply. 'You're in my way, Priss.'

Priss stopped slightly, his high crest almost brushing the trench roof.

Grek eyed his junior officer warily, pulled off his soaking boots and sat down on his bunk. 'Get me some new boots would you, lad, and a speecher if you can find one.'

Priss saluted and left. Was it Grek's imagination or had his more decisive tone made Priss's response a little more correct, his salute a little sharper?

He smiled, lay back on his bunk and gazed at the creaking ceiling. Outside, the ceaseless bombardment of Cutch shells punctuated the shushing of the rain.

The room was small and crowded, two bunks to each wall and a small cooking area. The open door in the far wall led into the network of tunnels which extended deep under the ground. It pleased Grek to have the well-defended trench just outside the main entrance and the warren of dark tunnels behind.

Grek's bunk had been inexpertly partitioned as a little gesture towards his rank, and ranged around it were various personal items. A battered mirror, a spare pistol, two very dirty dress tunics, a chipped basin and a long-abandoned bowl of wax with which Grek had once polished his crest and scales for parade. A thick layer of dust lay over it now.

Grek closed his eyes and let himself sink onto the scant comfort of the bed. The sound of the rain now seemed oddly comforting. There was a strong, pungent smell of wet leather and damp which recalled the mustiness of childhood visits to the Temple.

Weariness began to leak into Grek's brain and he felt, almost heard, his own breathing becoming heavier.

Dark, Dark and cold. Smell of old books. Stone pillars the size of giants. Plaster walls mottled with mould. Diffused sunlight through a coloured glass roof. Youngsters milling about. Crowds outside, laughing, talking. His mothers fussing around him. Pressing fruit and strange wine to his lips. Then the long walk towards the shrine.

The shrine. Taller than five men. Three open windows

24

*pouring light onto its cracked marble façade. Precious
stones cut into its pitted surface over generations. Sur-
mounting it, a curiously dull, discoloured rock, set in
copper and jet. Why was the least attractive stone given
pride of place? 'The most beautiful things are not neces-
sarily the best,' his mothers had said. More wine. More
food. Then the Induction. The Faith. His tiny, delicate hide
wrapped in layers of white muslin. Smell of incense and
damp. The Shrine bathed in sunlight. The old attendant
with the sagging crest and long grey face-hair. And that
night – when the headiness had left him and he had been
placed with the rest of the litter and the night-gas turned
on – his brother had crawled close and whispered in his
ear about . . .*

Grek shot out of bed with a cry, claw scrambling for
his pistol. Maconsa was standing by the bunk, smiling.
'It's over there where you left it, sir.'

Grek patted his old friend on the arm. 'Good job you're
on my side.'

'Isn't it?'

Grek picked up the least distressed of his tunics and
struggled into it. A series of cloth hoops were ranged
around the hem and he began to drop miniature grenades
into them as he spoke: 'Status, Maconsa?'

Maconsa dug his claws deep into the pockets of his
greatcoat. He had turned up the collar against the incessant rain and it framed his massive head like a cloth halo.

'I've got fifteen in the infirmary. Average of three new
cases every hour. I thought this armistice would give me
a little breathing space.'

Grek buttoned up his tunic. 'You know the Cutch, my
friend. They'll carry on to the very last minute. And the
armistice isn't definite yet.'

Maconsa nodded wearily. 'Most of the casualties are
from sniper fire anyway. Or shrapnel. Shelling seems to
be dying down.'

As if to confirm this there was a sudden lull in the

25

periodic *crump-crump* outside. Grek listened for a moment and then sat down on the bunk.

'Well . . . if we're patient and careful we might just get out of these jungles alive. So . . .' He looked around testily. 'Where is that idiot with my boots?'

Maconsa shuffled a little, uneasily. 'Grek, what if we still haven't heard from Porsim? What then? Would we have the authority to stop the war?'

Grek flexed his clawed toes, glad to have them dry, albeit briefly. 'We'll hear from the city. It's just a communications breakdown. It's happened before.'

'Ran says we've lost contact with Tusamavad and Arason too. How do you explain that?'

Grek said nothing, silently cursing his first officer's big mouth. The silence from all three major cities on Betrushia had been something he'd rather have kept from his men. For now.

'There's always confusion at the end of any conflict, Maconsa. Remember Dalurida Bridge? We were so scared we almost shot our relief column.'

'We were children.'

'And what are we now?' There was suddenly a hard, almost hysterical note in Grek's voice. His blue eyes blazed in agitation. 'Rotting in this hole for half our lives. There are more important things to do. And better ways to die.'

Maconsa looked down. There were pools of dark, muddy water forming on the planked floor. 'You don't have to try and convert me, Grek. There's . . . there's something else.'

Grek said nothing, merely fingering the collar of his tunic distractedly. Maconsa cleared his throat. 'Have you heard what they're saying?'

Grek turned. 'Who?'

'The men. Old Thoss. Everyone. There are stories filtering through.'

'Stories? What stories?'

Maconsa began to walk slowly up and down the dug-

26

out, his boots clomping on the rotten floor. 'They're saying that there's a reason why we've lost contact with Porsim and the other places. It was inevitable because it was written. The last book of the Faith. They're saying that *they* have come back.'

'Who?'

Maconsa met Grek's gaze. Grek frowned, then laughed, then clapped a claw to his forehead. 'You're not serious? The Keth? You think the Keth have come back? Good God, man, I thought you were a scientist! How can you believe . . .?'

'We all believed once, Grek, remember? In the Faith. In the Cause.'

'But as you've just pointed out, we were little more than boys.'

Maconsa's voice dropped to a low, grave rumble. 'The Faith flourishes in wartime. We all know that. And the texts do say the Keth will return one day.'

Grek punched his pillow merrily. 'Well, now I've heard it all. We're on the verge of ending the longest conflict this planet's seen in three centuries and all you can talk about is fairy stories.'

Maconsa ran a claw around the line of his jutting chin. There was four days' growth of spiny hair on it. An unthinkable lapse once upon a time.

'You'd be well advised to listen to fairy stories from time to time, Grek. There's often a lot of sense in them.'

Grek turned hollow, tired eyes to his old friend. 'What should I do?'

'Show the men some leadership. They're exhausted. Restless. Confused, even. They came out here to do a job and the politicians have denied them their victory. They need reassurance. If there's going to be an armistice then for God's sake let them all know. Tell them when they'll be going home. Tell them it hasn't all been for nothing.'

'How can I say that,' said Grek, his voice dropping to a whisper, 'when I don't believe it myself?'

Maconsa shuffled uneasily. 'I've got to go. Think about

what I've said. The troops will take refuge in anything familiar in times like this. Even old stories about the Keth. And if you aren't up to the job, remember there are plenty of others willing to take your place.'

The old surgeon saluted, turned on his heel and, bending low, exited into the rain-swilled trench.

3

The Eleventh Colony

The Doctor hummed a little tune as he strolled towards Ace's room, feeling more relaxed and confident than he had in an age. Several recent weeks had been devoted to tidying up some of the loose ends he'd spent most of his lives ignoring. Loose ends tend to pile up and there comes a time when not even a Time Lord can avoid a little spring-cleaning.

Now, with the chameleonic fluctuation sorted out he thought he might try a spot of redecorating. Shunt the interior dimensions about a bit. But all that could wait. First a little jaunt, and Bernice's idea of visiting a pleasant old world like Massatoris sounded just the ticket.

Smiling happily, he knocked on Ace's door and went in. The room was empty. Empty of Ace, that is, but not of clutter.

Since her return to the TARDIS after three years in Spacefleet, Ace had developed a precision and cleanliness which rather affronted the Doctor's bohemian sensibilities. The coverlet of her bed would invariably be turned neatly down and her collection of stout boots arranged in order of size by the door. She had managed to make a spartan white room seem positively austere.

But today something was different. The bed was a mass of unmade sheets, stray boots dotted about in the whiteness like chunks of coal in a melted snowman. The floor was stained with chemicals and, in a crumpled heap in the corner, resembling nothing so much as a sloughed-off crab-shell, lay Ace's body armour.

She had been wearing it less and less, the Doctor had been pleased to note, but to see what she had once regarded as her 'second skin' treated with such carelessness gave the Doctor pause.

He sniffed and ducked back into the corridor, closing the door behind him with a soft click.

Although the Doctor had wondered before, though never aloud, what exactly he'd been letting himself in for the day he took Ace aboard the TARDIS, things had recently gone swimmingly. The bright but somewhat disturbed teenager who had given way to a mature but somehow unreadable adult, seemed to have finally settled down. The three of them made rather a good team, in his considered opinion.

However, if the Doctor knew Ace, and he thought that by now he possibly did, then he had a pretty fair idea of where she might be.

There were fifteen doors in this particular corridor and he ran his fingers over each as he passed. The light was faintly blueish as though he were passing through some huge, translucent artery. The roundel-studded walls were thick with dust, and dust, the Doctor recalled, was ninety per cent shed skin.

A disconcerting thought fluttered through his mind. Was there, perhaps, someone else living inside the ship? With infinite size it was always so difficult to tell.

Grek stood in silence, his shoulders sagging. Then he started as Priss marched into his quarters, carrying a pair of boots in one claw and a curious brass and wood instrument in the other.

'At last,' cried Grek with what he hoped was the semblance of confident bluster.

He leant over his bunk and connected the instrument to a series of wires which hung slackly from the dug-out wall.

The speecher was in two halves and Grek placed the larger half – a round brass disc – to his small ear whilst rapidly turning a handle inset in the wooden casing.

Priss squatted on the floor and began to force the stiff new boots onto his commander's feet.

'Couldn't you get a better speecher than this old junk?' hissed Grek as a blast of whirring and static assaulted his ears. Priss had succeeded in getting one of the boots on.

'Most of them were destroyed in that big Cutch raid, sir.'

Grek nodded distractedly. There was a voice at the end of the line. Grek winced at another blast of static. 'Conference? Get me Portrone Liso.'

The TARDIS never ceased to amaze Ace. She had once spent several fruitless days attempting to map out the network of rooms and corridors which surrounded the console room but had given up in despair.

It wasn't just the corkscrew geography of the place. Sometimes, she swore, places she knew well simply weren't there when she looked for them. Asking the Doctor how he found his way around, he had simply winked and told her he had a nose for such things.

One day, though, whilst working her way back from a tiny, shuttered room mostly crammed with unwound clocks, she had found the Eighth Door. Found it, opened it, and felt her jaw literally dropping open in surprise.

It was a perfectly ordinary door and inside, the jamb connected to a perfectly ordinary dove-grey wall. Or, rather, the suggestion of a wall. For the wall simply faded away, its roundels bleeding into a lovely, rosy, sunrise sky, like an infinity of crescent moons vanishing into the dawn. And leading away from this mirage-like entrance was a wide expanse of beach, calm white water lapping at its pebbled edge.

Ace stood there now, dressed simply in T-shirt and chinos, gazing at the far-off sun which never seemed to rise. Her bare feet luxuriated in the cold water.

31

The Doctor popped his head around the door and cleared his throat. 'I thought I'd find you here. Having fun?'

She smiled languidly. 'Mmm,' she mumbled, her long, chestnut hair fluttering in the breeze.

The Doctor took a deep breath of the invigorating air and approached, hands behind his back, the tide sizzling around his shoes.

'Benny has an urge . . .' he began.

'She should see a doctor.'

The Doctor laughed lightly. 'She has. She wants us to visit a little planet called Massatoris. Likeable sort of place. Oceans. Forests. Culture. That sort of thing.'

Ace continued to gaze at the eternal sunrise, her face composed but unreadable.

The Doctor looked out towards the sea too, narrowing his eyes at the glare from the pinkish waves. 'People to do. Things to see. And some sort of colony which means absolutely nothing to me. Professor Summerfield, on the other hand, is quite intrigued by it. Coming?'

He extended his arm so Ace could take it. She smiled and nodded but refused his crooked elbow.

'I'll see you in the console room. Just want to stay here a bit longer.'

The Doctor let his arm drop. The smile faded slowly from his lips. 'Nothing wrong is there?'

Ace shook her head, her hair wafting across her eyes. 'I'll be there in five minutes.'

The Doctor smoothed down his cravat, nodded, and walked up the beach in silence. He closed the Eighth Door behind him and felt momentarily stifled by the change in atmosphere.

Walking back towards the console room, the Doctor's brow rumpled in concern. He didn't like this at all. Ace accepting an idea of his without a single murmur of discontent. Without one *bon mot* of Spacefleet-honed wit. No, no, no. Something was up.

Bernice was beaming triumphantly as he walked slowly into the room.

'I've found it. Massatoris. Shall I read off the co-ordinates?' she chirped.

The Doctor took his place beside her and nodded silently.

Bernice began to reel off a list of figures and the Doctor keyed them into the console almost without thinking.

It won't be long now.

'Are you all right?' asked Bernice.

The Doctor turned to her blankly and then smiled and nodded, his hand straying to the dematerialization lever. 'Massatoris, here we come.'

Ran and Liso crouched low over the table, their tiny ears clamped to the speecher sets. A mass of tangled cables, like wiry offal, spilled from the machinery in front of them. Valves flashed intermittently.

The operator seated by them was small and young, inwardly quaking in the presence of his superior officers. Liso, in particular, seemed to loom over him, his feral smell oppressing the operator's senses. He leaned closer to the machine.

'Ask them to repeat,' he barked.

The operator put his own speecher to his ear and pulled a brass tulip-shaped device closer to his snout.

'Say again. Say again, Porsim.'

There was a soft rush of static, like the crashing of an electric tide.

'Say again.'

Ran leant back slightly, his face twitching convulsively. 'Try once more,' he ordered.

'Porsim. Come in. Come in, Porsim.' The operator strained to hear a reply, his bright eyes glancing nervously about.

There was more static then, out of the rush of interference, a small, tinny, frightened voice.

'They have come. No time. They have come at last.'

There was a distant dull thud, more static and, finally, silence.

Liso grabbed the speecher and bellowed into it: 'Porsim? Come in! Come in, damn you!'

Ran bent forward and clicked off the transmitter with a gloved finger. 'It's no good, Liso. We've done all we could.'

Liso exhaled angrily and flung the instrument onto the table. The operator flinched visibly and tried to busy himself.

Ran clapped a hand on his fellow officer's shoulder. 'That's it then. No communication with the capital. Nor Tusamavad.'

'Tusamavad too?' Liso's voice was a strangled, disbelieving whisper.

Ran nodded. 'And that's not all.'

He walked over to one of the planked walls where a map had been stretched out. It showed, in some detail, the Betrushian land-masses; Ismetch-controlled countries in red and the smaller, diminishing Cutch in green. In addition, the southern hemisphere was dotted with little black pins, like cloves studding an orange.

'These represent communications breakdowns and sightings.'

'Sightings?'

Ran shrugged. 'We've had reports from various cities before losing touch. Things have been seen.'

Liso laughed humourlessly. 'What kind of things?'

'Nothing we can make sense of.'

Ran yawned wearily. 'It's just superstition.'

'Of course,' purred Ran. 'But it's getting worse. Rumours persist. Look at them, Liso.' He gestured at the forest of black pins. 'Something is heading our way. It's like a cancer. Spreading . . .' He seemed to lose himself in a reverie for a moment, his voice dropping to a whisper. 'Spreading . . .'

Liso stood and joined the smaller man by the map. He lowered his voice so as to be out of the operator's earshot.

'But it must be the Cutch, Ran. I mean, who else could it be?'

Ran shrugged. 'Who can say? But the Cutch? A demoralized people we're on the point of defeating? How could they possibly do it?'

Liso stroked his empty socket nervously. 'It's a plot to undermine the armistice . . .'

'Wouldn't that be nice?'

Liso looked up, gazing suspiciously into Ran's twitching face. 'What's that supposed to mean?'

Ran looked away, a small smile playing on his thin lips. 'Oh come now, Liso. I know that's what you want. This war mustn't end in diplomacy. It *can't* be allowed to.'

Liso leant even closer, whispering anxiously, 'But what can we do? And what does all this mean?' He gestured angrily at the map.

Ran folded his arms. 'We've lost contact with all the major cities in the south. If they don't tell us to stop fighting then we're quite within our rights to carry on, wouldn't you say?'

Liso seemed to consider this, his good eye shining. 'Go on.'

'Something's happening, Liso. There's more to this communications breakdown than meets the . . .' He glanced quickly at Liso's empty socket. 'Than . . . might at first appear. I have a feeling events are heading our way after all.'

'But Grek . . .'

'Grek is living on borrowed time. He was a gallant officer once. A great soldier. But different circumstances call for different attitudes. Different personalities.'

'D'you mean Hovv?'

Ran cocked his head to one side and pushed a large black pin into the dot which Porsim made on the map.

'Our old general has plenty of spirit left in him. Perhaps we might let him loose and . . . clear up a few of our problems along the way.'

35

He pushed the pin home and the dead city's name was obscured.

Liso turned away.

'We'll have to find him first.'

The TARDIS stood at a vaguely crooked angle on the slopes of a green hillside, bright sunshine playing off her battered exterior.

Bernice sat with her back to the doors, smiling to herself. Massatoris had proven to be everything she'd hoped for. A small, friendly planet with a rich and fascinating culture.

The Doctor had brought them there during the ascendancy of the Eleventh Colony and seemed absolutely delighted in his choice, first examining a strange badge which had, as predicted, reappeared on the TARDIS door panel (something to do with Sage-old ambivalence, she thought he had said), then running down to a crystal-clear lakeside with his shoes and socks in his hand.

Bernice herself had wandered off, to be greeted by an extraodinarily friendly group of local herdsmen who regaled her with bawdy tales and copious amounts of glutinous red ale which she had spent the best part of the afternoon sleeping off.

She closed her eyes and enjoyed the warmth of the sun on her face. The shadow of a bird fluttered over her face and she blinked into wakefulness.

Shading her eyes, she could just make out Ace wandering alone through the forest. What was wrong with her?

The Doctor had waved aside all Bernice's worries about their companion and concentrated on soaking his feet in the staggeringly cold water. Bernice, however, had remained troubled; a condition which only the local ale had managed to offset.

Now, though, as reality began to intrude unpleasantly into her mind, she called to the Doctor, her brow wrinkling into a concerned frown. He splashed out of the water, a delighted little-boy's smile on his pixie-like features.

'Where's Ace?' he said, wriggling his toes in the sunshine.

'Here,' said Ace, emerging from the forest.

'Ah, good. Well, that was very pleasant wasn't it? But we must be on our way. We've used up enough of these good people's hospitality.'

Bernice rose, somewhat unsteadily, to her feet and the Doctor slipped the key into the lock of the TARDIS.

'Erm . . .' said Ace from behind them. 'This is . . . erm . . .'

'What is it?' said Bernice.

Ace frowned, her long hair blowing into her eyes. 'This is difficult but . . . I think I'd like to use up a bit more of their hospitality.'

The Doctor looked at her thoughtfully, cocking his head to one side. He laid a hand gently on her shoulder. 'Alone?'

Ace nodded. 'Just for a bit. It's good here. It's . . . simple.'

'Are you all right?' asked Bernice, concern rumpling her brow.

Ace smiled warmly. 'Of course. I just . . .' She flapped her hands helplessly. 'I need time to think.'

The Doctor was silent. Ace cuffed him playfully under his pointed chin. 'I did the same for you once, remember?'

He grunted understandingly and rested his hand against the TARDIS.

'How about this, then?' he said at last. 'Bernice and I could pop off somewhere for a little while. Do a little sightseeing. Buy a few picture postcards. Then we'll come back for you. What d'you say?'

Ace nodded happily. 'I feel like you're picking me up from the disco,' she laughed.

The Doctor wagged his finger. 'Well, don't talk to any strange men, then, will you?'

'Story of my life.'

Ace turned to go. The dark green forest was only a few feet away.

'Are you sure?' Bernice's face set into a concnered frown.

'I'll be fine. Honestly. I just need a bit of a break. Nothing heavy.' Ace grinned and propelled Bernice through the double doors of the TARDIS. 'I'll be *fine*.'

The sun was shining weakly through a curtain of fine rain, steam billowing in clouds over the thick vegetation.

The incessant chirruping of insects abruptly ceased as a strangulated, grating whine disturbed the peace of the jungle.

A carpet of dead leaves stirred itself up into a little vortex, a large rectangle of air turned dark blue and, with a shuddering thump, the TARDIS arrived on Betrushia.

Immediately, the Doctor poked his head around the doors, regarding the rain-drenched landscape with an expression Bernice was rather afraid might be glee.

'Ah yes,' he exclaimed, breathing in lungfuls of the humid air. 'This looks like the place. Off by a few hours though. The rings always look best at night.'

'And even better when not totally obscured by clouds,' added Bernice, stepping from the TARDIS and shrugging on a raincoat.

'Don't fuss. I promise you, the rings of Betrushia are worth a dreching any day.'

After leaving Massatoris, the Doctor had chosen Betrushia, a nearby planet legendary, so he assured Bernice, for its spectacular ring system.

She leant back against the TARDIS doors and frowned.

'D'you think there's something wrong with her, Doctor?'

'Who?'

'Ace, of course.'

The Doctor shook his head a little too vehemently. 'Wrong? Oh, no, no, no. She's been a bit quiet for a while now. Nothing to get alarmed about. I was like that for a hundred and fifty years once.'

He glanced about at the drenched jungle. 'And we're

38

only next door, spatially and temporally speaking. 2148 AD plus two weeks into the future. Ace can put her feet up. Do her own thing. And we'll be back to pick her up.'

'Or pick up the pieces?'

The Doctor looked round. 'What d'you mean?'

Bernice put a hand on her hip, her dark eyes narrowing. 'I've noticed it too, Doctor. She seems so different these days.'

The Doctor looked down.

It won't be long now.

He stroked the TARDIS distractedly. 'Well,' he drawled, 'she's been through a lot. Uprooted from her own time, set down in another, uprooted again, plonked down in the twenty-fifth century and so on and so on. I'm surprised she doesn't show it more, to be honest.'

'I hope you're right.'

'Oh yes,' he grinned, 'I usually am. Have you remembered, by the way?'

'Remembered what?'

'About the eleventh colony of Massatoris. Whatever it was you knew about them as a child? That *was* why we went there in the first place.'

Bernice pulled a face. 'Oh. Well . . . no. The whole thing's rather slipped my mind.'

But the Doctor's thoughts seemed to be already elsewhere. He pulled his cream fedora low over his eyes but kept his umbrella furled, peering into the jungle.

Bernice grabbed at the umbrella, her face a mask of sulkiness. 'Well, if you're not using it,' she said, shooting a murderous look at the dismal sky.

'You know,' said the Doctor, not listening, 'there was something funny about the readings I took in the TARDIS.'

'About this planet?' queried Bernice. 'Funny? How?'

She followed him as he progressed through the clearing and further into the jungle.

'I'm not sure. Something's not quite right, though. I wonder whether . . .'

The Doctor was cut off, mid-flow, as a deep, rumbling tremor shook the ground. The towering cycads above their heads rocked back and forth and the Doctor clung to one until the moment passed.

He looked at Bernice and they stood in silence until sure of the ground beneath their feet.

'Quake?' asked Bernice.

The Doctor shrugged.

Bernice pulled the lapels of her coat closer to her neck. 'What's the . . . er . . . crack with this planet, then?' she asked, using a term Ace had taught her.

'Crack?'

'History. Civilization. All that. What d'you know of it?'

'Oh, very little.' The Doctor pushed aside a clump of huge, leathery leaves.

'Is that you being modest? I must write it down.'

'No, no. Honestly. I've seen the rings from space before but I don't know anything much about the planet's past. Or present.' He paused, looking at the leaf-scars which pocked a huge horse-tail tree. 'Or future,' he added, almost as an afterthought.

Clouds hung low over the jungle now, and Bernice found her boots sinking into the black mud.

The Doctor seemed cheerfully unperturbed, smiling beatifically at the swampy vegetation as rain coursed down his baggy linen suit.

'I don't know about you,' said Bernice at last, 'but I wouldn't mind waiting to see these rings from inside the TARDIS. Where it's dry. You remember *dry*, Doctor? As in ginger ale, wit and rain, opposite of?'

The Doctor smiled and nodded. 'You're right. We could, of course, nip forward in time a few hours. But the ship doesn't seem as good at those short hops as she used to be.'

He turned back the way they had come and joined Bernice under the umbrella. 'No, a decent malt and a game of nine-dimensional Scrabble should while away an hour or two. Or whatever they call hours on Betrushia.'

He slipped his hand surreptitiously around the handle of the umbrella.

Bernice's eye gleamed with images of warm towels and whisky. 'Now you're talking.'

She paused for a moment and realized the Doctor had gone off ahead, taking the umbrella with him. 'Nine-dimensional Scrabble?'

The Doctor talked over his shoulder as he headed for the TARDIS.

'Oh wonderful game, wonderful. Gives you a whole new slant. Still too many letter Qs though.'

He disappeared into the jungle, swallowed up by the rain-shadowed trees and hairy vines.

Bernice smiled and was about to follow when she heard a sound behind her. Whirling around, she stepped back in shock as first one, then another, then another, tall reptilian form emerged from the undergrowth.

They wore identical brown uniforms which covered every inch of them save for their crested, lizard-like heads. Bulbous eyes on serrated turrets gazed inquisitively at her. One of them opened its snout and hissed, revealing tiny, tiny teeth.

As one, the creatures fell upon her.

Oh dear, thought Bernice, and it had all begun so well.

4

Freaks

The orderly wiped sticky white sweat from Maconsa's grizzled head. The old surgeon grumbled at nothing in particular and ripped open the uniform of the soldier on the slab before him.

'Where was he found?' he barked, pulling at the cloth with rubber-sheathed claws.

'Eastern section, sir. Near to the dirigible plain.'

Maconsa harrumphed, his gaze taking in the numerous weeping wounds on the boy's hide with little interest. 'Shrapnel, I suppose,'

The orderly said nothing. Maconsa looked up. 'Well?'

'I can't say, sir. There were fragments of something all over him.'

'Let me see.'

The orderly wheeled over a steel trolley. A variety of small, discoloured objects had been arranged on a square of dirty cloth. Maconsa looked at them carefully.

'Stones?'

The orderly shrugged.

Maconsa picked up a pair of forceps and inserted them into the largest of the soldier's wounds. There was a muffled scream from the prostrate boy.

'Any more gas?'

The orderly shook his head. 'We're being restricted to emergencies only, sir, I'm afraid.'

'Well, never mind, never mind.'

Maconsa bent down so he was level with the soldier's

fluttering eyelids. 'Cheer up, son. We'll have you out of here in no time.'

He dug the forceps deeper and the soldier moaned in pain.

Eventually, after a series of frustrated grunts, Maconsa drew out the forceps and held aloft a sharp, bloodied fragment of stone. It was difficult to make out much in the dim gaslight. Blood splashed from the stone to the table.

Maconsa placed the fragment on one side and set to work on the next wound. As he operated he looked up at the orderly. 'Have there been any others like this?'

'Yes, sir. I took some similar stuff out of two troops only yesterday.'

'Survive?'

'No, sir.'

Maconsa grunted and plucked another stone from the soldier's hide. 'If this one does, try and get him to remember how it happened.'

He frowned briefly and then threw the fragment onto the trolley where it landed with a loud clatter.

Dusky light bled slowly into the Doctor's eyelids, revealing a letter-box view of the Betrushian jungle. His sight suddenly blurred sickeningly as he was swung back and forth by reptilian arms in black cloth uniforms. A pattern of jungle and mud swam before his eyes. He was being carried upside-down.

A sparkling golden light in the indigo sky seemed to be the first suggestion of the ring system creeping into luminescence but the Doctor was too aware of the terrible, dull pain in the back of his neck to care. Feeling his hair matting in the sticky black mud, the Doctor closed his eyes and sighed. Captured. *Again*.

He had some vague memory of reaching the TARDIS, finding Bernice gone, turning back to see where she'd got to, and then something heavy had come down onto his head and he had slid silently onto the marshy ground.

How long he'd been unconscious he couldn't tell, but his wrists and shins has been expertly tied together and a long wooden pole slid through his bonds. The smell of sap from the newly felled wood was overpowering.

There was a large fire somewhere nearby which crackled and spat damply, as the reptiles crowded around, warming their necks and upper bodies in a curiously cat-like fashion.

The Doctor opened his eyes fully, ignoring the pain in his head, and began to struggle against the ropes which bit into his flesh. Vainly, he tried to remember every muscle relaxation technique he had learned over the centuries, but his mind seemed fuzzy and unfocused.

He clamped his eyes shut as he felt himself being hoisted in the air and carried towards the fire. The downy hairs on his cheeks seemed to retreat into his skin as though afraid of the flames. There was a lurching movement and he was dumped onto the ground once more, mud splashing into his face.

There were soft footsteps in the undergrowth as someone else approached. The atmosphere changed palpably as the two reptiles standing over him stiffened to attention. Their boots creaked by the Doctor's prone face. He looked up cautiously.

A creature with one eye and wearing a pristine black uniform had approached, his claws behind his back. The other soldiers fell silent. He leant down to examine the TARDIS, his scaly face crinkling in puzzlement.

He passed his claw over the freshly restored St John's Ambulance badge and then straightened up.

The Doctor could see the alien looking curiously at him but was too woozy to make any sense of the situation. The reptile picked up the Doctor's hat with the Doctor's umbrella and peered at both unfamiliar items. Then he dropped them with a shrug, gave a little jerk of his head and walked off into the jungle.

The soldiers relaxed.

The Doctor found himself being lifted again and this time the flames danced closer before his eyes.

The image of the TARDIS swooped before him, shimmering in the haze from the fire. He seemed to be swooning in and out of consciousness, the darkness of the jungle, the heat of the flames and the animal stench of his captors assaulting his befuddled senses. He struggled weakly with his bonds and felt them biting agonizingly into his exposed wrists. The heat increased steadily.

The hem of the Doctor's coat flapped into the flames as the two soldiers hoisted him onto a spit. He screwed his eyes tightly shut and struggled feverishly with the coarse twine which bound him. If he could only shout out, convince these creatures he was more than just a dumb animal. But his voice seemed to die in his throat as waves of heat pounded at his skin. His eyes stung with sweat, and hot rising air burnt the insides of his nose and throat. It felt like he was breathing fire. Panting desperately, the Doctor made one last effort to pull himself away and then the night closed in around him.

Bernice stuck out her tongue. The tall reptilian creature guarding her didn't react. Instead, it looked away, as though embarrassed. Bernice rested her head on one hand and sighed, looking around bleakly at the bare walls of the room.

'How long do you intend to keep me here?'

The guard's turreted eyes widened in surprise and what looked like fear. He shuffled a little and then straightened up at a noise from the doorway.

A smaller, older reptile came into the room, his brown uniform covering a full, round frame, his squarish head covered in slicked-back grey bristles.

The guard saluted his superior and then said, in a disbelieving whisper, 'Do you . . . do you think it just mimicks us, sir?'

The older man smoothed back his greasy spines over his stunted crest. 'No, no, Utreh. I think it can talk.'

45

'What, *really* talk, sir?'

Bernice shot to her feet, her fists rising confrontation-ally. 'Of course I can talk. What do you take me for, you bloody iguana?'

Both men stepped back in shock, then the elder one burst out laughing.

Eventually, a little shamefacedly, Bernice sank back into her chair.

'You will forgive us, I'm sure,' said the officer with mock graciousness. 'We're not used to talking ... er ... creatures here. My name is Imalgahite. You are ...?'

Bernice looked straight into his lively blue eyes. 'Pro-fessor Bernice Summerfield.'

Imalgahite rolled the unfamiliar name around on his small black tongue and then huffed contentedly. 'Are you ... are you a male or a female of the species?'

Bernice tried to remain calm. 'Female. What about you?'

'I am commander of the Cutch forces in this part of the jungle. What are you doing here?'

'I'm ... I'm just visiting.'

'Is that all?'

'I'm tired, wet and very annoyed, too,' said Bernice testily.

Imalgahite seemed to consider this in the same rumin-ative fashion. 'Dear me, you are a curiosity, aren't you? I wonder what we should do with you?'

'I'd be ever so grateful if you could let me out of here. I have this thing about confined spaces.'

Imalgahite looked up with interest. 'You are afraid?'

'I'm not afraid of anything,' said Bernice in a voice which didn't even convince herself.

Imalgahite clapped his claws together delightedly. 'Excellent! What a brave little ape she is!'

Bernice rolled her eyes. This wasn't getting her anywhere.

'Look, if you'll just let me go I can find the Doctor and

46

we'll leave you in peace. We only came here to look at the rings anyway.'

'Rings?' said Utreh, nervously fingering his rifle.

'You know, the rings which go round your planet. Surely . . . ?'

Imalgahite held up a claw. 'We are aware of our planetary phenomena, Professorbernicesummerfield.'

'It's three words,' said Bernice, smiling in spite of herself. 'Just Bernice will do.'

'As you wish. But you say you came here to look at our . . . er . . . rings. Came from where? From the jungles? From Porsim?'

Bernice folded her arms. 'What's Porsim?'

'You don't know?'

Utreh leant towards his leader conspiratorially and grinned. 'She is only an ape, sir.'

'I am not an ape!' shouted Bernice, her wide eyes blazing in fury. 'And if you must know, I came here from another planet, not too far away from here, called Massatoris, and before that . . .'

She felt her anger receding. 'Well . . . before that, it's a little difficult to explain.'

Imalgahite eyed her a little more warily. 'My dear Bernice. I have no doubt that you are very clever and imaginative, for a mammal, but the idea of life on other planets is patently ridiculous. You'll have to come up with something better if I'm not to have you shot.'

Bernice sat up straight in alarm. 'Shot?'

'Oh yes. You could easily be an Ismetch spy. We are at war. Or didn't you know that either?'

She sank miserably into her chair and rolled her stiff neck around, gazing at the low ceiling. 'There seems to be a lot I don't know.'

Liso was staring into space, the recently slammed-down speecher humming on the table beside him. A couple of engineers, who had been poring over maps, stared at him, having witnessed an extremely vocal argument the Portrone had just had with Grek upon his return to the dug-out.

Liso scowled at them. 'Get on with your work.'

They sank back into the shadows as though trying to make a smaller target for their superior's wrath.

'Damn you, Grek,' hissed Liso under his breath, drumming his claws on the table.

The conference room was the largest in the base, built into a natural cavern in the rocks. Three of its walls glistened with moisture, the fourth was made up of familiar wooden struts.

Half a dozen long tables, their surfaces plastered with maps, log-books and measuring equipment, took up most of the space. This far from the entrance the incessant rain and shell-bursts formed a distant background annoyance, like the tick of a clock Liso had long since learned to ignore.

His one good eye seemed feverishly active next to the calm black socket of the other. He had insisted upon seeing Grek in person. Something had to be done about that *thing*.

Grek marched into the conference room looking infinitely more confident than he felt. Liso was already on his feet and saluting.

'I thought I made my instructions clear on the speecher, Portrone,' said Grek.

'Yes, sir. But I don't see . . .'

'I don't want it shot. Not yet.'

Liso put his claws behind his back in his familiar way. 'It's an abomination, sir. What's the good of keeping it alive?'

Grek smiled. 'It interests me, Liso. I've never seen anything quite like it before and I find my curiosity has been . . . aroused. I was a scientist once, remember?'

Liso remembered. It was at the military college in Porsim that they'd first met. Grek had been everyone's hero then.

The younger man put his memories aside and cleared

48

his throat. 'There's nothing you can learn from it, surely sir? And I can think of less important times to start keeping pets.'

Grek looked around at the clusters of men, studying their maps with an intensity only his presence could explain. 'Where is it now, Liso?'

Liso sighed. 'In the cell next to the infirmary.'

'Sir,' said Grek quietly.

Liso stood up a little straighter. 'Sir!'

Grek was silent for a moment. 'Well.' He cocked his head to one side. 'I think I'll go and see it.'

Liso frowned. 'Is that wise, sir? You know they can turn on you without warning.'

'Oh, I think I'll manage, Mister Liso, I think I'll manage. Carry on.'

Liso snapped to attention as Grek left the room but his shoulders relaxed almost immediately. The flames of the gas jets glittered in his solitary eye.

Grek strode along the corridor, his too-tight boots fixing a pained smile on his face.

He passed the mess room, then the infirmary (covering his snout at the stench of formaldehyde and decay) before reaching a small metal door, a spyhole cut crudely into its battered surface. He crouched down and peered inside.

The beast was hideous, to be sure, but Grek found his scientific training overwhelmed his distaste.

It had intrigued him so much that he had prevented his men from doing unspeakable things to it after its capture in the jungle. Quite what he would do with it, Grek didn't know.

Perhaps if he got home alive, if the damned armistice were ever signed, he might make a name for himself as the creature's discoverer.

It was small and pale, its horribly smooth flesh peeking out from wherever its white cloth garments didn't cover it. It had a mound of dark hair on its hideous head and strange, tiny, dark eyes. There wasn't a crest or scale anywhere on its repulsive body.

Crouching in a wooden cage in the corner, the beast looked, if Grek hadn't known such feelings were beyond a mere mammal, downright disconsolate.

It peered through the darkness as the bright blue Betrushian eye appeared at the spyhole and sighed.

Like Grek, the Doctor just wanted to go home.

Maconsa blinked and picked himself up from the ground.

Moments before, the jungle had been heaving as though the ground had turned to water and the acres of jungle were merely storm-tossed flotsam. He had watched through cupped claws, listening to the deafening, thunderous roar as the tremor took hold.

Now, as the last peal died away, he paused a moment, watching the tops of the trees as they continued to sway in agitation.

He frowned. The eastern jungles were not an earthquake zone. Never had been. There was no tectonic activity this far north at all. Arason had the odd rumble but that was only to be expected as it was so near the great trench of the Isthmus Sea. If they were now faced with earthquakes on top of everything . . .

Maconsa stiffened suddenly, his claws half-way into the crescent-shaped pockets of his greatcoat. There was a distant whispering sound creeping into the very edge of his senses.

He looked about, tiny ears pricked, and felt a cold wave of fear steal over his flesh.

The whispering sound was tantalizingly close, like a snatch of melody just out of earshot.

Maconsa cocked his head, eyes darting about in their deep sockets.

What was that?

The answer came, unexpectedly and terrifyingly, from the sky.

There was a great rending crash and a firework screech

as something thudded into the ground at Maconsa's feet. He cursed and stepped backwards, head jerking heavenward in alarm.

He couldn't make anything out in the bleary white sky, and was about to stoop and examine the missile when another hit the marshy ground, sending a great plume of mud high into the air.

This time, Maconsa threw himself into a ditch, covering his head as a rain of projectiles screamed down from the cloud-heavy sky.

His blue eyes widened in shock as the ground was pocked repeatedly. Steam hissed from the saturated ground.

After a few moments, Maconsa eased himself gingerly from the ditch.

The black, puddled soil was studded with small rock chips about the size of his fist.

He edged towards the impact craters and pulled on his gloves. Warily, he bent down and plucked one of the fragments from its muddy grave. It glinted dully in his palm.

He sat on his haunches for some time, remembering the rocks he had taken out of the young soldier's hide in the infirmary. A large gob of rain splashed onto his claw and he blinked out of his contemplation. This meant more bad news for Grek. And he wouldn't welcome it.

The Doctor had come to inside a small wooden cage which was, in turn, inside a dingy cell, its four black stone walls glistening with moisture.

He had looked down miserably at his ruined suit. The jacket was gone, and the waistcoat and trousers were singed and mud-blackened.

In a pool of filthy water by his side lay his hat, floating like a sad cream jellyfish.

He had fished it out and, tut-tutting, began to examine himself for breakages. There seemed to be nothing amiss.

Quite how he'd escaped from the fire, however, was a mystery.

Extending a sore hand, the Doctor had tested the strength of the cage. It was fashioned from saplings but seemed more than up to the job of keeping him imprisoned.

He had tried to sit up straight but the cage was too small.

On the point of muttering a particularly colourful Gallifreyan oath, the Doctor had suddenly stiffened at the sound of approaching footsteps.

He had peered through the gloom as the cell's spyhole opened and a large reptilian eye looked in on him. The eye disappeared after a while and there was a series of clanking noises as the heavy iron door was unbolted.

Framed in the doorway was a tall, slender figure, his crested head silhouetted against the weak, greenish light from the corridor.

For a moment, the Doctor took him for the one-eyed reptile he had seen next to the TARDIS, but when this one spoke his voice was almost gentle.

'Well, well. What a funny little thing you are,' said Grek. 'Where the devil did you spring from?'

'If you'd get me a glass of water,' said the Doctor, brushing himself down, 'I'd be delighted to tell you.'

Grek's leathery jaw dropped open.

Imalgahite had seemed such a decent sort, thought Bernice. But now, as she tramped through the ugly wet jungle, giant leathery leaves slapping at her legs, she was beginning to think otherwise.

After considering a number of more likely stories, she had finally decided to tell the absolute and undivided truth.

Being wholly honest did not come naturally to Bernice and she was annoyed that the Cutch leader failed to respond to her gesture with appropriate gravity.

He had, in fact, sighed in exasperation and given a

whispered command for her to be taken out into the jungle and shot. Perhaps the idea of travelling through time and space inside a blue box with a double-hearted Doctor did sound a little fanciful but he could at least have given her the benefit of the doubt.

Utreh, the guard who thought Bernice no more than a clever primate, poked her in the back with the barrel of his rifle.

'Come on. Keep moving.'

Bernice's mind began to race. There had to be a way out of this. Something she could do. But if she ran off into the jungle they could pick her off with ease, even though it was getting quite dark.

She was only alive now because Imalgahite wanted the body of an 'Ismetch spy' to be found in enemy territory. The armistice might be in preparation but he could still show them how the Cutch dealt with 'filthy mammal trash'.

The increasingly petrified filthy mammal trash called Bernice Summerfield tried slowing down her steps, anything to buy her time. But Utreh noticed and pushed her in the small of the back with his claws. His two Cutch companions were glancing about nervously, seeing enemy bogymen in every inch of the shadowy jungle.

Inevitably, it began to rain and Bernice heaved a tremendous shuddering sigh, all kinds of thoughts flitting through her mind.

It couldn't end like this. Surely.

'All right,' barked Utreh. 'This'll do.'

His words went through Bernice like cold steel. She dug her fingernails into her palms and shivered.

'Turn around.'

Bernice spun on her heel, her mind literally reeling in shock and terror. She glanced about desperately into the dark jungle for any sign of rescue.

She would run for it, she decided, and at least go down fighting.

Utreh and the other Cutch raised their rifles in silence.

* * *

53

Grek marched the Doctor through a network of tunnels towards the conference room.

Soldiers stared in blank astonishment at the funny little creature in the filthy white clothes but the Doctor did his best to ignore them, inwardly relieved that Grek didn't have him on a lead.

The Ismetch leader's long legs made swift progress along the gloomy passageways and the Doctor struggled to keep up, the ripped turn-ups of his linen trousers catching on his shoes.

'Commander Grek,' he called breathlessly. 'Where are we going?'

'You've got some explaining to do, beast,' said Grek without looking back. 'And I'm not going to interrogate you in that filthy cell.'

'Interrogate?' The Doctor sounded affronted.

'In here,' barked Grek, propelling the Doctor into the now-empty conference room.

The place stank of gas. The Doctor cleared his throat noisily and sat down in a canvas chair, mopping his perspiring brow with a silk handkerchief.

Grek began to pace up and down and the Doctor watched him with some amusement. 'Aren't you going to shine a light in my face? Or haven't you had the electricity laid on yet?'

Grek spun round, his face a picture of anger and puzzlement. 'What?'

'It's one of the hoarier cliches of interrogation, in my experience.'

'How do you do that?'

'Do what?'

'Talk!'

The Doctor laughed lightly. 'Second nature. I've been doing it all my lives. As an aid to communication it's quite without parallel.'

Grek bent down and gazed into the Doctor's impenetrably dark eyes. 'What kind of beast are you?'

The Doctor gazed back levelly, unblinking. 'I'm not a

beast. I'm the Doctor. And if you'll stop treating me like an exhibit in a circus, I'll explain myself to you.'

Grek stood up sharply, shaking his head in disbelief. 'No. No, it's impossible. You're some kind of freak.'

'I did know some Siamese twins once,' said the Doctor, glancing introspectively at the low ceiling. 'And the odd hermaphrodite. Very odd, in fact. But I wouldn't count them amongst my closest aquaintances.'

Grek turned slowly, his pearly teeth biting into his lip. 'You're a spy, then. Some sort of experiment the Cutch have devised. Get behind the lines, gather intelligence . . .'

'I'm a little conspicuous for a spy, wouldn't you say?'

'Then what are you?' hissed Grek, grabbing the Doctor by the shoulders.

'I've told you. I'm the Doctor. I'm just passing through.'

The two men were silent for a long moment, as though daring each other to move. Then the tension was broken by a light, rattling sound.

The Doctor glanced up and saw that the gas jets were shaking in their housings. Grek spun round as the map instruments on the long tables rolled onto the floor.

The room suddenly shook as though it had been rammed, and Grek tumbled into the Doctor's arms.

'Get down!' shouted the Doctor, leaping from his chair and pressing Grek's head towards the planked floor.

The walls were shuddering now, struts bursting asunder, sending rivulets of black mud cascading into the room.

'We must get to the surface!' screeched Grek, attempting to stand. He buckled instantly at the knees as the ground swayed beneath his boots.

'No! Stay down!' shouted the Doctor above the increasing din.

Grek ignored him and crawled across the floor towards the lurching doorway. The gas-frames creaked ominously.

Grek had almost reached his goal when the floor buckled under him, sending him crashing into the corner. Above, the fragile ceiling beams groaned as mud pressed down from the surface.

The Doctor shot a glance at the splintering beams above the dazed Grek and made a split-second decision. With surprising strength, he upturned the long refectory table and tipped it over Grek.

The Ismetch leader looked up confusedly as the table blocked his view. Almost immediately, a great corner of the beamed ceiling came crashing down, thudding onto the table and littering it with timber, mud and masonry.

As the tremor rolled to an end, the air was filled with dust and gas. Grek peered through the murk, the table shadowing his dazed face, and saw the Doctor smiling down at him.

'Well, Commander,' said the little freak, 'I think I just saved your life.'

Night was coming on fast. The jungle was disappearing in an inky haze, trees and foliage rustling like restless, shadowy giants. The chirruping of insects continued unabated.

The sentry looked around uneasily. The rain had let up but there was now an incessant dripping from the soaked jungle canopy which did nothing to calm his nerves.

He adjusted the strap of his rifle and began his regular patrol, boots sinking deep into the marshy ground. A falling star caught his eye and he looked up at the cloudless night sky in wonder, his vigilance, for the moment, distracted.

The sky was profoundly dark, a rich, midnight blue but so crowded with stars that it quite took the sentry's breath away. There were recognizable constellations, of course, and dense clusters which he couldn't name but, most astonishingly, there were the rings.

Of course, viewed from Betrushia's surface they didn't look like rings, although the sentry had seen artist's impressions back in his schooldays in Tusamavad of how they must appear.

From his point of view, however, they were spectacular enough. A great, broad diagonal line like a pointillist rainbow, its colours shifting and merging endlessly, took up half the sky; stars peeking occasionally between illuminated dust-clouds.

As darkness drew on, the rings would shimmer gloriously, the light from Betrushia's sun gaining in strength as night turned to day. Then, just before dawn, shafts of sunlight would set the rings ablaze, transforming them into an incredible display; a sky-bound ocean of glorious colour.

It never failed to move the sentry even though he had grown up with the phenomenon. Since joining the army he was also awake for many more dawns than during his childhood.

Something made him look down and, for a moment, he could see only blackness. The great dark trees whispered slightly in the breeze. He looked down at his feet, conscious of a deep, rumbling sound somewhere at the edge of his perception. He cocked his head inquisitively and the light from the rings glanced off his crest.

The sound came again, like behemoths whispering far below the surface. The sentry strained to make out the sound, his warty face crinkling with the effort.

Then he felt it, a slight, rocking sensation, as though the jungle had been delicately pushed to one side. His knees gave slightly and he had to struggle to keep standing.

The sentry had quite forgotten the rings now. He didn't even notice a pattern of falling stars which lit up the far horizon. His every sense, every instinct was trained on the low trembling beneath his feet.

In one movement, he stripped off his rifle and grenade belt and threw himself down onto the soft jungle floor. Wet leaves and mud slapped onto his uniform.

He was tempted to put his ear to the ground but decided this was too ridiculous and contented himself with crouching on his haunches, ears pricked.

There was another tremor. The sentry felt himself sway slightly, his boots creaking as he rocked on his heels.

Around him, the sounds of the night continued undisturbed.

This had to be reported, the sentry decided. If it were some kind of earthquake then the officers would need to know; and if the Cutch had developed some new device, perhaps to sabotage the armistice, then he might just get the Pelaradator's Star for spotting it first. He stood up excitedly.

If he had been a little more vigilant, his mind not filled with dreams of glory and shining medals, the sentry might have seen the thing that burst suddenly from the jungle and tore him to pieces.

5

Raining Stones

There was a fragrant, dusty smell about the place as the woman rose in silence from her bed.

The room around her, though icy, held something of the feel of winter sunshine, its blank stone walls hard and pale and cold.

Shivering, she pulled the rough hessian robe over her head, twitching involuntarily as the material brushed against her skin. There was no mirror in which she could check her appearance; in fact, no decoration of any kind in the room, save for the plain golden cross, its shaft entwined with gilded flames, which hung crookedly on the far wall.

The woman pulled a basin and jug from under the bed and gazed at her reflection in the frozen water. It would have been nice if the place had been a little warmer, she conceded, but such comforts were hardly the Chapter's way.

Decisively, she punched at the block of ice and it loosened, slipping about in the basin. Another blow and the liquid water beneath was freed.

She scooped up a couple of handfuls and splashed them onto her face. Her eyes widened in shock at the cold.

Somewhere, distantly, a bell tolled. The woman slipped into her sandals and clopped across the stone-flagged floor to the doorway.

Running a hand over her completely shaven head, she stepped into the corridor. It was time to worship.

* * *

Grek was still on the floor, the Doctor bending over him when Priss came careering around the corner, almost falling into the conference room.

'Sir! Are you . . .?'

The young soldier caught sight of the Doctor and gave a little screech of alarm. He pulled his pistol from its holster and trained the weapon on the Doctor.

'Don't move, sir. It won't attack if we're calm.'

'Priss . . .' began Grek.

'Move towards me, sir. Slowly. I'll try to get it between the eyes.'

'You'll do no such thing, Priss,' said Grek, getting to his feet. 'The Doctor here just stopped me from being flattened under that lot.'

He pointed to the rubble on the floor and took Priss's gun from him in one easy movement.

'But sir . . .!'

'No more complaints, Priss. This person isn't just a dumb animal. It . . . he knows things.'

'Knows things, sir?'

Grek clapped a claw onto the Doctor's shoulder. 'Yes. I'm not quite sure why, but I suspect he may prove rather useful.'

The Doctor smiled. 'Well, you know, anything I can do.'

Priss peered at the talking wonder in abject amazement. Grek began to brush mud and dust from his tattered uniform.

'Any idea what all that was, Priss?'

Priss pulled himself to attention. 'No, sir. I mean . . . Some sort of earthquake, I suppose.'

Grek frowned, as conscious as Maconsa had been of their distance from any known earthquake zone. He smiled at his subordinate. 'I thought for a minute the Cutch had brought up their big guns.'

'Yes, sir. Oh, sir, there was something else. A communication from Porsim.'

Grek's reptilian face lit up. 'Excellent! At last. Are they all right?'

Priss looked down uneasily. 'It was from the Pelaradator, we think, sir. Repeated. Over and over.'

He handed Grek a small square of discoloured paper.

The commander looked at it, his expression unreadable
in the flaring light of the gas jets. He crumpled the paper
into a ball and tossed it dismissively into the corner.

'That'll be all, Priss.'

Priss clicked his heels and marched smartly from the
room, already miserable at the prospect of clearing up
the mess.

In silence, the Doctor and Grek pulled the table into
the middle of the room and sat down at opposite ends.

'Why did you come here?' said Grek at last.

The Doctor ran a hand through his mud-matted hair.
'Sightseeing, to be honest. We came to see your planet's
ring system. It's very spectacular, as I'm sure you're
aware.'

'We?'

'My friend Bernice came too. I'd just lost her when
your men found me. I've been meaning to ask where
you've been keeping her.'

Grek stood up. 'We found no one else, Doctor. You
were taken by a scouting party.'

The Doctor felt a growing sense of dread. 'What do
you mean?'

Grek's exhaled breath hissed between his teeth. 'You
were way beyond the front line. A section of jungle near
the plains. It's Cutch-occupied.'

'Cutch?'

Grek turned away and his face was plunged into
darkness.

'They're the real beasts, Doctor. If the Cutch have your
friend then she's as good as dead.'

Bernice felt panic rising through her. Her throat constricted and her stomach flipped over.

Come on, Summerfield! Don't let it end like this! Think!

61

Sweat dripped down her back. She felt her legs begin to move.

Adrenalin coursed through her body. The rifles were being cocked.

Her feet began to move.

A volley of shots rang out with a multiple crackle like the snapping of burnt twigs.

Bernice stumbled and crashed to the jungle floor, her face slamming into the yielding black mud.

'You must find her!'

The Doctor banged his fist on the table, rattling the few remaining instruments which the earthquake had not dislodged, and biting his lip in an effort to conceal the sudden pain in his hand.

Grek folded his arms and fixed the Doctor with an unwavering stare.

'It's impossible, Doctor. I can't risk my men on a suicide mission into Cutch territory. The war is almost over. I'd never forgive myself if those lads were killed over a . . . a . . .'

'Over an animal?' said the Doctor.

Grek shrugged. 'Yes! I accept that you're different to the ones we're used to but it'll take a lot to make me trust you. If your friend was taken by the Cutch then I'm sorry, but there's nothing I can do.'

The Doctor put his damp fedora onto his head, hoping this might lend him an air of authority.

'Then I insist I be allowed to return to my ship. I'll find her – even if you won't.'

Grek straightened his tunic and winced as his boots cut into his clawed feet. 'I'm afraid that's impossible. You must stay here, now. I may need you.'

'Then I'm still a prisoner?'

Grek scratched his crest irritably but said nothing in reply. Finally, stepping over the debris on the planked floor, he turned. 'Don't try anything stupid, will you? My men are awfully keen to get you back on that spit.'

The Doctor sat down on the table miserably. 'You'll at least ensure they don't put me in a kennel, I hope.'

Grek frowned, then, grasping the Doctor's meaning, smiled. 'I'll see what I can do.'

He stepped out into the corridor, locking the conference room door firmly behind him.

The Doctor sighed and took off his hat. Disconsolately, he began to root through his waistcoat pockets for anything of use. He huffed disappointedly at his collection. Some nutcrackers and an autographed picture of Disraeli wouldn't get him far.

Then, struck by a thought, the Doctor crossed the room and began to fish about in the shadows. With a little cry of triumph he picked up the ball of crumpled paper which Priss had given to Grek.

He returned to the table where the light was better and flattened out the paper with a couple of strokes of his hand. He peered closely at the hastily scrawled message from the Pelaradator and frowned.

Bernice opened her eyes.

She breathed in tightly, experimentally, feeling the air catching in her shuddering throat. There was nothing wrong with her.

Moving cautiously, her face sliding through the wet black mud, she looked over her shoulder.

The bodies of Utreh and the other Cutch lay sprawled in the undergrowth. Thick, pasty blood oozed from bullet wounds in their hides.

Standing over them, like a hunter with a brace of bagged pheasants, was another of the reptiles. He seemed somewhat different to those she had already encountered. His blue eyes were recessed into his skull and his crest rose proudly from the wide ridge of his snout.

Also, noted Bernice, he had the worst twitch she'd seen since one of her professors back at college. The reptile's face convulsed as though something were actually crawling about under its skin.

He hooked his rifle over the shoulder of his black uniform and gazed at Bernice. 'Well,' said Ran. 'You'd better come with me.'

Grek lay on his bunk with his eyes firmly closed. Next to him, sitting on a canvas chair was Maconsa, his massive head resting on his arm. Standing somewhat wearily to attention was young Priss.

'. . . structural damage to all areas. Damage in third level limited to gas leak, sir. Entrance to dug-out now restricted to Number Seven shaft,' he concluded breathlessly.

Grek shot a glance at the firmly closed door at the far end of his quarters. No way through to that reassuring maze of tunnels now. He passed his claw over his face and yawned. 'Any firm idea what caused it?'

Priss cleared his throat. 'No, sir. I mean . . . Has to be some sort of tectonic activity.'

'Here?' cried Grek. 'Not very likely is it?'

'A last-ditch manoeuvre by the Cutch then, sir?' said Priss brightly.

Maconsa grunted. Grek turned to him. 'You have a comment, Maconsa?'

The old man got up, and jerking his head to one side, dismissed Priss. Once the two men were alone, he began to speak.

'I was out there yesterday, Grek, when the quake hit. There was something else. It followed the tremor almost immediately. A meteorite shower.'

'A what?'

'Shower of what appeared to be meteorites. Look.'

Maconsa pulled one of the stones from his pocket and tossed it at Grek who caught it deftly in one claw. The stone glinting dully in the weak light.

Grek blinked repeatedly and shivered as a strange sense of familiarity stole over him. The spines on his neck rose rapidly, like flower petals in time-lapse.

'I watched them come down,' continued Maconsa. 'And I've taken similar shrapnel out of three troops recently.'

Grek propped himself up on his elbow.

'With all due respect, Maconsa, I have rather more pressing problems than interesting astronomical activity. In case you've forgotten, we've lost touch with all our major cities. And Hovv . . .'

'I haven't forgotten.' Maconsa sat down wearily and rubbed his jutting chin. 'But Grek, I don't think this is just a coincidence. I think the events are linked.'

Grek looked at the stone in his palm and half-smiled. 'What is it the Faith says? "When the ground turns over in its sleep and the rain turns to stone"?'

' "Then the Keth shall come again",' whispered Maconsa.

' "And come. And come".'

They sat in silence for some time, the sound of the streaking rain outside the only interruption.

Grek suddenly shook himself from his reverie.

'Where's Ran?' he said.

For the second time that day, Bernice found herself being frog-marched. Ran, however, seemed less keen than her previous captors to prod her with the end of his rifle.

'Thank you,' she said, craning her neck to look round.

'For what?'

'Saving my life.'

Ran's twitching face crinkled with laughter. 'Don't get too optimistic. You may be a rare one but I did find you in Cutch territory. You're living on borrowed time.'

Bernice shrugged. 'Borrowed time is better than no time at all.'

Ran peered at her closely as they tramped through the jungle towards the Ismetch encampment. 'Our commander has another one like you.'

Bernice's eyes lit up. 'The Doctor?'

'What?'

'Is he called the Doctor?'

65

Ran frowned, his expression somewhere between puzzlement and delight. 'You even have names for one another,' he trilled. 'How quaint.'

Bernice made a mental note never to patronize another lifeform if she ever got off Betrushia alive.

Ran lashed at an overhanging liana with his rifle. 'I'm afraid I don't know its name. Grek keeps it in a cage or something.'

Bernice stepped over a clump of wet, mossy plants and narrowed her eyes. 'You're not like the others are you? Like the "enemy", I mean.'

Ran didn't look up. 'The Cutch are barbarians.'

Bernice frowned. 'Cutch? Yes, they mentioned that. So you must be . . .'

Ran stopped suddenly and pulled himself up to his very impressive seven feet. 'I am Ran of the Ismetch, Portrone to Commander Grek and hero of Dalurida Bridge.'

Bernice cocked an eyebrow witheringly. 'Really?'

Ran laughed, a strange, whinnying laugh. 'You must forgive me. I've been listening to the propaganda so long it's become my second language.'

Bernice considered her next question carefully. She pulled aside a clump of spiky ferns. 'And you're at war?'

'Of course we're at war. For the Greater Glory of the Ismetch. My Country or my Soul. I took an oath.'

'An oath to destroy the Cutch?'

Ran's scalp retracted slightly which Bernice took for a nod. 'But why?'

'Isn't it obvious?'

'Obviously not.'

Ran strode on, his breeches becoming soaked by the onslaught of the rain-drenched undergrowth. 'I would have thought you'd developed quite an insider's knowledge of them by now. If what you told me was true.'

'It is true. I was captured. I'm not a spy.'

'Well, well. We'll have to see.'

He cocked his head slightly, returning to his theme:

66

'We are at war with the Cutch because they are racially inferior.'

Bernice sighed, feeling a rush of anger rise to her cheeks. 'I see.'

'They're less intelligent. Devious. Filthy. Aggressive. And they breed like *mammals.*' Ran looked at her and laughed. 'No offence.'

Bernice stood still. 'And you're at war with them to keep them from . . . from infecting the Ismetch race?'

'Keep moving,' barked Ran suddenly. 'Yes. That's it essentially. Have you been listening to the broadcasts too?'

Bernice said nothing, concentrating instead on ploughing through the jungle.

Ran came up behind her. 'And now it's all over. Fifteen years of conflict. Peace. Now we can all go home.'

Bernice looked at him closely. For a battle-weary soldier, he didn't sound awfully pleased about it.

'There is one thing I'd like to know,' she said at last.

'Oh yes?'

'What were you doing out here?'

Ran's pale blue eyes regarded her steadily before breaking up into an erratic spasm of tics.

Imalgahite squinted through the twin barrels of the telescope towards the jungle. The crested helmet he had jammed onto his head sparkled with a coppery sheen in the fine rain.

Around him, the Cutch trench was almost knee-high in muddy black water. He glared disgustedly at the rat-like mammals swimming in V-shaped ripples through it, and leant his elbow against the duckboards propping up the trench wall.

A thin soldier with mangy, blackened scales sloshed through the water towards him and saluted. Imalgahite acknowledged him with a grunt.

'Well?'

'Nothing, sir. Utreh and the others have failed to report back.'

Imalgahite turned back to the twin telescopes and spoke in a low murmur: 'So, unless they've gone over to the Ismetch, it's safe to assume they're dead.'

The soldier gazed down at the water lapping at his knees. 'I'm afraid so, sir.'

Utreh had been a good friend. The whole brigade had found Imalgahite's orders to take the mammal female out into enemy territory bizarre. And now the inevitable had happened. Three good Cutch dead.

'And if I know the Ismetch mentality,' rumbled Imalgahite, 'the mammal will have been taken back to their base – dead or alive.'

'Sir?'

Imalgahite gazed levelly into the soldier's eyes. It was a shame about Utreh, he reflected, but brave soldiers could find only glory in a premature death.

'I made sure she was taken into Ismetch territory for a very good reason, soldier.'

He ducked into an alcove and pulled out a small, square box, its grilled front exposing a complex of wires and valves at its heart.

Carefully, Imalgahite plugged the machine into one of the speecher cables and then crouched down as a series of whistles and squeaks erupted from it. He turned three or four dials, his clawed fingers moving with surprising dexterity.

Finally, a single high-pitched note bled into the rush of static. Imalgahite gave one last turn on the dial and the note rang out, high and pure. He turned to the thin soldier, a smile playing on his scaly features. 'Can you get a fix on that?' he said.

After an uneventful journey through a series of gloomy corridors, Ran passed Bernice into the custody of young Priss. Her twitching captor had, in any case, become totally uncommunicative as soon as they had entered the Ismetch

68

base, no doubt embarrassed to be seen in the company of a mere mammal.

Priss, now getting quite used to talking animals, was more forthcoming, but his preferred dialogue seemed to consist of 'Move!' and 'Shut up!' for the most part.

At the door of the conference room, Priss looked about, his eyes glinting in the dismal light of the gas jets. 'Don't try anything. There'll be trouble.'

Bernice set her jaw fiercely. 'You're dead right. What're you going to do with me, anyway?'

'Portrone Ran says you are to be restricted inside the conference chamber. The chamber is through this door. You must proceed.'

'I *am* proceeding,' she squawked as he pushed her through the doorway and slammed the door shut in her face.

She banged furiously on the door. 'If you'd stop treating me like . . .'

'Please don't shout,' cut in a soft voice. 'I've got a headache.'

Bernice whirled round. Concealed by the shadows, his feet up on the table and his fedora over his eyes, sat a familiar figure.

'Doctor!'

'Yes,' he drawled, sitting up and smiling. 'In person. You know, I'm inordinately pleased to see you. Commander Grek seemed to think your chances of survival were extremely slim.'

'They nearly were. But I was . . . er . . . rescued.'

'Rescued? By whom?'

Bernice shrugged, trying to remember Ran's pompous description of himself. 'The first officer. Ran. Poltroon or something.'

The Doctor tapped his fingers against his chin. 'Ah, yes. The man with the twitching lids. I've seen him about.'

Bernice sank wearily into a chair, rubbing a knot of muscle which had developed in her shoulder. 'What are our chances of getting out of this bloody swamp?'

The Doctor fiddled with the buttons of his filthy waist-coat. 'That depends. Seems to be a particularly vicious civil war taking place.'

'Genocidal more like,' murmured Bernice, 'if you believe the rhetoric old Twitchy was coming out with.'

The Doctor sighed. 'Same old story. Everywhere you go. An unreasoning, irrational hatred of other races.'

'Mind you,' she smiled, 'they may not be far wrong about the Cutch. They did send me off into the jungle to be executed.'

The Doctor looked up. 'Did they indeed?'

'Yes. They thought I was an enemy spy or something.'

'Mmm. Same thing this end.'

'But they also said the war was almost over. Twitchy said so, too.'

The Doctor brushed a lock of mud-caked hair from his eyes. 'There's a lot going on here that doesn't make sense. Remember those readings I took in the TARDIS?'

Bernice nodded. 'Funny, you said.'

'Indeed. Since we arrived there's been another tremor. I don't like it. I don't like it at all.'

Bernice got up and laid a gentle hand on the Doctor's arm. 'Just for once, couldn't we leave these people to sort it out for themselves?' I mean, it's war. And unless you've got any heavy artillery up your sleeve, there's probably very little we can do to help, one way or the other.'

The Doctor's face rumpled, and he smiled. 'Perhaps you're right. We could find a way out and go back for Ace. See how she's getting along.'

He stood up and made a vain attempt to brush the dried mud from the remains of his suit. 'There's one thing that bothers me, though. You say the ... the Cutch isn't it? The Cutch sent you out into the jungle to be executed.'

'That's right.'

'But why? Why not do it right there?'

Bernice shrugged, pulling her coat closer around her against the chill. Recessed in the left lapel, a tiny brass and crystal stud glittered and winked quietly.

* * *

70

'All right,' said Grek, swinging round to face his officers. 'I want opinions. Where do we go from here?'

He was looking quite impressive, his tunic freshly sponged by a couple of press-ganged orderlies. Liso, however, still managed to look more alert and confident, even stooping slightly to prevent his crest from brushing the low ceiling. Ran stood next to him, one claw behind his back in his familiar fashion and Maconsa, head sunk on chest, was almost standing to attention. Priss, ever eager, had his chest pushed out as though he were expecting a medal.

'The female mammal isn't saying anything,' said Ran. 'If she's a spy then she's a very good one.'

Liso snorted contemptuously. 'Kill them. Kill them both, that's what I say. Filthy animals. They're not the issue here.'

Grek glanced sideways at him. 'And what is?'

'There's no question of ending hostilities now, sir. No armistice to sign. No peace.'

Grek inclined his head a little. 'Yes, well, if you could put your glee to one side for a moment, Portrone, perhaps you could address the question: why?'

'Why, sir?'

'Porsim, mister. Tusamavad. Why haven't we heard from them? What the hell is going on out there?'

Ran cleared his throat. 'A cursory study of the facts, sir, shows that something is systematically cutting off all our links with the major conurbations.'

Grek looked at them all and heaved a desperate sigh. 'So what do we do?'

Unexpectedly, Priss piped up, his voice cracking with nervousness: 'If I may be so bold, sir.'

The others looked at him in surprise.

'Go on, Priss.'

'If they don't contact us, why don't we go to them?'

Liso flexed his gloved claws in irritation. 'Go to them? What are you suggesting, boy?'

Priss glanced about anxiously. 'An expedition, Portrone.

71

A dirigible. Perhaps two or three. They could be over Porsim in a day or so. And we're bound to find out what the problem is. One way or another.'

There was a thoughtful pause in the dug-out, then a slow smile crept across Grek's warty face. 'Excellent! Excellent, Priss! We'll make a first officer of you yet.'

He clapped a claw on the young reptile's shoulder and moved towards the speecher, which still lay on his bunk. 'I'll organize it at once.'

'Permission to speak, sir . . .' began Maconsa.

Grek eyes him warily, knowing the uncomfortable facts he was to draw to his fellow officers' attention.

'Denied,' he said simply.

'Grek . . .'

'Permission denied, Maconsa. I want you back in the infirmary. Priss, I'm putting you in charge of the search for General Hovv.'

'Sir!' cried Priss delightedly.

'And Liso . . .' Grek paused a moment, regarding his one-eyed nemesis with measured calm. 'Liso, I want you to take command of the expedition to Porsim.'

Liso's good eye blazed in fury. 'But you can't pack me off to Porsim now!' he bellowed. 'I'm needed here!'

'You will do exactly as you're ordered, Portrone.'

'I will not!' Liso marched up to Grek, his thin lips curling into a snarl. 'It's obvious you want me out of the way. You're afraid.'

'Afraid?' laughed Grek. 'Afraid of what? Of you? A child?'

Liso's claws flew out into angry fists. 'No! You're afraid of the truth. Because you know the men have no respect for you any more. They look to me for leadership, Grek. Try and deny it. Go on! Try!'

In one sudden movement, Grek's claw flew to his shoulder-holster, pulling out his pistol and training it on Liso. The barrel came to rest inches from Liso's enraged face.

'I should hate to have to blow out the other eye, Liso,'

hissed Grek. 'Now, until further notice, I am still in command here. You will report for embarkation at once or I'll shoot you down where you stand.'

The other officers stood stock-still. Priss could feel cold sweat trickling down the knobbly ridge of his spine. Grek cocked the gun, his hand, surprisingly, rock-steady.

Liso's hand stole to his face, caressing his empty socket. Then he spun on his heel and stalked from the room.

After a moment, Ran and Priss followed him in silence.

Grek uncocked the pistol and blew out a grateful sigh. 'Well. Thank God that's over.'

Maconsa grimaced. 'Is it, Grek? Is it?'

Grek tossed the gun onto his bunk. 'I've already told you, Maconsa. I can't have your superstitious rubbish spreading to the men. Morale is low enough as it is. How you can – '

'Listen!'

Grek strained to hear. 'What?'

'There. Outside. It's the same sound.'

Grek shrugged but then, just at the edge of his hearing, made out a strange, low, whispering.

'Come on!' barked Maconsa, shifting his bulk with surprising speed towards the dug-out entrance.

Grek ran after him into the trench. The rain had stopped but the sky was still a bleary gun-metal grey.

Maconsa looked up in anticipation. 'Here they come!'

In a rush, like a sudden, drenching rain shower, a hail of meteorites slammed into the ground all around them. Maconsa and Grek ducked back into the entrance for shelter.

For a few moments, the air was alive with missiles, thudding into the jungle and the wet, muddy ground. Grek put his claws on his hips and blinked. 'I think I'll have a word with the Doctor,' he said at last.

Utreh opened his eyes. The constant chittering of the living jungle around him filtered gradually into his brain. He could taste mud in his mouth.

73

Above him, the sky was a greasy palette of cloud and mist.

He flexed a leg and then tried to haul himself onto one elbow. He gasped in pain.

Ran's bullet had passed straight through his side. There was a lot of blood staining his uniform but nothing vital seemed to have been touched. His comrades, however, had not been so lucky. They lay where they had fallen, limbs already stiffening, clouds of flies busily at work on their flesh.

Utreh gritted his teeth and shunted himself into a sitting position, his breath coming in painful grunts.

Wherever that dirty mammal female had got to, she would pay for this outrage. The Cutch did not forget.

Now, if he could only make his way back to the encampment, everything would be all right. His side felt like it was on fire and blood continued to seep from the ugly wound.

He stumbled forward through the thick undergrowth, claws scrabbling at the mass of unyielding grass and impacted turf.

Then he stopped abruptly. There was someone close by. He couldn't see who it was. Not properly. But they were coming out of the jungle. And coming fast. But not a person. Not a Cutch, nor an Ismetch. Not even one of the talking mammals . . .

Utreh held up his arms in a pathetic effort at protection as it screamed out of the trees and enveloped him.

6

Church Triumphant

The Doctor had succeeded in opening the conference room door. The earthquake seeming to have somewhat challenged the integrity of the locking system, he had made short work of pulling it apart.

Bernice peered into the darkened corridor and was about to step out when the Doctor pulled her back.

'Ah, no,' he said. 'You stay here.'

Bernice frowned. 'Erm, this isn't a child you're talking to here, Doctor.'

'Yes, yes,' muttered the Doctor testily. 'I know that. It's just a question of bearings. There's a maze of corridors out there and until we know how to get out, there's little point in us both getting lost. I'll have a quick recce and be back in five minutes.'

Bernice looked at her watch. 'Five minutes? And then what do I do? Go off without you?'

The Doctor grinned. 'You could give me another five.'

'It's a deal. Don't be long.' She pushed him out into the corridor.

He crept through the gas-lit passageways, looking about furtively and carefully stepping over the piles of debris left by the earthquake.

He recognized the site of his cell and what was, judging by the smell, either the infirmary or the morgue. Taking a right-hand turn down another wooden-propped tunnel, the Doctor became conscious of another odour in the

dank air. Raising his eyebrows in surprise, he smiled.
'Flowers?'

He walked slowly down the tunnel and then stopped
sharply at a large metal door.

It was clear that this area was much older than the rest
of the dug-out. In fact, the blend of wood and stonework
seemed to indicate that the Ismetch base had been built
around it. The metal door was framed by a crumbling
stone arch and had a huge brass ring set into it.

The Doctor pressed his ear to the door and then, acting
on impulse, threw it open.

A set of winding stone steps led down into dank gloom,
a few blossoms of yellow candle-light the only islands of
brightness. The Doctor walked slowly down the steps, his
shoes clattering in the icy hush. The walls, made up of
massive stone blocks, were coated in slimy moss, moisture
running in rivulets down the dressed faces.

The Doctor reached the bottom of the steps and looked
around.

It was a fairly large chamber with a flat ceiling, its
corners blurred into pitch darkness. And the atmosphere
was unmistakable. As familiar here as in any Gallifreyan
hall, English college or Balanystran learning block. A
place of worship and neglect. An admixture of forgotten
books, unaired clothes, damp dormitories. Church. Or
whatever the Betrushians liked to call it.

In one corner, the Doctor spotted a hideous gargoyle,
its face seeming to move in the flickering of the tall,
spindly candles. He jumped. The face *was* moving.

It belonged to one of the reptiles. He stepped out from
the shadows, holding his candle aloft in one gnarled claw.
'Oh,' he wheezed, rheumy eyes taking in the Doctor's
small frame with some distaste. 'You've come at last.'

The Doctor was, to say the least, somewhat taken aback.

Ran gazed at his reflection in the mirror. Behind him he
could see the scant comforts of his room; the draped
partition which separated his bed-space from the cooking

76

area. The twin standards of his old legion and the battered copper case in which he kept his medal from Dalurida Bridge.

But none of these caught his attention now. His eyes stared back at him and they were weary eyes, the scales below them hanging in unhealthy bags, the warty flesh of his face beginning a tendency towards jowls. And then there were the tics.

He remembered the day they had started. Two years previously. A particularly bad Cutch bombardment, an incessant rain of shells. Banging and shuddering. The screams of the injured and dying. All these he had learned to cope with over the long years of his military life. But not Testra. Testra had been different.

Ran had met her when he was on leave. General Hovv had been visiting the front line and, pleased with recent successes, had granted unexpected leave to all of Grek's officers.

Whilst Liso and Maconsa had gone back to Porsim in the first available dirigible, and young Priss to the coast, Ran had opted for a period of rest in the little town of Jurrula.

He'd been there before, of course, in the early days of the war, when the reputation of its whore-house was near to legendary. As a young soldier, he had cheerfully added his voice to those who said Jurrula was the closest an Ismetch got to heaven this side of the Veil.

All that had been years before, however, and he knew how much the charming old town, positioned high in the hills above the jungle, had suffered. Even a veteran like Ran, though, was shocked by the extent of the devastation. The wonderful old High Temple (in which he'd said prayers the night before the battle of Dalurida Bridge) was nothing but a pile of rubble. The old town square with its florid statues and fountains had vanished in a vast bomb crater. The whore-house, even, was gone, he'd noticed with a sad smile.

Then, in a tiny eating-house, its once-elegant facade propped up with sheet metal, he had found Testra.

She had been waiting at table, sullenly, but he soon discovered what a lively, intelligent and very funny woman she was. Ran liked her at once. She served him at his battered table with a coquettish grin and a certain impudence rarely seen in provincial Ismetch. Ran was used to being treated as almost everyone's superior and this girl's attitude intrigued and amused him. When asked her name she had stated, clearly and boldly, 'Testra,' earning a look of disapproval from her father in the kitchen.

In the automatic scheme of things, Ran would have taken her as his lover. But she refused to respond to any of his wooing. Even, he was delighted to discover, the possibility of money and advancement.

As the days of his leave ticked away, Ran became increasingly obsessed with Testra, eating at the place three or sometimes four times a day, his blue eyes appealing to her to show some mercy.

Testra would merely smile; the fine, graceful lines of her hide tantalizingly revealed by the cut of her clothes.

On the last night of his leave, Ran had lain in his room, determined not to embarrass himself any further. He had to admit that, for once, his charms had failed him.

Then there had been a light knock at the door. He opened it to reveal Testra, grinning broadly, dressed in a splendid, plain peasant garment, a jug of fruit wine in her claw.

She'd pushed past him, slipped out of her clothes, into the bed and blown out the candle in one fluid movement.

From then on they kept in touch constantly. He took her to Porsim, which she had never seen, delighting in the naïvity of her awed reaction. He helped to pay for the repairs for her father's business and, on subsequent leave, enjoyed eating there all the more, knowing that it was mostly down to him that the place looked so inviting and whole once again.

Ran could see Testra now if he closed his weary eyes.

78

Feel his lids, heavy, heavy, sealing shut, cutting off the pain of reality. Testra laughing until her hide shook. Wine spilling from her wide, beautiful snout.

But then the other image would come to mind no matter how much he screwed up his eyes and wept. Him running down the streets of Jurrula as the Cutch bombs smashed into the dusty ground around him. The stench of smoke and blood. Children crying out until they were hoarse. And Testra lying in the shell hole with her chest blown open, her eyes wide with terror. Screaming, screaming, screaming.

Ran opened his eyes and slammed his fist into the mirror. The shattered glass split his reflection into a dozen fragments, each one twitching as if it now possessed a mad, solitary life of its own.

He had struggled to maintain his composure. Discipline had to be maintained. He could never show weakness in front of the men.

The tics had begun under his right eye, slowly, then growing, week by week, until his whole face was a mass of writhing muscles.

Sometimes he wanted to plough his claws into his own flesh. Anything, anything to stop the infernal, incessant movement in his face.

That had also been the day when he really began to believe in the Cause. To wipe those bastard Cutch from the face of Betrushia. For the Greater Glory. And for revenge.

Grek marched down the dingy corridors, inordinately pleased with himself. He had taken a firm grasp of the situation and appointed personnel to deal with it.

The earthquakes and meteorite showers were something else entirely but a deep, almost instinctual feeling told him that the beast called the Doctor might be able to shed some light on things. If it really did have something to do with the Faith then old Thoss from the Temple might be the man to consult but for now –

Grek stopped dead at the sight of the conference room door, suspiciously ajar. He pushed at it with a clawed finger and it creaked open.

Bernice looked up sheepishly as Grek was revealed in the doorway.

'Ah,' she said. 'Hello.'

'Where is he?' hissed Grek.

'Who?'

Grek strode into the room, peering into the shadowed corners, all his good humour evaporated.

'Don't play games, beast,' he spat, upturning a chair with a sweep of his arm. 'I am Commander Grek. I ordered him to stay here. He may be . . . needed.'

Bernice sat down on the edge of the table, defeated. 'To be honest, he hasn't gone far. We're . . . we were trying to find a way out. We've had rather enough of your planet.'

Grek looked up. 'You were trying to escape?'

'Prisoner of war's prerogative, isn't it?' said Bernice, half smiling.

Grek put his claws behind his back and breathed in deeply.

'Your . . . Doctor knows a good deal more than he's saying.' He gazed curiously at Bernice's smooth face, like a puzzled zoologist.

'He'll be returning for you, no doubt?'

'I sincerely hope so.'

'Good. Good.'

Grek plugged in a speecher to the mass of wires hanging from the wall. He powered up the device with a few turns of the brass handle.

'This is Grek. Get me Portrone Liso.'

He clapped the speecher to his chest like a telephonist asking a caller to hold. 'I'm arranging a little trip for you.'

'What?' Bernice was immediately worried.

Grek put the speecher to his snout. 'Liso? Yes. Hold on a moment.'

He turned back to Bernice and contorted his face into

80

what she took to be a smile. 'I have to ensure that the Doctor co-operates.'

He put one half of the instrument to his ear and spoke confidently into the other: 'Liso. I have a surprise for you.'

'It's always nice to be expected,' said the Doctor, doffing his hat. 'Have you baked me a cake?'

The old reptile shuffled out of the shadows, a garland of pale blue flowers in his claws. He advanced towards a monolithic structure at the end of the chamber, but it was so shrouded in darkness that the Doctor was unable to make it out.

'I'm Thoss, by the way,' confided the old creature in a high, piping voice, chomping at his lower lip. He began to relume a host of yellow candles.

The Doctor rushed to his aid. 'May I help?'

'No,' said Thoss evenly. 'Only an anointed representative of the Temple can do these things. I imagine you are not anointed?'

'Not to my knowledge. I'm the Doctor. Tell me . . .' He gazed about the darkened room and up at the monolith as it was revealed by increasing candle-light. 'Tell me how you knew I was coming.'

Thoss let out a little squeal of amusement. 'Don't flatter yourself. It wasn't you I expected but one like you.' He bent down to light a particularly stubborn candle.

'A stranger?'

'In a way. A mammal certainly. It is spoken of in the Faith.'

The Doctor pulled a face. 'Commander Grek doesn't know his scriptures then. He found me very surprising.'

'It is a forbidden text,' muttered Thoss, 'known only to the Inner Temple. Not for the likes of the military.'

The Doctor put his hands behind his back. 'I see.'

The monolith was revealed now in all its glory, standing perhaps nine or ten feet tall, its surface encrusted with precious stones.

'Some kind of shrine?' offered the Doctor.

Thoss turned to him slowly, examining the Doctor with his cool blue eyes. 'It is a monument to God. A symbol of the Faith. Don't you know anything?'

'I'm new,' said the Doctor. 'Tell me more about the Faith.'

'Of course,' said Thoss. 'You must have more primitive beliefs.' He narrowed his eyes. 'If you are who you claim to be.'

'I don't claim to be anyone.'

Thoss rubbed his palms together in contemplative fashion, making a sound like rustling leaves. 'The Faith is central to the Ismetch race. It is the foundation of all systems of justice and truth. One God and one chosen people.'

'And no room for anything else?'

'Blasphemy even to think it. That's why the Cutch can't be allowed to spread their heinous beliefs over the world.'

The Doctor cocked his head to one side, the candle-light turning his eyes into shadowed hollows. 'The Cutch don't believe as you do?'

'They have a number of strange little gods,' said Thoss with a dismissive wave of his claw. 'Gods for this. Gods for that. They are a most curious people. I find them intriguing.'

The Doctor smiled humourlessly. 'But not intriguing enough to let them survive?'

Thoss turned his gaze to the little stranger and, for the first time, there was a trace of steel in his voice.

'A war has been fought, Doctor. A war the Ismetch have won. We are not barbarians. If the Cutch wish to survive they must adapt to our practices.'

The Doctor rubbed his eyes tiredly. 'Well, conversion of heathens aside, Thoss, you may have other problems. When I arrived here, I noticed a few anomalies in your planet's readings . . .'

' "When the earth turns over in its sleep and the rain turns to stone",' interrupted Thoss, his voice dropping to a whisper. ' "Then the Keth shall come again. And come. And come".'

The Doctor's eyes brightened. 'The Keth?'

Thoss straightened up as much as his crooked old back would allow. 'All this was foreseen thousands of years ago, Doctor. The texts speak of it. The war. The round engines filling the air. The end of all things.'

'That's what I wanted to tell you,' said the Doctor gravely. 'You may not be far wrong.'

Bernice Summerfield felt sick. A prickling sensation stole over her scalp as she gazed at the sight before her with ill-disguised terror.

'You're not getting me up in that thing,' she breathed hoarsely.

The young soldier appointed to deal with her merely grunted and dragged her further into the clearing.

An area about half a mile in diameter had been cleared, the horse-tail trees and fecund outcrops of giant-leaved plants cropped or incinerated.

In the centre of the scorched earth stood the dirigible, three bladder-like balloons strung together under a kind of coppery mesh. A fragile-looking gondola was slung underneath.

As Bernice advanced gingerly towards it, the dirigible began to hover upwards, the motion of its brass propellers flattening the new shoots of the already recovering jungle.

The soldier pointed to the gondola with his claw. 'Inside.'

Reluctantly, Bernice clambered through a hatchway into the gondola. It was about the size of her old room back at college, with panels of unreassuringly crude instrumentation taking up most of the space. She thought briefly of the mechanical splendour of the Silurian airships and decided that technology, no matter how alien, always made her feel more secure.

As if to confirm her fears, the dirigible gave a sudden

lurch, slightly unbalancing the five other Ismetch who were fussing at the controls.

Only one stood aloof, his broad back turned defiantly away from her. Liso spoke without turning round.

'I am ordered to return to Porsim, our capital, in order to find out what is going on there. I am ordered to take you along with me to ensure the co-operation of the animal known as "Doctor" and because, I am led to believe, you may prove useful.'

He swung round suddenly. Bernice took an involuntary step backwards, overwhelmed by his presence and the stench of his reptilian body.

'However, I have voiced my disapproval regarding both these orders and if you step out of line, just once, I shall have no compunction in throwing you off this ship. Do I make myself clear?'

Bernice thought of a smart retort. It was bubbling to her lips even as she thought better of it and nodded, slowly and obsequiously.

Liso scowled. 'I do not understand the gesture.'

'Yes,' whispered Bernice.

Liso turned back. 'Helmsman. Take us up.'

The gondola rocked again as the dirigible's engines roared into full life.

Bernice slid silently into a chair, looking glumly out of the window at the vista of endless green. The ship juddered into the air.

Darkness was bleeding into the sky and she noticed, for the first time, a suggestion of the fabulous ring system. Broad bands of gold, like a gilded spectrum, were peeking through the indigo sky. It was certainly impressive, she conceded, but had it really been worth all this trouble? Wistfully, she wondered whether the Doctor even knew she was gone.

The woman sank to her knees in supplication and then stretched out fully on the freezing stone floor.

The cathedral was immense, its walls, carved from

blocks of pale stone, were hung with faded tapestries. Two sets of double doors flanked a central aisle at the head of which, at the very top of a flight of steps, stood a plain wooden throne. Another smaller door was inset in the opposite wall. Sunlight gushed through the cathedral windows.

Next to the woman, a naked man lay curled in a ball, sobbing inconsolably. She noticed the livid weals on his skin and pressure sores on his knees glinting red and wet. Appeals for forgiveness tumbled insanely from his cracked lips.

She thought for a moment of helping him, but such actions belonged to the old life. Now he would have to fend for himself, trust in the Chapter and hope that his sins would be absolved. She sat up straight and pressed her hands together, intoning the words she had been taught in a low, tremulous whisper.

The man next to her rolled over onto his side, groaning. His back was a mass of suppurating cuts. In one hand he clutched a three-pronged whip, its tentacle-like thongs terminating in tiny metal ball-bearings. Without hesitation, he began to move off down the aisle on his knees, the healing sores bursting appallingly. The volume of his chanting rose in correlation to the increasing pain.

After every third or fourth word he brought the whip down onto his bleeding back, flagellating the livid flesh.

The woman quailed at the sight but then remembered that such feelings should now be beyond her. If her faith wasn't strong enough then perhaps she might have to undergo such a ritual.

For now, though, she squeezed her eyes shut and prayed with all the fervour she could muster. If the Magna were to discover her weakness –

light – light and heat – trees splintering – soil burning – melting – turning to glass – houses flaring – bursting – men crying – screaming – lungs hurting with effort and smoke – smoke – then running – running – water bubbling – steaming – darkness closing over it – girl falling – begging

– help me! – help me! – heat – light and heat – washing over – fire – the fire – oh god the fire! –

The woman blinked slowly in the dazzling sunlight of the cathedral. She was breathing quickly, frightened and puzzled by the vision which had risen, unbidden, into her mind. She looked about. The flagellant was lying in a pool of blood, the whip limp in his exhausted arm. There was a slack, contented, almost post-coital smile on his face.

The woman stood up, smoothing down her hessian robe. In the recessed shadows she caught a glimpse of something purple. But the Chapterman had not seen her. Her vision had not betrayed her. She was safe. For now.

The Doctor looked up at the shrine with renewed interest. Candlelight glinted off the jewels studding its surface. He frowned, stepped down from the dais and began to pat his pockets. His waistcoat revealed the square of crumpled paper which Grek had thrown into the corner of the conference room.

Old Thoss was sitting in the corner, his white-spined head nodding up and down as he drifted in and out of sleep.

What had he said? All this was foretold? The war, the earthquakes, even the meteorite showers. And perhaps something else. The Doctor smoothed out the paper in his hand.

'What have you got there?' asked Thoss, glancing over.

The Doctor passed the paper to the old man who squinted his bulbous blue eyes in concentration. The dim light revealed the three words of the Pelaradator's last message.

KETH   KETH   KETH

7

Pale Horseman

The small gondola of the Ismetch dirigible was studded with tiny windows, like square portholes, the glass in them curiously thick and crude. Bernice rubbed at the nearest with the sleeve of her coat.

It was badly steamed-up and the endless vista of rain-forest below was distorted by the glass, so that huge trees seemed to be bent inwards as though skulking in fear.

The dirigibles slid past with only the thrum of their engines to break the oppressive silence.

Ignored for the moment, Bernice strained to look at the other two ships hanging in the air behind Liso's craft. She rubbed the back of her neck and blew air out of her cheeks, aware of the tense and unpleasant atmosphere in the gondola, as though a furious argument was about to erupt.

The crew of five remained at their posts as the dirigible fleet crawled towards the city of Porsim. Liso's helmsman had said they were making good progress but Bernice found it difficult to see any difference. Whenever she looked out, the jungle seemed the same. Only the shadows of the three ships on the tree-tops appeared to move.

Liso was looking out of the gondola's bow, his monocular gaze darting back and forth as though desperate to detect any change, any sign of enemy intrusion.

In spite of her fear, Bernice felt sorry for the Portrone. All kinds of dreadful thoughts must be passing through his mind. The fate of his family, if he had any. And the fate of the place he knew and loved so well.

'What do you expect to find in Porsim?' blurted Bernice, almost as though the words had forced themselves out of her.

As before, Liso's broad back remained turned towards her.

'Portrone,' said Bernice with a weary sigh, 'I realize I'm a burden to you but . . .'

'I did not give you leave to speak, beast,' hissed Liso.

Bernice ruffled her dark hair and set her jaw angrily. Enough was enough.

'If you could just accept me for what I am and treat me with a little respect . . .'

'*Respect?*'

Liso swivelled his head round, his eye bulging in fury. 'How do I know you're not in league with the Cutch? Or that you don't have some filthy mammal interest in this situation? Maybe I'll find Porsim overrun with an invading army all like you.'

Bernice walked boldly towards him. 'Not very likely, though, is it?'

Liso said nothing.

Bernice thought for a long moment as the glare of green from the jungle below reflected off her sweating skin.

'I'd honestly like to help you, Portrone. I'm no good to anyone stuck in the corner. If there's anything I can do . . .'

Liso stroked his socket, his long nails scraping on the exposed bone. 'I told you I'd have you put off the ship –'

'Well, why don't you, then?' blazed Bernice. 'If you're so grand and clever. Why don't you?'

Liso turned to her with an interested eye.

This was it, thought Bernice. The moment when he realized that B. Summerfield gave as good as she got. That no talking lizard could play these kind of status games with her and expect to . . .

Liso gave a little jerk of the head and Bernice found herself being lifted up by two of the crew. They carried her bodily towards the stern of the gondola. One of them held her by the throat whilst the other slid open the largest window at the stern.

The dirigible's engines roared deafeningly and freezing air streamed into the gondola, sending papers and loose mapping instruments slapping against the far wall. Bernice felt her heart leap into her mouth.

The guards clutched at her wrists and began to bundle her towards the window. She thrust out her legs and rammed them under the brass frame, gulping at the pressure of the soldiers' claws around her throat.

All she could see was green. A great carpet of green, hundreds of feet below, swaying in the downdraught from the Ismetch vessel.

The corridor was long, narrow and gloomy, its wooden walls stained a strange dark crimson as though through long exposure to blood. The vaulted roof was heavy with cobwebs.

The woman was walking slowly along it on her way back to her cell when a pattering of feet made her turn round.

Out of the darkness stepped a tall man with a large face and bright, rather appealing eyes. His features were fixed in a permanent, beatific smile and he was swathed from head to foot in silk robes, which glinted the purple of arterial blood in the half-light of the corridor. His shaven head, topped by a purple skull-cap, was already showing signs of re-growth.

The woman bowed low, touching her temples in a familiar gesture of supplication.

'Chapterman Jones,' she breathed nervously. 'How may I serve?'

The Chapterman's smile did not falter. 'Not me, child. You are required by Parva De Hooch. He wishes to speak to you.'

The woman's eyes widened. 'Parva De Hooch? Am I to be punished for something?'

'That is not for me to say, alas. But be comforted that if punishment ensues it will be a good and just punishment with much letting of fluids in the name of the Chapter.'

The woman's face seemed troubled. 'Yes,' she said quietly.

'In peace,' murmured Jones, turning and melting back into the shadows.

'In peace,' replied the woman in a small, scared whisper.

More than anything, she wanted to go back to her room to get some rest. The gruelling round of prayers and fasting she had recently endured had left her exhausted. But exhaustion and misery were part of the joy she had found in the Chapter and, most importantly, the Parva was never to be disobeyed. She must go and see him at once.

Her sandalled feet scraped over the stone-flagged floor as she wound her way through the maze of corridors, their cloistered environs heavy with sickly-sweet incense.

The woman found herself troubled by the vision in the cathedral. The pictures she had seen, the feel of fear, of panic, of all-consuming dread, had been familiar. Yet how could they be?

There had been a time before initiation into the Chapter, but the scholars had told her any remembrance was impossible. The old life was dead. Her soul belonged to Saint Anthony.

The woman stopped before the massive limestone arch of Parva De Hooch's rooms.

The door was imposing, carved from one huge piece of oak with a smaller, metal-banded door set into it. Black marble pillars bordered it on either side. On close inspection, the woman noticed they were packed with fossilized coral, exposed like frozen flowers in the dull black stone.

The small door opened and another Chapterman, whom she had never seen before, lean and intense-looking with acne scars on his shaven head, came out.

'What do you want, child?'

The woman shuffled uneasily, shivering as a draught

from the great empty cloisters fluttered through her robes. 'Parva De Hooch wishes to speak with me.'

'Does he indeed?'

The Chapterman poked his head around the door. There was a brief exchange of words and then he came out again.

'You're right,' he said with some surprise. 'Wait here and he will call you.'

The woman looked about for a chair but, of course, there were none. Comforts of any kind were forbidden. Instead, she rested her weary body against the cold stone arch, feeling the rough surface scraping at her skin.

Although her mind was unfocused and her memory foggy, she knew she had never seen the Parva before, let alone been summoned to meet him. It was almost as extraordinary as meeting Magna Yong himself.

Perhaps, if the Parva favoured her, then this honour too might not be beyond her reach.

She was mentally chiding herself for considering such an eventuality, unworthy as she was, when a high, brittle voice called, 'Come!'

Silently, she stepped through the small door into the room.

Maconsa drank a little more of the sugary liquid. It tasted vile but at least it was warm. He swilled it around inside his snout and cast a glance across the infirmary at Ran.

'Lost it? How?'

Ran was gazing at the ranks of groaning soldiers, thrashing in pain on their filthy mattresses.

'Cleverer than he thought, it seems. Made short work of the lock and disappeared.'

Maconsa laughed. 'And the other one, the ... er ... female?'

Ran rubbed his twitching face. 'Grek's sent her off to Porsim with Liso. He hopes it'll bring the other one to heel.'

'I bet Liso's happy,' chuckled Maconsa.

Ran attempted a smile. 'Meanwhile, I've been detailed to find this Doctor creature before he runs riot.'

He smoothed down the front of his tunic. Maconsa looked at him.

'Something on your mind, Ran?'

Ran sniffed and extended his long tongue, licking his protuberant eyes with its wet, glistening point.

'When Grek refused you permission to speak . . . you know, when Liso nearly got his head blown off?'

'Yes?'

'What was it you wanted to say?'

Maconsa turned stiffly and cleared his throat.

'Ah, well. That's a little difficult, my dear Ran. It's a question of faith, do you see?'

Ran rubbed his scrawny chin. 'You've heard the rumours too, then. How did Grek react?'

'How do you think?'

'I should say he dismissed it out of hand as superstition. That there are more likely explanations than the return of the Keth.'

Maconsa sighed. 'You're exactly right.'

Ran folded his arms. 'And what about you? Are you a superstitious man, Maconsa?'

'I've seen too much recently for me not to be. I don't pretend to know what's happening, Ran. But something is very, very wrong here.'

Ran stood by him now, his twitching gaze flicking over the old surgeon. 'Have you noticed the weather recently?'

Maconsa was momentarily taken aback. 'The weather?'

'Mmm,' mused Ran. 'The rain has taken on a rather petrified feel, wouldn't you say?'

In the gloom of the Ismetch Temple, unaware that he was missed, the Doctor was sitting across from Thoss, his arms folded and his deeply lined face set in a thoughtful frown.

Eventually, he shook the old man's arm and pulled the Pelaradator's message from his gnarled claw.

Thoss lifted up his head and looked into the Doctor's eyes. 'You again. Have you not had enough?'

'Far from it,' said the Doctor. 'Tell me what this means.'

Thoss made a low groan and champed anxiously on his thin black lips. 'You wouldn't want to know.'

'But I do want to know,' insisted the Doctor. 'And if your books speak of people like me living here in the past then I want to know about that as well.'

Thoss struggled out of his chair and crossed to the shrine, caressing it lovingly with a gnarled claw.

'The Keth are the agents of our destruction. The bringers of Armageddon. The – '

'Yes, yes,' muttered the Doctor. 'Every world has a similar legend.'

'Really?' said Thoss. 'How fascinating.'

'What's different,' said the Doctor, 'is that most people's four horsemen of the Apocalypse don't ride into town in person. So . . .'

He put out his hands, palms upwards, pleadingly. 'Tell me about the . . . Keth.'

Thoss stroked his bearded face and made a contemplative sucking sound in his snout. 'They were here in the Time Before.'

'The Time Before what? Before you, you mean?'

Thoss inclined his head. 'Before all things. The Ismetch. The Cutch. All things. They laid waste to the land and everything on it.'

The Doctor clasped his hands between his knees and leant forward in his chair. 'But if they were here before . . . everything . . . how do you know about them? I mean, if they destroyed whatever civilization existed before yours, how do you know about them at all?'

Thoss blinked slowly. 'You know, Doctor, that's a very good question.'

The Doctor sighed. For a fount of all knowledge, Thoss was proving remarkably stupid.

* * *

93

Bernice held her breath as she tottered on the brink of death, air streaming past her face.

This really is becoming intolerable, insisted a voice in her head. Threatened with death twice in two days.

Bernice tried to tell the voice to shut up whilst, at the same time, struggling to think of a way out of her predicament. Her eyelids fluttered in the updraught from the dirigible's propellers and her cheeks flapped slackly as though she were experiencing G-force.

The Ismetch soldiers stood on either side of the brass window-frame and began to force her through it. She lashed out, catching both on their powerful forearms, and attempted to gain purchase on the polished glass, to no avail. Jamming her feet just below the sill, her mouth opening and closing in panic, she struggled desperately to pull herself back inside.

'Sir!'

The helmsman's call cut through the atmosphere in the cabin.

All eyes, including those of Bernice's guards, turned back towards the interior. Liso glanced over and jerked his head.

'All right. That'll do.'

Bernice was dropped to the floor where she sank to her knees, hugging herself in relief. Then she dragged herself into the corner, slapping the firm floor beneath her with grateful hands.

Liso marched to the prow of the gondola and peered out, following the line of the helmsman's outstretched arm. He swallowed anxiously, his larynx bobbing up and down in the skinny column of his leathery throat.

Billowing over the horizon, like the terrible bloom of a funereal flower, hung a vast pall of smoke.

Liso's claws dug into the wooden balustrade.

'Porsim,' he breathed.

The crew were silent for a long while. Liso's eye remained fixed on the image before him.

'Helmsman,' he whispered. 'Best speed.'

94

The helmsman, shocked, mumbled his assent. Liso turned back towards Bernice and stalked towards her. She shied away, having had quite enough for one day, and threw up her arms for protection.

'Is this your doing, animal?' hissed Liso.

He closed a claw around her arm and dragged her to her feet. Bernice cried out in pain.

'That is my home!' spat the Portrone. 'You and your Cutch masters are going to pay for this.'

Bernice shook her head violently. 'It's got nothing to do with me. I swear it. Why won't you listen? I'm just as much in the dark as you are.'

'You deny you know what's happened to Porsim?'

'Of course! How could I know? Surely it . . . it could just be the Cutch blitzing the place. I mean, you are at war.'

Liso seemed to consider this, but then remembered Ran's words. 'The Cutch are on the point of defeat,' he snarled. 'They couldn't possibly muster the firepower to do this.' He gestured towards the plume of black smoke.

'All right! All right!' cried Bernice, thinking desperately. She had to come up with something or she'd be out of that window again in no time.

'Forget about me and the Doctor. And the Cutch. Couldn't it be something else?'

Liso's eye closed in weary anger. 'What?'

'Another power. I mean, just how many people are there on this planet? Another power bloc could've intervened. Even an offworld one.'

'Offworld?' snorted Liso. 'So that's your great theory is it? Aliens? I suppose they come from the fourth planet!'

Bernice frowned. 'Where?'

'That's where our fairy stories say aliens live. The fourth planet in our solar system.'

'You mean Massatoris!' cried Bernice. 'It's practically next door. We came from there to here. There are people there! People like you and . . . well, like me anyway. Honestly. I don't think they have space technology but . . .'

She stopped suddenly and her face fell.

For all his bluster, Liso seemed disturbed by this. 'What is it?'

Bernice sank slowly into her chair.

'We left a friend there. For a rest.'

'So?'

'I've just remembered why the eleventh colony of Massatoris is so famous.'

'A race memory, then?' urged the Doctor. 'That would explain it.'

'I don't understand you, Doctor,' confessed Thoss. 'I only know what the Faith tells me. There was another people here before ours. A people resembling yours.'

'But what happened to them?' said the Doctor, getting to his feet and pacing about.

'I've told you. The Keth came and wiped them out. And now, just as the Faith foretold, they have come again.'

'So it's the end of the world as you know it?'

Thoss shrugged philosophically. 'It happens. There is no sense in fighting it when it comes.'

The Doctor put a hand on the old man's shoulder. 'That's where you're wrong, my friend. There's always something to fight for.'

'That's easy for you to say,' mumbled Thoss. 'I'm an old man. I'm tired. Things seem a lot less complicated at my age.'

'Believe it or not,' said the Doctor, turning to look at the shrine, 'I know how you feel.'

He craned his neck and gazed at the tall marble structure which extended upwards into the darkened ceiling of the Temple.

'That stone at the top.'

Thoss glanced towards the shrine. 'The Keth-stone, Doctor. Most precious of all.'

'Seems a bit out of place, though. Amongst all those rubies and diamonds.'

'Another secret of the Temple, I'm afraid,' murmured

Thoss. 'When the shrines were built, they all had the Keth-stone set into the top.'

The Doctor peered into the gloom at the dull stone surrounded by glinting gems. 'All the shrines are from the same date then?'

'For the most part. This . . . construction of the army's is built around an old temple. I was brought here to give spiritual succour to the men. But they seem to have little use for religion these days.'

The Doctor put his hands in his pockets and tut-tutted thoughtfully.

'Well, back to the matter in hand, Thoss. I don't know whether it has anything to do with the return of the Keth but your ideas about the end of the world – '

Thoss held up his claw. The Doctor's ears pricked at the unmistakable sound of the outer door opening.

'Someone's coming!' hissed Thoss.

He dashed across the flagstones with surprising speed. 'Quickly, Doctor. In here!'

The Doctor followed him, looking around in puzzlement.

Thoss pressed one of the jewels in the shrine. There was a low grumbling sound.

'In where?' quizzed the Doctor.

Thoss pushed him in the small of the back and the Doctor suddenly saw a flight of stone steps which had appeared in the floor. They wound down beneath the shrine into ever more stygian darkness.

The Doctor shot one last glance at Thoss and then half-stumbled, half-fell down the steps. Thoss pressed the shrine with a skeletal digit and, with the same grinding protest, the floor resealed.

He placed a couple of candlesticks atop the stone just as Ran and two soldiers emerged from the top stairs.

Thoss held up a candle and gave his sweetest smile. 'Why, Portrone, what an unexpected pleasure. It's a long time since we've seen you in Temple.'

97

Ran's face twitched into an embarrassed and faintly guilty smile.

The three dirigibles in the Ismetch fleet finally passed over Porsim, in silence save for the constant drone of the motors. Each of the crew stood at their posts, gazing in horror at the devastation below.

The beautiful city, jewel of their race, was an inferno. Scarcely a structure was not consumed by enormous, wind-fed flames.

Bernice had seen fire-storms before, conflagrations so intense that the very air itself seemed to catch light. But she had never seen anything so terrible as this.

Shattered, blackened skeletons of once-proud houses, vast civic buildings reduced to ashes, trees and parks like miniature bush-fires, erupting into crimson life. Above it all snaked the column of greasy black smoke, like an evil genie revelling in its freedom.

Bernice sat very still in the corner of the ship, aware that any false move on her part might incur the wrath of these justifiably angry people.

She resisted every impulse to say 'sorry' and merely gnawed at her knuckles in agitation. Having remembered about Massatoris, it was imperative that she told the Doctor and they went back for Ace before ... well, before the inevitable happened. She only hoped she had got her dates mixed up or something and that Ace was fit and relaxed and having a good time. If she was wrong ...

Liso scanned the ruins of his birthplace with gloved claws clenched tightly behind his back.

The thick, oily smoke billowed into the dirigibles' path as they hovered over the city. Liso watched until it obscured the view and then turned smartly to his men.

'It may seem appropriate to say a prayer,' he said in clipped tones.

The men began to bow their heads but he continued: 'It may seem appropriate, but it isn't. Our people have been slaughtered. And the best way we can remember

98

them is to forget about the pathetic crutch of religion and avenge them! Cover their blood with the blood of their murderers!'

The back window suddenly shattered and the cabin lurched with a rending screech of metal. Bernice hit the wall with the side of her face and stumbled into the corner.

Liso looked around fearfully, his bony head whipping back and forth.

'Portrone!' gasped the helmsman.

Liso swung round just as the whole room was plunged into shadowed darkness. A deep, resonant throb assailed their senses.

Bernice glanced upwards, her throat drying in fear. Something was out there. Waiting.

Ran stood aloof, arms folded, as his men searched the dank gloom of the Temple.

'You'll forgive the intrusion, I'm sure, Thoss. Commander Grek was most insistent that the beast be captured.'

Thoss held up his claws. 'Don't worry about it. I mean, we can't have dangerous animals running loose in the place, can we?'

Ran smirked. 'Quite.'

The soldiers emerged from the shadows. 'Nothing, sir.'

Ran sighed. 'I thought not. Well, sorry to have troubled you, my friend.'

Something in the corner seemed to catch his eye but he turned back to Thoss almost immediately. 'I shall endeavour to get to Temple before too long.'

Thoss smiled. 'Good, good. No doubt for the victory celebrations, eh Ran?'

Clicking his heels smartly, Ran ascended the stairs, followed closely by his men.

Thoss waited a full minute before reopening the hidden stairwell.

The Doctor was shivering with cold and sitting on the

second step. The others stretched away like rotten piano keys into the darkness.

'That was close,' said Thoss. 'Now, I want you out of there in case they come back.'

The Doctor glanced back down the steps as he clambered out. 'Where do those lead?'

'Never mind that. Out. Out!' Thoss flapped his claws in agitation.

The Doctor tried to calm him down. 'But we need to speak, Thoss.'

'Later, Doctor, later. The Temple is not a thoroughfare. There will be time enough . . .'

'No!' shouted the Doctor gravely. His face was so stern that Thoss was immediately silenced.

'There won't be time,' said the Doctor. 'That's what I've been trying to tell you. The earthquakes are symptomatic of a far greater problem. Those readings I took in my ship together with everything I've observed lead to an inescapable conclusion.'

Thoss's eyes twinkled wetly. 'Well?'

'Your texts are right, Thoss. Betrushia is dying. It may only have a matter of days.'

8

Servus Servorum Dei

Parva de Hooch tapped his pudgy little fingers on the elaborately carved wooden cabinet at his side.

Dressed in purple robes like a swaddled pig, he was a dwarfish man, his nose wide and ugly, his feverishly bright eyes like beads of black blood in the clammy little balloon of his face.

The room around him was large and, by the standards of the seminary, decidedly cheerful. Mahogany niches housed crumbling marble representations of a thin, ascetic-looking man, his white eyes rolled heavenwards, his delicate hands held out before him in supplication.

Sunlight streamed through the open, diamond-patterned windows. Bright, clear bells tolled gently. Somewhere a swallow was trilling.

De Hooch opened the cabinet and felt around in the musty darkness until his childlike hands rested on something. Swiftly he pulled out the object and concealed it beneath the folds of his robes. Then he crossed to his desk and sat down on the padded chair, its seat piled high with cushions in an effort to increase his inconsiderable height.

'Come!' he called, adjusting the skull-cap which was clapped tightly onto his totally bald head.

The woman came in, her head bowed low so that she could not see him. She seemed to be watching her feet, measuring every step as she advanced towards De Hooch.

He regarded her coolly with his pinprick eyes.

'Very well, child. You may look upon me.'

101

The woman lifted her head.

De Hooch noticed the rather cruel line of her mouth and the potential of fire behind her eyes. He rather liked that. She had promise.

'I am honoured indeed, Parva De Hooch,' said the woman in a reverent whisper. 'To be seen by the Magna's second is . . .'

'Yes, well, never mind about that,' muttered De Hooch with some irritation. 'It is not of the Magna that I wish to speak.'

The woman looked at him. 'No, my lord.'

De Hooch twisted around on his cushions, wiping a sheen of sweat from his brick-like forehead. 'I want to talk about you.'

The woman felt a thrill of alarm run through her, mixed with unease and not a little excitement.

De Hooch criss-crossed his fingers. 'I've been watching you, and you have made excellent progress. In the very short time since your initiation you have studied hard, prayed hard and done great service to the Chapter. You are to be congratulated.'

'Thank you, my Lor – '

'Were not the notion of personal gratification completely alien to our way of life,' concluded De Hooch with a fat little smile.

The woman bowed her head. 'Of course.'

De Hooch hopped off his chair and walked towards her. He strutted about on the cold stone floor, hands behind his back, gazing appreciatively at the woman's firm arms and the suggestion of flesh revealed by her rough hessian robes.

'However, in recognition of your progress, I have decided to confer this upon you.'

His fat hand stole to his gown.

For a moment the woman flinched, then her face relaxed as De Hooch produced a small, simple wooden box on a heavy pewter chain.

He pressed it into her hands until she felt the edges digging into her skin.

'It is a holy relic, child. One of the most precious in my collection.'

'My Lord?'

De Hooch slid open the lid. Inside the box was a strange, gnarled black lump.

'It is the sacred, uncorrupted tongue of Saint Anthony,' breathed De Hooch excitedly. 'Wear it with pride and do not disgrace it.'

He ran his hand over her thigh. 'You will serve the Chapter well, my dear. Rest assured.'

The woman shuddered in spite of herself and looked down at her feet, closing the lid of the box in silence.

The dwarf gave a sickly little smile and returned to his chair.

'You may go,' he said loftily, turning his attention to the pile of parchment on the broad desk before him.

The woman bowed low and walked backwards out of the room. The metal-banded door closed after her with a solid clunk.

De Hooch rocked back and forth in his chair, sucking his fat little fingers.

The first suggestion of a gale was rippling through the jungle, setting the trees swaying in agitation. Lightning flashed across the darkening Betrushian sky, illuminating the rain-washed Cutch trench.

Imalgahite looked up briefly and then back down to the tracking device. The beeping signal was now extremely faint.

The thin soldier at his side gave an angry sigh. 'Fading fast, I'm afraid, sir. She must've moved on.'

'Yes,' said Imalgahite slowly, 'but she was in one place long enough for me to be sure. The Ismetch base must be at these co-ordinates.'

He waved a scrap of paper in the soldier's face.

'Get the cartographers onto this and pinpoint the exact location. When we're sure . . .'

The thin soldier's eyes widened in expectation.

'When we're sure,' continued Imalgahite, 'then we go in, in force.'

He began to move off into the trench, calling over his shoulder as he waded through the filthy water.

'If we're going to lose this war we might as well take as many of those bastards with us as we can.'

The thin soldier watched his commander disappear, his face suffused with pride. This was the Cutch way. No armistice for them. Only death or glory. He ducked inside, the precious co-ordinates held tightly in his claw.

The Doctor had climbed half-way up the shrine, his hands splayed wide on the smooth marble facade, his feet placed gracelessly on Thoss's back.

'This is sacrilege, Doctor,' moaned the old man. 'I can't think why I'm letting you do it.'

'Because,' muttered the Doctor, his penknife clasped between his teeth, 'I need to find out everything of relevance here. And this stone,' he gestured upwards with his hand, 'intrigues me.'

'I've told you. It's the Keth-stone. Apart from religious attachments, I can't see what bearing it has on the situation.'

The Doctor sighed, his words indistinct through his teeth.

'I know you're taking all this in your stride, Thoss, but I dare say your fellow countrymen quite fancy surviving this particular holocaust. I'd like to help if I can.'

Thoss looked up, his face pained. 'And where does the stone come into it?'

The Doctor's face rumpled.

'Ah, well, I don't know that just yet. But there's more to this Keth business than meets the eye.'

He gave a final heave, his shoes scraping on the shrine's surface, and found himself perched on a ledge towards the top. The discoloured stone shone dully in the candle-light.

The Doctor poked experimentally at its corners and found the stone yielding easily to his knife.

'The important thing,' he grunted, ramming the blade home, 'is to find out how long this planet's got left to live. And precisely why it's in the state it is.'

Thoss straightened up and rubbed the small of his back, drifting into the shadows with a grimace fixed on his snout.

'It is the Keth,' he said simply.

'Well, more likely an instability in the planet's core. I've seen it happen before. Ah!'

The stone popped out of its housing and into the Doctor's palm. He examined it carefully. It was flat and smooth but had not been cut like the others in the shrine. Strange, scratchy indentations seemed to have been scoured onto it.

The Doctor frowned and then almost fell from his perch as the outer door was flung open and Ran and his men clattered inside.

'Just as I thought,' shouted Ran, scooping up the Doctor's incriminating hat which he had noticed earlier. 'Not only do you flout the orders of Commander Grek, beast, but you vandalize one of the greatest relics of our culture!'

The Doctor shrugged and smiled. 'I don't know what I like but I know a lot about art.'

'What?'

'There's more to this shrine of yours than you think. I need to speak to Grek urgently.'

The Doctor slid down the façade of the shrine and slipped the stone into his waistcoat pocket.

'Take him,' ordered Ran.

The Doctor seemed quite unperturbed. The guards slid their claws around his arms and marched him up the stairs.

Ran regarded Thoss with an amused look, the thin flesh of his eyelids slipping into a spasm.

'Aiding a Cutch spy carries the death penalty, old man.'

'He's not a Cutch spy,' sighed Thoss. 'He is the one

105

whose coming is written of. Now, get out of my way. I must speak to Grek.'

Ran barred his way. 'Suddenly everyone wants to see Grek.'

He smiled and held up a talon theatrically as though struck by an idea. 'I tell you what, Thoss, I'll arrange for you to see the commander just after I've demanded the Doctor's execution. How about that?'

He turned on his heel and clattered up the stairs.

Thoss sank down at the base of the shrine and passed a claw over the concealed entrance to the passageway. He gazed thoughtfully at the stone-flagged floor.

The low, heavy clouds flared with electricity as Grek looked out over the lip of the trench. Thunder boomed in the distance, rolling over the rain-drizzled jungle. He raised dispirited eyes heavenwards.

Priss waded through the trench towards him and attempted a salute.

'Sir.'

Grek shivered. He had become accustomed to bad news but there was something about his junior officer's bearing which disturbed him.

'What is it, Priss?'

Priss was literally wringing his claws, his eyes swivelling in their large sockets. 'Sir, we've lost contact with the dirigible fleet.'

'What?'

'They were almost at Porsim, according to the messages.'

He stuffed a sheaf of thin papers into Grek's claws. The information seemed all the more real and frightening in the terse staccato of the telegraph.

Grek cast his eyes quickly over the papers and looked up. 'And then?'

'They reported the city destroyed, sir. Totally. That was the last we heard.'

Grek let out a low groan and rubbed his crest in naked

despair. 'Has ... has Ran found the Doctor yet?' he managed at last.

'I don't know, sir.'

'And you? What about General Hovv? Have you done anything?'

'Sir, I ...'

Grek's blue eyes flashed. 'What is going on here? Is this a command or a shambles? Do I ...'

He sighed, his sudden fury abating, and placed a kindly claw on Priss's shoulder.

'I'm sorry lad. Just keep me informed. All right?'

Priss saluted and then shrank back as forked lightning lashed the sky.

'Looks like quite a storm coming,' said Grek, lowering his eyes.

The Doctor trotted in front of his captors, hands above his head. Ran smiled grimly as they moved down the corridors.

'Sedition. Espionage. Sabotage. It's all becoming clear, Doctor.'

The Doctor puffed angrily. 'Really, I haven't time for this nonsense. The situation is far more important than your petty little war, Portrone.'

They rounded a corner and approached a ladder which rose up into the roof and out onto the surface. It was Number Seven; now the only way into the maze of Ismetch tunnels.

'We'll have to go this way,' said Ran. 'The earthquake has blocked the other route.'

The Doctor was forced up the rickety ladder, its rungs slimy with moisture.

The ladder emerged through a rough hole in the muddied field. Barbed wire was ranged around it in effort at camouflage.

Ran reached the surface first and scowled as rain lashed down onto his crested head.

'Come on!' he ordered, dragging the Doctor off the ladder.

The guards emerged behind him and all four set off across the blasted landscape towards the main trench and Grek's quarters. Rain sliced through the sticky air. Lightning bleached the sky.

The Doctor kept his head down, his shoes disappearing in the liquid soil. Ran continued to berate him above the howl of the storm.

'I shall have that old fool Thoss shot too. And that female when she returns.'

The Doctor looked over. 'Bernice? When she returns from where?'

Ran smiled, his twitching face it up by flashes of lighting. 'Of course, you can't know. Your friend has gone on a little trip.'

The Doctor looked suddenly furious. He glared gravely and threateningly into Ran's twitching eyes. 'I should get that seen to if I were you.'

'Really, Doctor. I'm above these little jibes of yours.'

The Doctor jumped over a clump of wire. 'Portrone, I'm not here to insult you, but to warn you. Look around. This planet's days are numbered. If your people are to survive then you'll need my help.'

Ran blinked away the rain which coursed down his face. 'A few earthquakes and meteorite showers don't constitute a terminal crisis in my book, Doctor.'

'It's more complicated than you think. Can we talk inside?'

He gazed levelly at Ran. The Portrone considered the Doctor's words and then, shrugging, pointed ahead.

The Doctor bowed his head as the wind howled around them and made to move towards the crescent-shape of the main dug-out.

Suddenly, he was pulled up sharply by Ran's claw on his arm. The two soldiers had also stopped and were listening attentively. Apart from the familiar crump of shells, the Doctor could hear nothing.

108

All at once, Ran pushed him into the mud as a meteorite screeched through the clouds and hammered into the soil, sending a spray of super-heated water into the air.

The Doctor rolled over and curled into a ball, his hands cupped over his head. Ran was craning his neck upwards and throwing anxious glances towards the dug-out.

'Move!' he ordered, grabbing at the Doctor's shirt-sleeve.

The two soldiers scurried anxiously behind, all the time gazing at the rain-heavy clouds.

A hail of meteorites began to crash all around them. One soldier yelled as he was hit on the back of the head. He slid into the mud, blood pouring from his shattered skull.

The Doctor moved to help him but Ran propelled him towards the dug-out.

'Inside! That's an order!'

Reluctantly, the Doctor scrambled towards the ladder.

Meteorites screamed down all over the field, crashing into the bales of barbed wire. The second soldier fell with a cry, clutching his face in agony.

As Ran and the Doctor neared the lip of the dug-out, the familiar face of Priss appeared over the edge. He flapped his claws encouragingly and grabbed at Ran's uniform, almost toppling his superior officer into the trench.

The Doctor grabbed a handful of mud and stuffed it into his pocket, then scurried down the ladder, his shoes slipping on the rotten wood.

'This way,' called Ran. He glanced over his shoulder. 'When it's clear, Priss, see if you can get out and help those men.'

Priss saluted and pulled himself gingerly up the ladder. He peered out onto the surface which was now covered in large, steaming craters.

The dead soldier's body, slumped in the mud, jumped occasionally at the impact of yet another projectile. His injured colleague, blood streaming from a wound in his

109

face, held up his arms in an effort to fend off the deadly rain.

Priss found his breath coming in agitated bursts. He had to get out there and help the soldier, but the bombardment continued unabated. The jungle beyond was blurred by the drizzled atmosphere and the almost solid curtain of fist-sized missiles slamming into the ground. The air was alive with a high-pitched squealing sound.

Priss crawled from the trench, his boots scraping on the duck-boards. He jerked back his arm as a meteorite landed close by, its red-hot surface hissing with steam.

The wounded soldier was sitting upright now, but swaying dazedly, one claw clapped to his wound. The course fabric of his uniform was spattered with dark blood.

Priss looked up at the sky and decided to try for a rescue.

He vaulted onto the surface, boots whacking into the saturated soil. Mud shot up his uniform.

He zig-zagged across the battlefield towards his injured comrade, avoiding the bales of wire and fresh craters alike. He was almost there when the ground before him erupted in a plume of mud as though a Cutch shell had exploded.

Priss was thrown backwards.

He felt his legs ramming into the ground and then a horrible, sickening snap as he went over on his ankle. He screeched in pain and bit savagely into his lower lip, rolling over and over into the mud. Vomit rose in his throat and he clutched at his leg with his claws.

Reeling with shock and pain, Priss looked up and gasped at what he saw.

The wounded soldier and his dead friend were sliding slowly backwards through the soil, carving a muddy trench towards the jungle. All around them billowed a strange, miasmic haze. A sickly yellow, ectoplasmic thread wormed from inside it and slipped over the contours of the soldiers' hides. With a sudden rush, it shot down their snouts and over their eyes.

The wounded Ismetch cried out in alarm and tried to

110

pull himself away. The corpse next to him was flung violently over and rolled into a ball, the dead limbs snapping and constricting as the vile yellow contagion spread over it.

Priss caught the wounded soldier's eyes in hopeless appeal. He tried to move his broken leg but it hung, slack and useless, in the mud.

Whimpering with fear, the wounded man began to claw his way towards the trench but was whipped backwards with tremendous force. The strange gossamer was forming a sticky sheen over his body.

He thrust out a claw towards Priss, trying to form words as his mouth filled with the yellow ooze. He screamed silently as it bit into his flesh.

Priss shuddered and pushed himself backwards as far as his leg would allow. He made out the wounded soldier's claws flying to his agonized face before the substance covered him completely.

In an instant, caught and enveloped in the retracting tentacle, the bodies of the two soldiers vanished into the jungle.

There was a sudden and awful silence.

Priss looked about in agitation. The hail of meteorites had ceased. But what had happened to his comrades? And what was that *thing*?

Priss had heard the rumours. The men were telling old, old stories about the return of the Keth. Could it be that Priss was the first Ismetch to see them? If he could only return to the trench . . .

He tried to stand but his shattered ankle crumpled under him and he fell flat on his pain-wracked face.

Moaning, he attempted to sit up. A sound behind him made him crane his exhausted neck around.

A yellow tendril was returning from the jungle perimeter, spreading a ghostly light over the meteorite-pocked ground.

Priss gave a little yell of terror and hauled himself bodily through the mud, his leg flapping behind him. He

111

clenched his tiny, pearl-like teeth as nausea and agonizing pain coursed through his body.

He looked back and saw that the tendril was only feet away.

Desperately, he told himself to concentrate on the journey to the trench. If he looked back again he would be lost.

He slammed his claws into the soil and pulled himself forward, his tunic filling with mud as he progressed. He could hear himself sobbing with terror and the rustling of the storm-tossed jungle and the horrible, sickening sucking sound of the yellow effervescence as it glowed towards him.

Priss's claws found the lip of the trench and, with a supreme effort, he tumbled over, hitting the stagnant water below with an agonized howl.

He moved his arms and one good leg. There was silence.

Priss sighed heavily in relief. He was safe. The thing had not followed him.

Grunting in pain, he sloshed through the trench towards the ladder and began to drag himself back towards the surface, using his uninjured leg alone to push his body upwards. He had to be sure it had gone.

Priss elbowed his way to the top of the ladder and gazed out over the steaming ground.

Nothing. The ticking of insects was gradually returning and the grooves gouged by the dead soldiers were rapidly filling with murky water.

He was about to turn back and negotiate the ladder a little more carefully when a flash of something in the corner of his eye made him look again.

The whole of the top of the trench was suddenly alive with the yellow ooze, glowing and crackling with terrible life.

Priss let out one long scream as it swamped him and then his body shattered into scaly fragments, dropping down into the trench water like lumps of offal.

Instantly, the mustard-coloured haze drifted down into

the trench and absorbed Priss's remains. Slowly, almost thoughtfully, it retreated into the darkening jungle.

The Doctor and Ran emerged into Grek's quarters but the commander was nowhere to be seen. Ran punched the wall in frustration but the Doctor laid a calming hand on his arm.

'Look,' said the Doctor. 'I want to show you something.'

He fished about in his trouser pocket and pulled out the lump of mud he had scooped from the battlefield. Placing it carefully on the wooden planked floor, he pulled several chunks of rock from out of it.

'Are those some of the meteorites that just came down?' asked Ran, his scaly brow furrowing.

'Yes.'

The Doctor put his hand into his waistcoat pocket and produced a single clean fragment.

'But this stone,' he advanced towards Ran, holding the object between thumb and forefinger, 'this stone I took out of your shrine with my penknife.'

Ran looked worried. 'It's a Keth-stone isn't it? I remember them from when I was a child.'

The Doctor picked up one of the meteorite fragments and held the two stones together. 'Two peas in a pod. They're unquestionably from the same source.'

Ran folded his arms, his twitching face settling a little. 'So my ancestors used meteorites in their shrines. What of it?'

The Doctor pocketed the fragments, feeling like Alice with her two halves of mushroom. 'Why are these prized above all the jewels in the shrine? And why are they called Keth-stones?'

'They must have some old association.' Ran shrugged. 'I don't know. I'm a soldier, not a theologian.'

The Doctor cleared his throat. 'I'll be frank, Ran. I need your help. I have a theory about all this but, like all theories, it has to be put to the test. I also have something to tell you about Betrushia.'

113

'What are you suggesting?'

The Doctor smiled slightly. 'Well, since Bernice has set a precedent, why don't we take a little trip?'

Grek pushed open the heavy door of the Temple and paused before the flight of stone steps. The darkness was overwhelming.

For a moment, he was a child again, in the Temple. The places were sometimes so unfriendly. So cold. So oppressively heavy with the weight of history.

He straightened up, feeling his too-tight boots creaking under him, and closed the door.

Grek had never had much time for religion, save for the odd prayer before battle. Now he had found himself wandering through the winding corridors of the dug-out towards – what? Reassurance?

Moving carefully, he began to negotiate the steps.

The complete darkness concerned him. The Temple was almost always occupied. He could feel damp clinging to the walls as he groped his way downwards. Fragments of rotten stone came away in his claws. He crumbled them between his talons with distaste.

'Thoss?'

His voice carried, echoing, into the darkness. 'Thoss, it's me. Grek.'

He almost fell as the steps abruptly ceased and he advanced across the flagstones.

There was a strange, dull scraping sound and then a sudden flaring of candle-light. Grek jumped in shock as Thoss's face appeared, up-lit by the candle clutched in his claw. The old man looked distracted, perhaps frightened.

Grek frowned. 'Thoss? What is it? What's the matter?'

The old man's cracked black lips were trembling. He watched as his candle flame flickered and died.

Then he opened his mouth and his sepulchral voice whispered through the blackness.

'*Old* things. *Moving.*'

9

Infernal Machines

High above the burning remains of Porsim, the fleet of Ismetch dirigibles struggled to stay airborne. An incredible force pressed down from the darkness outside, growing ever stronger as the three craft began their unwilling descent.

Liso's crew had begun to panic as the walls of the gondola vibrated and a pounding, throbbing sound rose out of nowhere. It increased steadily to an unbearable volume, sending the instruments haywire.

The helmsman, a thread of spittle hanging from his snout, and eyes wide with terror, suddenly abandoned his post and careered across the rocking gondola.

In an instant, Liso's pistol was in his claw. 'Get back! Get back, mister!'

Whimpering with fear, the helmsman staggered reluctantly back to the wheel.

There was a roar of power from beyond the skin of the dirigible and the whole cabin was plunged into impenetrable darkness.

Bernice pulled herself upwards and felt the side of her face where she had connected with the wall. She winced, knowing it had bruised badly but, for the moment, she was more concerned with whatever was outside. Even in the pitch black, it was obvious that their nemesis was incalculably massive.

The heavy glass of the gondola windows began to rattle in unison as the throbbing sound rose in waves.

Liso reholstered his gun and ran to the bow, craning his neck in an effort to see above and below. The fiery light from the burning city reflected off the banks of machinery and the scared faces of the crew.

'What is it, sir?' asked one of the crew, his claws flexing in agitation.

Liso said nothing but bolted towards the helmsman. 'Take us back. We're too close to whatever it is to see.'

The helmsman obeyed, spun the wheel, and the dirigible began to turn.

'In all seriousness,' said Bernice, cradling her cheek, 'do you have any lifeboats?'

Liso ignored her and passed a claw over his weary face. Droplets of sticky sweat were collecting in his empty eye-socket.

The ship pulled back and around. Bernice crossed to the windows and pressed her face to the glass, trying to make out something in the shadowed darkness. Under the blanket of night, Porsim blazed spectacularly, fire washing over the disintegrating architecture of the once-proud city.

She glanced quickly over her shoulder, just able to see Liso standing to attention, his claws behind his back, shadows flickering over his face.

The cabin lurched again as though buffeted by a hurricane.

'This is nothing to do with me,' said Bernice at last.

Liso regarded her with his eye and bit into his thin black lips. 'No. I don't believe it is.'

'What're we going to do?'

Liso stroked his socket in his familiar way. 'If we can get sufficiently far away to see – '

'But it's following us!' she cried. 'Whatever it is. Don't you have any weapons? Or was this purely a pleasure cruise?'

The helmsman swung round, peering into the darkness. 'It's ... er, she's right, sir. It's shadowing us. As soon as

116

we move back it seems to alter its position. I could bring the starboard guns to bear.'

'No,' said Liso flatly. 'It's pointless unless we know what we're firing at.'

Bernice stiffened suddenly. 'What's that? Can you – '

There was a tangible change in the atmosphere.

'It's getting hotter,' said the helmsman.

Liso looked about, his crest bathed in glutinous sweat. 'The fire from Porsim, that's all. Bound to affect us.'

'No,' said Bernice in a frightened whisper. 'Look.'

Outside the window, a strange, ghostly light was refracting off the rattling glass like a torch beam. In an instant, the glass fragmented and the beams of light shot through, prodding at every available surface.

The helmsman threw a terrified look at his commander. Liso looked round wildly and then bellowed, 'Take us down! Quick, man!'

The cabin was suddenly alive with shouted orders as the crew surged around the gondola.

'No good, sir. It's forcing us down. We'll crash before we can make landfall.'

Liso clenched his claws together, his gloves creaking. With a hiss of anger, he spat out his next order: 'Very well. You know what you must do.'

The crew stood suddenly to attention at their posts and saluted.

'Try and get to ground level,' said Liso with regret. 'Good luck.'

'For the Greater Glory!' chorused the crew. Liso saluted and walked swiftly to the rear of the cabin.

'Hang on!' shouted Bernice. 'Where're you going?'

Liso ignored her and opened up the hatchway which led into the heart of the balloon.

Bernice looked at the stoic faces of the crew, illuminated red by the fires of Porsim below.

'There's a distinct whiff of martyrdom in the air,' she muttered to herself. 'I think I'll stick with the winning side.'

117

Without further hesitation, she dashed after the one-eyed Portrone, squeezing herself through the hatch and entering a gangplanked area of enormous size. In the darkness, she could just see the gas-filled balloons which held the ship aloft glinting dully beneath a fine mesh of copper, similar to that which covered the exterior skin of the vessel. Four catwalks spread through the chamber towards the ceiling.

Bernice squinted and gave a little cry of satisfaction. Perched on one of the catwalks was Liso.

Another hatchway was fixed into the outer skin of the dirigible. As he threw it open, wind howled through the ship and the tremendous roaring of their unknown assailant blocked out all other sound.

Liso swung his legs through the hatch and began to clamber outside.

Bernice raced after him through the darkness, tottering over the narrow catwalks, the deadly bags of gas only a few feet below. She clambered hand over hand to the hatchway.

'Hang on!' she called. 'I'm coming with you!'

Liso looked back and almost smiled. 'I'm sorry, beast. I must return to my command. The men can take their chances. It is the received wisdom that officers must survive.'

Bernice staggered towards him, her hands gripping the hatchway determinedly. 'But we don't know what's happening.'

Liso looked out into empty air, at the fire raging below and, finally revealed, at an impossibly vast black ship, hovering half a mile above them.

'Don't we?' he said in an awed whisper.

Bernice swallowed hard.

The ship was phenomenally sized, its sleek structure mottled with strange spiny protuberances. Massive engines took up most of the stern but the bow was shaped into a kind of clawed hollow like a crab's pincer. The

118

smoke-filled night air was swirling like diabolical sulphur all around it.

Bernice looked down out of the hatchway. Another dirigible was directly below them. The third, above and to the right.

'How do we get off this thing?' she cried above the roar of the engines.

Liso pulled himself to his feet and swung out of the ship by holding the hatchway with his claw. He pointed upwards.

Bernice poked her head out, the wind screaming around her, and gazed over the copper mesh to the broad, flat back of the dirigible. Attached to the outer skin was a small, compact machine like a gyrocopter. Its brass rotor blades and wooden, concave hull did not inspire much confidence in her.

'Ah,' she said, the wind flapping through her hair. 'Lifeboat.'

'Come on then, if you're coming,' said Liso, grasping her hand. Bernice was surprised at its warmth.

They struggled out of the hatchway onto the surface of the vessel, clinging onto the copper mesh until it bit into their hands. Climbing upwards was surprisingly easy and Bernice was soon able to flop onto the back of the dirigible and catch her breath.

The copter was tantalizingly near. Bernice rose to her knees and could see Liso staggering over the mesh towards the small craft. Two parallel brass rails covered the whole of the larger ship's spine, presumably acting as some kind of runway for the escape vehicle.

Bernice managed to stand and cast a fearful look upwards, but the ship was all but invisible now in the night sky. The reflected flames of Porsim merely hinted at the ship's enormity. It was like glimpsing the base of a huge, rusty storm-cloud, she thought.

Liso was already climbing into the copter. Bernice was about to follow when a change in the pitch of the relentless throbbing made her turn her head.

119

The vast black ship was bearing down on them at incredible speed. Bernice felt irresistible pressure on her head and back as she was pushed downwards by the approaching ship. She scrabbled at the collar of Liso's tunic and pulled him bodily from the copter. 'Look out!'

They tumbled back against the mesh and rolled almost to the edge of the dirigible, just as the pincer of the black ship scraped over the surface of the balloon.

There was an immediate rush of escaping gas. Bernice stumbled away from the copter, shielding her mouth with the sleeve of her coat.

The world dropped like a stone. Her stomach lurched and she fell to her knees, gripping the copper wire with shaking hands.

Senses reeling wildly, Bernice slipped her arms through the mesh and clung on for dear life as the dirigible began to fall.

'Liso?' she bellowed, looking round.

He had rolled to the edge of the balloon's broad, flat back and was hanging on by one arm, seemingly unconscious.

Bernice looked back immediately towards the copter. The impact of the great black ship, still hovering massively above them, had crushed the escape vehicle. With upsetting speed, it was easing free of its moorings.

Bernice sighed hugely as their only means of escape flopped out of its housing and plummeted towards the ground in a mass of twisted metal. She watched it explode as it hit the city below, one more fire in the inferno which had been Porsim.

'I thought I'd find you here,' said Maconsa as he clomped down the temple stairs.

Grek was sitting at the base of the shrine, a circle of candles around him giving fitful illumination. Thoss was asleep at his side.

Grek grimaced. 'Don't imagine I'm taking refuge in religion, Maconsa,' he said defensively. 'I was just ...'

He faltered, looking across at the old man's sleeping form.

'What's the matter with him?' asked Maconsa.

'I don't know. If I didn't know better I'd say it was shock. But it seems deeper. Almost as if he were possessed.'

Maconsa allowed himself a weary smile. 'Possessed? And I thought you weren't getting religious.'

Grek stood up decisively. 'Yes, well I've been thinking. Maybe Liso was right. I *have* let things slip.'

He straightened his tunic and cleared his throat. 'It all stops right now. I'm taking a firm grip of the situation. How's the infirmary?'

'Oh, the infirmary's fine, Grek. The Cutch shelling has stopped completely. The rest of the men are holed up in their quarters.'

'Yes. On my orders. We're going to sit tight until we know what's going on.'

Maconsa rubbed his brow. 'All the men except for Liso and his crew, obviously, with whom we have lost contact . . .'

'Maconsa . . .'

'General Hovv and the whole eighteenth brigade. Ran and that Doctor creature whom I've just seen running loose . . .'

'Maconsa, I'm sick of your sniping!' barked Grek. 'If you're not happy with my command then just tell me straight. And if you can think of any better ideas then I am extremely open to suggestions!'

Maconsa fell silent but then lowered his head and mumbled. 'And Priss of course.'

Grek looked up, frightened. 'Priss?'

Maconsa felt in his pocket and pulled out Priss's metal name-tag. He threw it at Grek. 'This was found in the trench.'

Grek sank down on his knees. 'Oh God.'

'If you'd listened to me . . .'

Grek was suddenly furious. 'What? What would I have

done? How do you suggest we fight this ... whatever it
is? By praying?'

Maconsa sat down next to Grek. 'The first thing we
have to do is admit we're in trouble. Pool our resources.
Forget about the Cutch and the war. There's something
else out there.'

He put his head in his claws. 'I think the Faith is right,
Grek. The Keth have returned. And if we're going to save
ourselves we'd better start thinking fast.'

'Too late. Far too late,' said Thoss, suddenly, blinking
his eyes. His lined face was filled with messianic fervour.
'Betrushia is finished.'

The Doctor and Ran had made their way out of the dug-
out and were carefully threading their way towards the
jungle. The night air was heavy with electricity and
the strange, fevered cries of the jungle's mammalian
inhabitants.

The Doctor was gazing with no little excitement at the
glorious display the rings made in the indigo sky.

'Breathtaking,' he concluded.

Ran did not look up. 'You get used to them,' he said.
'Now, Doctor, you said you needed my help. How?'

The Doctor shivered in the night air, missing his hat
and coat. 'Ah ... yes. Can you lead me back to where I
was found? The place where your comrades were going
to roast me. It was a kind of clearing.'

Ran frowned and then his twitching face cleared. 'Yes,
I know where you mean, I have a ... I mean ...'

He faltered momentarily and then said decisively, 'I
know where you mean. Why do you want to go back?'

The Doctor smiled enigmatically. 'I have some ... er ...
equipment there. I need to do some tests on those
meteorites.'

'Very well.'

The Portrone led the way into the jungle, starlight
making his uniform glow dully.

The thick jungle loomed oppressively around them, the

122

sharp electric tang in the air, which the Doctor could only attribute to the planet's numbered days, blending with the heady fragrances of a hundred different flowers. He gazed around sadly as they made their way through the dense foliage.

'Here we are, Doctor.'

They had reached the clearing at last. The Doctor trotted up to the TARDIS and gave his ship an affectionate pat. 'Hello, old thing.'

Ran was looking at the tall blue box suspiciously, his features glittering in the reflected light of the rings.

'This is where you keep your equipment?'

The Doctor produced his key. 'Well, yes and no. Strictly speaking, this *is* my equipment.'

He opened the TARDIS doors and went inside. In an instant he popped his head back around the door. 'Coming?'

Ran walked slowly towards the strange box. The Doctor's voice carried back through the still night air: 'Wipe your feet.'

Ran disappeared inside and the door closed behind him. For a man who had become blasé about the wonders of his own world, he was about to get a very big surprise.

Grek and Maconsa marched swiftly through the corridors towards the conference room, their impassive faces now bright, now dark, in the irregular light of the gas jets. In one claw, Grek held Priss's bloodied name badge. Almost knocking the damaged door off its hinges, he powered into the room.

'How many troops do we have, Maconsa?' he asked.

The old surgeon, somewhat revived by Grek's newly confident mood, cleared his throat. But the news was not good.

'Hard to say, sir. We lost a good few in the last meteorite shower and with the casualties already in the infirmary – '

'I want answers, Maconsa. How many can we get into the trenches?'

123

Maconsa shrugged. 'Walking wounded, around twenty I suppose. And about thirty five on active service.'

Grek's scalp contracted as an affirmation.

'All right. I want you to get as many as you can in a fit condition to fight. And before you ask, I don't know what they'll be fighting. I just want them to be ready.'

Maconsa smiled. This was the Grek he knew and remembered before the weary inertia of war had eroded his soul. He saluted crisply. 'Right away, sir.'

Grek dismissed him with a gesture. Maconsa left the conference room, feeling a new vigour flooding through him. He rounded the corner and, with surprising ease, clambered up the rickety wooden ladder of Number Seven onto the surface.

It was completely dark now and the rings blazed spectacularly in the sky like forks of frozen lightning. Maconsa could feel a strange, disquieting rumble very deep in his bones. Thoss's doom-laden prophecy refused to go away. The old man had not elaborated, merely repeating over and over that the planet was dying.

Well, be that as it may, Maconsa was first and foremost a soldier. And bold recognizable military thinking was the greatest solace he knew. If he could organize the wounded into an efficient fighting team then at least he would feel he was contributing something.

He ploughed through the muddied ground which was still steaming from the meteorite impacts. Reaching the lip of the trench he swung himself over and began to descend. His face was set with a kind of fiery intensity. Perhaps this terrible war might prove to have meant something after all.

Maconsa was on the fourth rung of the ladder, his face already turned towards the trench, when a bullet spat out of the darkness and punched a big black hole through his leathery throat.

He stood very still for a long moment, blood fountaining from his neck, and then toppled forwards into the trench, vanishing into the filthy brown water.

124

His greatcoat blossomed like a huge lily.

At once, the night was filled with a high, almost hysterical battle-cry as Imalgahite's Cutch forces screamed out of the jungle, their rifles high above their heads.

On his way towards the ladder hole, Grek heard them coming and was almost knocked off his feet by a knot of soldiers running along the tunnels towards the surface.

'What's . . .?' he began.

'Cutch! Cutch!' someone screeched distantly.

Grek felt faint and sick and strangely exhilarated all together.

'Get out there!' he bellowed.

The Ismetch troops sprinted for the ladder.

The air was suddenly filled with gunfire, echoing terrifyingly from every corner of the dug-out.

Grek knew there could be men in the trenches by now, but if the Cutch forces were sufficiently sized then the Ismetch would soon be overwhelmed.

He dashed back to the conference room and skidded towards the speecher. Snatching it up, he plugged in the instrument and barked hoarsely into the receiver: 'Now hear this! We are under attack. All units to surface immediately!'

He thought briefly of adding some words of personal encouragement but realized there simply wasn't time.

Throwing down the speecher, he pulled his pistol from its holster. His crested head shone with sweat in the glow of the gaslight.

If Maconsa had reached the infirmary and managed to galvanize some of the wounded then they might just have a chance. He cursed his own inactivity. The dense jungle terrain had kept the location of the dug-out secret for so long he had become complacent. An attack was inevitable, he supposed, but why now? Why now when there was so much more at stake?

Grek pelted out of the room and back into the gloom of the tunnels. With Priss and Liso gone, both probably dead, his only remaining officers were Maconsa and Ran.

He breathed deeply. It was up to him now. Finally, all up to him. This was the decisive moment of his command.

He reached the ladder to the surface and immediately threw himself into a corner as a pair of unfamiliar booted legs descended into the dug-out. Two Cutch soldiers dropped warily into the tunnels, waving their rifles about uncertainly. They advanced a little way and then Grek stepped out of hiding, shooting them both expertly in the backs of their heads. The soldiers slumped to the floor.

Grek put two more bullets in his pistol and hurriedly shouldered both the dead soldiers' rifles. He glanced about quickly and decided his only choice was to go over the top. He needed to be with his men and that was impossible, cut off by the collapsed tunnels. Rung by rung, he rose cautiously into the night.

The misty battlefield was in turmoil. A dozen Cutch were weaving their way through the barbed wire towards the trench. A volley of shots rang out and three Cutch crashed into the mud.

Grek's fist rose involuntarily into the air. Good lads! They were fighting back.

At once, another six Cutch were streaming from the jungle, their snouts wide open as they bellowed their harsh and unfamiliar battle-cry.

Grek brought down two of them with his pistol and then rolled over in the mud. It wouldn't do to get shot by one of his own men.

He scrambled across the saturated ground, feeling the meteorite fragments beneath his skin, and pulled himself over and into the trench in one expert movement.

A rifle was instantly cocked at his ear.

'It's me! It's me, Grek!' he cried, holding up his claws.

The soldier looked surprised but rather pleased. 'Good to have you with us, sir.'

Grek smiled. 'How many of them are there?'

The soldier reloaded his rifle hurriedly. 'Can't say, sir. As soon as we hit any, more come out of the jungle.'

Grek looked up the darkened trench. There were perhaps twenty-five men with their rifles pointed over the edge towards the jungle. The trench was half filled with the corpses of their comrades.

Grek knew he didn't have much time. If the dug-out was vulnerable to a stealthy invasion, as through the Number Seven ladder-hole, then they would soon be overrun. If they could keep the advancing Cutch at bay then it would at least buy them some time.

Grek looked into the soldier's eager face.

'Break out the explosives, soldier. I've got a job to do.'

'Sir.' The soldier saluted and vanished into the puddled blackness.

Grek pulled two grenades from his belt, looked quickly over the edge and tossed them into space.

The night was suddenly illuminated, magnesium-bright, as though the noonday sun had risen. Two virtually simultaneous explosions ripped through the atmosphere. The trench shook and great clumps of mud splashed into it.

Grek looked again. There were no more Cutch advancing. He nodded to himself, satisfied.

Now he had to make sure their backs were covered. The blocked tunnels gave them some security but as long as Number Seven was open, they were vulnerable.

The soldier came back with the explosives and placed them in Grek's claws.

'Right.' He looked the soldier in the eye. 'I'm going back to seal off the rest of the base.'

'Sir?'

'It's a gamble, I know. But it's only temporary. We can fight them on only one front and it has to be this one.'

The night was suddenly alive with firecracker explosions as the Cutch rifles renewed their assault.

Grek turned as he climbed the ladder, hanging on by one claw. 'Good luck, soldier.'

He was back on level ground in an instant and scrambling through the mud on his elbows, his head jerking back and forth as Cutch bullets sang over his head. He had to make it back to the ladder. If he could blow up the hole they would lose the conference room for a while but at least the Cutch couldn't get into the tunnels.

Grek started as a flare lit up the night.

A Cutch soldier was standing over him, his rifle shaking in nervous hands. For an instant, the two soldiers stared at one another, then Grek jumped to his feet, cracked the soldier across the jaw, pulled the rifle from him and bayoneted him viciously through the heart. He twisted the blade and pulled it out with a grunt.

Immediately Grek fell, panting, to earth, clutching the precious explosives to his chest.

He pulled himself forward towards the bales of barbed wire until his claw met empty air and he realized he was back at the ladder-hole. He looked down cautiously. The bodies of the two Cutch he had killed were still sprawled in the jade-green gloom of the tunnel below.

He stood up, breathed in and then gasped as he felt a sharp kick in the small of his back. The ladder shot past his startled eyes as he fell heavily through the hole and into the corridor below, the box of explosives shattering and spilling out over the floor.

Grek lay on his back, winded, and looked upwards.

Silhouetted in the hole crouched an ample, brown-uniformed figure, his pistol trained on Grek's completely vulnerable body.

'At last, Commander,' said Imalgahite with relish. 'I've been so looking forward to this.'

128

10

Attack from the Unknown

The Doctor was already at the console when Ran slipped into the TARDIS.

The brilliant white glare of the room and its baffling dimensions achieved something which long years in the trenches could not: it temporarily stopped Ran's twitch. His gaze swept around the chamber in undisguised awe.

The Doctor looked up but didn't smile. 'I'm afraid there's no time for explanations, Portrone. We've got work to do.' He fussed around the console, rapidly punching a course into the navigation circuits. The time rotor shushed steadily up and down as the TARDIS dematerialized.

Ran looked hard into the Doctor's face. 'Are we moving?'

'Oh yes.'

Ran let his claws brush lightly over the instrumentation. 'Now, Doctor. You said you had something important to tell me about my planet's future?'

The Doctor swallowed, looked at his muddied fingernails and then took a very deep breath. This was going to be difficult.

The great black ship ploughed remorselessly forward, the booming of its engines sending waves of nausea through Bernice. It was all she could do to hang on to the outer skin of the dirigible as the ground seemed to jump up at her from hundreds of feet below. She cast an anxious glance at the alien ship and then looked over to Liso who was slowly coming round. He blinked twice and cried out in pain, the copper mesh cutting through his sleeve and into his arm. He flexed his muscles and managed to shove his other arm through the mesh.

'Are you all right?' called Bernice over the throbbing of the engines.

Liso's blue eye clenched tightly shut, his breath hissing between his teeth. 'I think so.'

He looked down into the great empty darkness, felt his stomach lurch and then jerked his crested head towards the position of the escape craft.

'No,' said Bernice softly, the wind making her hair stream in a short black column behind her. 'We lost it.'

The immense shape above them continued to hover menacingly nearby.

Liso looked down once again. The second of the descending dirigibles was now less than twenty feet below them. He bent forward, his entwined arms straining on the mesh and then turned to Bernice, his scrawny neck taut like bunched rope. 'We've got to jump for it.'

Bernice's eyes widened. '*What*?'

Liso winced as wind buffeted his face, and soot and smoke blasted into his eye. 'There's no other way. This ship's finished. If we can get to the other dirigible . . .'

Bernice shook her head. 'You're mad. We'll never make it.'

Liso eased himself forward. 'No choice. If we stay here, we die.' He slid his arms out of the mesh, took a deep breath and fell into empty air.

Bernice, clinging tightly to the airship, held out a hand in a gesture of mute horror. 'No!'

She closed her eyes and then tentatively looked down. Just visible thanks to the fire-light from Porsim, Liso was sprawled on the broad back of the lower dirigible, scrabbling desperately at the mesh with his claws and booted feet.

He looked up. 'Come on! Come *on*!'

Bernice's face fell into shadow as the black ship

130

descended still lower, as though taunting her. This close up she could make out the polished metal plates of its hull, the gargantuan engine flues and the masses of spiky proturberances which covered almost the whole surface. It was like some gigantic mutated sea-urchin, drifting slowly through a dead sea.

'Quickly!' Liso screamed up at her. The throbbing roar of the black ship and the fire-storm hundreds of feet below raged at her senses.

Bernice looked from right to left, to Porsim beneath, and then straight out in front of her.

'Well,' she mumbled to herself, 'it's not been a bad life. Quite interesting in places.'

She hurled herself off the dirigible. There was a brief, giddy, horrifying moment which seemed to last forever, her arms and legs windmilling as she dropped. The night and the stench of smoke shot past her and she slammed onto the back of the other dirigible.

Immediately, she hooked her arms and legs into the mesh, struggling for purchase. She almost bit into the balloon's outer skin.

Suddenly there was an arm around her waist. Her eyes flicked upwards. Liso was holding her.

'You made it,' he whispered hoarsely. 'Well done.'

He was on his feet in an instant, crouching low as he made his way towards the rear of the vessel.

Bernice stayed where she was for a while, breathing in grateful sobs of air, then scrambled to her feet, feeling inordinately pleased with herself. She ran towards Liso, her flushed face bathed in a sheen of sweat.

Liso was already at the copter, checking over its wooden and brass structure as best he could in the near darkness.

'Is it coming any nearer?' he asked.

Bernice couldn't help but look up, although the black ship was virtually indistinguishable from the night sky. The pounding throb of its engines, however, made its presence all too obvious.

'I don't know,' confessed Bernice. 'I think so.'

131

Liso's claws fumbled over the copter's moorings. 'There's not much time. Get in.'

Deciding that she could no longer be fazed by anything, Bernice clambered into the rear of the three seats inside the copter. The same short runway of parallel brass tracks was laid out over the back of the balloon. As Liso hopped inside the machine and started the engines, they slid along them towards empty air.

'Hold on!' he called. Bernice clung to her seat, gritted her teeth and screwed up her eyes. The tiny craft trundled towards the edge of the dirigible, its blades chopping noisily through the air.

In the middle of a fervent prayer, Bernice realized they were airborne.

Liso swung the craft downwards and they swooped over the devastation of Porsim, leaving the three dirigibles to their fate.

The light from the fires made the Portrone's face light up warmly. 'Are you all right?' he asked, twisting round in his seat.

'Yes. Yes, I am,' said Bernice with relief. It could have been her imagination, but was that genuine concern in Liso's voice?

pain – hard cold pain – arms held down – tight – too tight – hurts – cold stone – water – dripping – somewhere – somewhere – someone – screaming – hands over hands – digging – scraping – pressure – on eyes – behind eyes – deep pain – pain – black pain – lightning – fire – oh, the fire – christ the fire!

The woman sat bolt upright in her tiny bed, breathing in great choking gulps. She pressed a hand to her face and forced herself to calm down. She could feel her eyelashes brushing against the sweating palms of her hands.

Where were these visions coming from? Had she so sinned, so offended Saint Anthony that she was to be tortured by demons now?

The woman stretched and got out of bed. As her bare

feet clapped onto the stone floor, she noticed the livid bruising on her wrists and ankles. Could these have anything to do with her visions?

Something nagged at her mind, something terribly important that she should not have forgotten.

The door was suddenly flung open and, framed in the doorway, stood the tiny figure of Parva De Hooch. He flexed his sausage-like fingers as his beady eyes took in the woman's nubile body.

She made a grab for her hessian robe but then remembered that personal modesty was a sin. Instead she stood bold and upright, her head bowed slightly in the Parva's presence.

'That is good, my child. We are all of us naked in the eyes of Saint Anthony.'

De Hooch smiled slightly, horribly, his puckered features bunching together. 'Now, then, you have learned the precepts?'

'Yes, Parva.'

He brushed a little dust from his purple robes. 'And what are they?'

The woman raised her head, her mind still clogged by her strange visions. She cleared her throat and began.

'I will honour Saint Anthony, hammer of the heretics, through endless pain and suffering. I will offer not only my soul, but the sacred egg and the sacred salt as token of my faith. I swear to uphold His name, unworthy as I am . . .'

She stopped, her mind suddenly blank. Blinking furiously, she clenched her hands together.

'And?' said De Hooch in a threatening whisper.

'I . . . I . . .'

'Yes?'

She hung her head defeatedly. 'I can't remember, Parva.'

De Hooch walked up to her and rubbed the nape of his fat neck. 'You can't remember, child?' His eyes blazed with sudden fury. 'You can't remember the most important of all edicts?'

'I'm trying . . .'

De Hooch slammed his tight little fist into her stomach and the woman lurched backwards, retching, onto her bed.

'Get up!' spat De Hooch.

She stumbled to her feet.

De Hooch grasped her face in his tiny hand and dug his nails into the flesh until she bled. 'I . . . am . . . pledged . . .' he recited, emphasizing each word by forcing her head further and further back.

'I am . . . p . . . pledged,' she stammered.

'To bring Saint Anthony's Fire to the heathen hordes,' concluded De Hooch.

'T . . . to bring Saint Anthony's Fire to the . . . the heathen hordes,' she gasped. The dwarf flung her back onto the bed.

'Dear me,' said De Hooch, looking with curiosity at his bloodied finger-nails. 'And you were doing so well. I'm afraid you'll have to see the Magna.'

The woman's eyes widened in stark terror. 'No, my Lord. Please. I meant no harm. It won't happen again.'

De Hooch laughed and traced a sticky circle over his lips with his small pink tongue. 'No. It won't.'

He slammed the door behind him as he left and the woman could hear it echoing endlessly through the vaulted chambers of the seminary.

She clutched her burning stomach and rested her head against the cool wall of the room. Every instinct in her seemed to cry out for . . . what was the word? *Revenge.* Yes. That was it. She wanted to pick up that vile dwarf and throw him against the wall. But this was not the way. It was forbidden. Forbidden.

She screwed up her eyes until she felt hot tears coursing down her face.

Grek coughed, a hard, black, bitter cough until there was

an iron-like taste in his mouth. He felt his bruised ribs through his uniform and winced.

Around him in the dismal, flaring light of the conference room were the pathetic remnants of his small force of men. He had counted fourteen, most of them little more than boys. His heart sank when he realized Maconsa was not amongst them.

Three Cutch were guarding the door, their rifles cocked in constant readiness. Grek looked around sadly at his dispirited comrades and sighed. The decisive moment of his military career hadn't gone too well.

The damaged door opened and Imalgahite marched in, an infuriating smile on his round, warty face.

'We shan't detain you long, Commander, I can assure you of that.' He pulled out a chair from under the long table and sat down.

'Please.' He extended a claw.

Grudgingly, Grek took his place on the opposite side of the table and folded his arms defiantly.

Imalgahite seemed to think for a long moment and then looked up, his eyes bright with triumph. 'Well, Grek, here we are. Two soldiers . . .' He laughed delightedly. 'Two soldiers quite literally on opposite sides of the table.'

'It's my table,' said Grek quietly.

'It was.' Imalgahite rubbed his chins thoughtfully. 'The dilemma is, Grek, what am I going to do with you?'

Grek rubbed his eyes exhaustedly. 'Listen. The war is over. The armistice was about to be signed when . . .'

'When what?'

Grek took a deep breath. He had nothing to lose by telling his enemy the whole truth. 'We've lost contact with all our major cities.'

Imalgahite's answer was not what Grek expected. 'You too?'

'What?'

The Cutch leader leant closer across the table. 'We've heard nothing in days. No orders to proceed. No orders to retreat.'

Grek's eyes widened. 'But we assumed it was you. I mean, who else could it be?'

'Who indeed?' said Imalgahite, leaning back in his chair.

'But this simplifies everything.' Grek sat up excitedly, his claws gripping the edge of the table. 'If we know it's an outside force then we can pool our resources to fight it.'

Something about Imalgahite's smile did not inspire confidence.

'Oh that would be so easy, Commander, wouldn't it? That's just what you'd want.'

Grek sighed. 'Don't be a fool, man. There's something out there that none of us understand. Something strange. We can't let our own petty differences – '

'Petty differences?' exploded Imalgahite, jumping to his feet. 'May I remind you that we didn't start this war. It was you and your filthy Ismetch religion. I've heard the propaganda, my friend. Every single word the Pelaradators ever said about us.'

He pointed a threatening talon into Grek's face, his eyes livid with fury. 'The Cutch are a proud people. A noble and ancient people. And we have a right to survive!'

Grek looked down, ashamed. 'Listen . . .'

'No, Grek, you listen. I don't care what excuses you may have or what clever ploys you've thought up to confuse us. We shall have revenge on you bastards for all the misery you have inflicted upon us.'

He paused, breathing heavily, angrily. 'You wanted genocide? All right. I'll give it to you. I won't rest until every Ismetch is wiped off the face of this planet!'

He stalked from the room. Grek sank into his chair and put his head in his claws.

As Portrone Ran sank down against the TARDIS console, overwhelmed by the news of his world's imminent destruction, the Doctor laid a kindly hand on his shoulder.

Ran looked up, his eyes filled with horror. 'You're sure?'

The Doctor pointed to the readings on the console.

'There can be no doubt, I'm afraid. I've run a few hypo-
theses. At best, Betrushia has three days.'

Ran's face convulsed. 'But why?'

The Doctor frowned and stuffed his hands into his
trouser pockets. 'That's the question, Ran. I thought it
might be a familiar planetary phenomenon. Unstable core,
something like that. But these readings worry me.'

He grunted, his bottom lip jutting out in concentration.
'I have a theory but it's so . . .' He shook his head and
rattled the collection of meteorite fragments in his
pockets.

The time rotor came to a halt with a soft chime. 'We're
here.'

Ran twisted round. 'Where?'

The Doctor flicked a switch and the scanner screen
flared into life.

For a moment, Ran saw only darkness. Then the view
seemed to shift and he could make out thousands of tiny
points of light. Suddenly the screen was brightly, vividly
coloured. A cloud-swirled globe, encircled by a luminescent halo, sprang into his startled vision.

'Is that . . .?'

'It is.' The Doctor held up his hand. 'Behold, Betrushia.'

Ran gasped, scarcely able to comprehend the beauty of
his world.

The Doctor disappeared into the corridor and returned
a moment later with a bulky, padded grey garment and a
transparent bubble-like helmet.

'What are you doing?' asked Ran, tearing his twitching
eyes away from the screen.

'Well, isn't it obvious?' muttered the Doctor, struggling
into the pressure-suit. 'I'm going outside.'

Thoss picked his way through the debris-strewn corridors
towards the ladder-hole. His face was curiously blank as
though a sudden, certain peace had come to him. He
glanced dispassionately at the corpses of the Cutch sol-

diers Grek had killed, and began to clamber onto the ladder, his old claws shaking with effort.

Blissfully, unaware that the dug-out had been captured by the Cutch, he pulled himself to the surface and stood in silence for some minutes, looking out over the night-black battlefield.

The bodies of the dead lay strewn around in craters of churned-up mud. A low mist drifted over them, collecting in eddies and pouring over the lip of the trench some distance away.

Thoss bent down and retrieved one of the meteorite fragments, weighing it carefully in his cupped claw. He looked over towards the edge of the field where the jungle began. A light wind was whispering mournfully through the treetops.

Thoss craned his neck, his jaw dropping open as he took in the majesty of the night sky and the brilliant, blazing rings. Soon it would all be gone. Forgotten.

His head snapped sharply back as he felt a low, low rumbling beneath his feet. The ground suddenly convulsed and he was sent toppling headlong into the mud. He felt the acidic soil sting his eyes and impact into his mouth and ears.

Getting up, Thoss found the ground trembling all around him. In the jungle, dozens of trees crashed noisily to the ground. With a startling boom of shattering rock, a great fissure opened up in the battlefield, mud and soil vanishing as sediment stabbed like broken fingers from the earth.

The ground was shaking violently now and Thoss had to spread his legs wide in an effort to remain standing. He looked across towards the shuddering jungle and gasped.

From out of the cleft in the earth, a huge yellow ooze was belching into the atmosphere, threading its way through the jungle and around the swaying trees like a restless ghost. It sped through the mud, whorling into a vortex, leaving a mucoid essence which sparkled like a snail's trail.

138

Thoss gawped at it and teetered backwards.

With sudden purpose, he began to struggle back towards the dug-out. The earth-tremor ceased as rapidly as it had begun but as Thoss ran over the battlefield, the yellow ooze began to rocket towards him, sloshing over the bodies of the fallen soldiers and pulling them into its core.

Thoss tripped, fell and was at once on his feet again, his exhausted old limbs humming with pain.

More corpses disappeared into the yellow ooze, their uniforms flapping and shredding. Thoss could see them swirling round inside, as though being digested within the sparkling, membranous interior.

The old man reached the lip of the trench and managed to clamber down the ladder. He shivered involuntarily as he hit the icy, stagnant water but waded on desperately towards the dug-out entrance.

His leg hit something and he recoiled as Maconsa's body rolled, belly-up, into view. The luminescent ooze poured over the edge into the trench and scooped up Maconsa's body like so much driftwood.

Thoss whimpered in terror and bolted through the door of Grek's quarters, attempting to slam it behind him. The ooze pressed against the woodwork and Thoss rammed his body at the door.

As it shut, he caught one last glimpse of the thing. What he saw within the ooze made him scream out loud. He was still screaming when two Cutch soldiers found him and dragged him out, through the Number Seven ladder-hole, to the conference room.

High above the jungle canopy, Bernice found herself lulled into sleep by the trill of the copter's brass rotor blades. She had wrapped her feet and hands into the leather straps which hung just inside the fuselage and felt comforted by them.

When she awoke, she could just make out Liso's broad

back as he steered the craft through the bleary dawn. She prodded Liso and he turned round.

'Good morning,' she said.

'Is it?' queried Liso, then, grasping the meaning of the greeting, smiled.

'I'm sorry about Porsim. Truly I am,' said Bernice with feeling.

'Thank you.'

The wind streamed past them as they descended and hovered low over the steaming green jungle.

'Do you know what might have happened, Liso? What that ... that ship was?'

The Portrone did not look round but his grave whisper was audible above the noise of the engines. 'It is the Keth. There can be no doubt.'

Bernice cocked an eyebrow. 'The what?'

'They devastated this world an eternity ago. The Faith always said they would come back.'

She considered this. 'I see.'

Something made her turn round in her seat and a *frisson* of terror leapt up her spine. 'I don't want to worry you, Liso,' she said, 'but I think the Keth may be coming back sooner than you thought.'

Liso turned his head and squinted with his solitary eye.

A few miles behind them, but clearly distinguishable, the great black ship was heading remorselessly after them, shepherding the three Ismetch dirigibles in its path.

Grek stood up sharply as Thoss was thrown unceremoniously into the conference room. He cradled the old man in his arms as Thoss sank to the floor, wide-eyed with terror.

'Keth! Keth! Keth!' he mumbled, foam flecking his black lips.

Grek laid a soothing hand on Thoss's brow. 'All right. It's all right, Thoss.'

Thoss grabbed at Grek's wrist and pulled himself upright. 'No! There was a face. A face!'

He went glassy-eyed as the last image of the yellow ooze returned to his mind.

Grek frowned. 'A face? Where? Whose face?'

Thoss swallowed. 'Inside it! Inside ... It was ... it was ... General Hovv!'

11

The Rings of Betrushia

Swirling with misted cloud like a great blind eye, Betrushia blazed emerald green in the light from its adjacent star.

The rings encircled the entire globe, glittering fabulously; every icy fragment, every captured asteroid or particle of dust catching the light of the sun and refracting it into a dazzling white light.

By contrast, the old blue paintwork of the TARDIS glinted dully as it hung amongst the rings, just one more block in the countless fragments of debris which made up the greatest wonder of Betrushia.

Inside the TARDIS, Ran had sunk into a padded armchair which the Doctor had provided for his comfort. His twitching eyes were fixed with a kind of blank horror on the scanner.

The Doctor had clambered into the pressure-suit and was balancing the transparent helmet on the edge of the console whilst his other hand danced over the controls.

'Now, Portrone,' he concluded, his dark eyes flicking over the console readings. 'Once I've sealed off the internal dimensions you'll be quite safe in here.'

Ran blinked and looked up. 'But why are you going out there, Doctor? My world is dying! We have to do something about it!'

The Doctor held up a gloved hand. 'We are doing something about it, Ran. I think my problem and your problem are related. If I can solve the one, then . . .'

Ran leaned back in his chair. 'Can I help?'

The Doctor pointed to the console. 'This display shows how Betrushia is getting along. Just keep an eye on it. I'll be relaying readings back to you, so stay alert.'

In the palm of the pressure-suit's glove was an arrangement of fibrous wires. The Doctor made a fist and steam hissed from the back of the suit.

'Good.' He smiled. 'That's all in order.'

He locked the helmet onto the top of the pressure-suit and turned to Ran.

'Oh, in case I don't come back, the controls are pre-set to take you back to Betrushia.'

Ran wondered grimly whether he really wanted to go. A return ticket to a doomed planet did not hold much appeal.

The Doctor pressed down a row of buttons and then pulled at the door lever. Ran stepped back involuntarily as the great double doors swung open and then closed behind the Doctor as he vanished across the dimensional threshold.

Ran heaved a huge sigh and rubbed his claws over his face. His muscles twitched beneath his sweaty palms like butterflies trapped in a net.

He glanced down at the console display where a computer image of Betrushia shone with brilliant intensity. All around the screen, various panels indicated the state of the planet's behaviour. Almost without exception the displays, which Ran couldn't pretend to understand, were clearly veering towards danger level.

But there was something he could do. A small chance of survival. For it to work he had to return to Betrushia, preferably with the Doctor. And soon. He looked again at the red displays. Soon.

Imalgahite walked slowly into the bottle-green, funereal light of the conference room, his face fixed into a troubled frown.

Grek looked up as he entered. 'Nothing to do? It's all

very well having power, isn't it? Question is, what do you do with it when you've got it?'

Imalgahite ignored his taunts and eased his bulk into a nearby chair. 'We've checked out the speecher lines to Porsim. You were right. There's no response.'

'I told you. And there'll be nothing from any of the other cities either. Look.' Grek stood up, the defeated Ismetch troops clearing a path for him, and jabbed a talon at the map on the wall.

'See these black pins? That's the extent of their advance two days ago. God knows how far they've got now.'

Imalgahite smiled humourlessly. 'They?'

Grek took a deep breath. 'I . . . well . . . Something we know nothing about.'

Imalgahite nodded slowly. 'Those mammals perhaps?'

'No. At least, I don't think so.'

Imalgahite ran a talon over his lips thoughtfully. 'There is something out there, Grek. My men have seen it.'

Grek returned to his chair, frowning. 'What do you mean?'

Imalgahite rubbed his brow, commas of greasy spines falling forwards over his face. 'It . . . leaves things behind.'

He beckoned to a guard who produced a wet sack and laid it out on the table. Inside was an ominous lump.

'Go on,' said Imalgahite. 'Take a look.'

Grek felt around inside the sack. Something cold and wet met the touch of his fingertips. Gingerly, he closed his claw over part of it and pulled the thing out.

He retched as a head tumbled onto the table before him. His claw flew to his mouth and his eyes bulged in disgust.

The head had been clumsily severed so that several vertebrae dribbled slackly from below it. The blue eyes were misted over and the once-proud crest was cut and battered.

'It's Maconsa,' gasped Grek, feeling bile rush to his throat. 'My surgeon.'

144

He managed to pluck at the gelatinous stuff which coated the grisly relic. 'What's this?'

Imalgahite shrugged. 'We have no idea.'

Grek pushed back his chair and flung the sack over Maconsa's head. He pointed across the room at the recumbent Thoss.

'This man – Thoss – he's the keeper of our Temple. Last night when you brought him in here he was raving about something he'd seen. Out there in the jungle. He's not made much sense since then but he claims this thing had the face of one our generals. Inside it.'

'General Hovv, was it? Yes, I've read your reports. He went missing didn't he?'

Grek leant forward. 'Yes. With a whole brigade. For a while I thought he'd just taken himself off because of the armistice. Always was a die-hard. Now I'm not so sure.'

Imalgahite's expression softened. 'What do you think, Grek?'

Grek looked around at his dispirited men and their suddenly frightened Cutch conquerers. Every one seemed to be hanging on his words. 'You and I have different religions. That's what this war was all about. But there is one common thread in both.'

Imalgahite nodded. 'Go on.'

Grek took a deep breath. 'I think ... I think the Keth have returned.'

Imalgahite closed his eyes and folded his claws neatly together on the table. 'So do I,' he whispered.

Magna William Hon Yuen Yong stretched his shapely, elegant fingers across the table and sighed. It had been a long and desperately tedious day.

He had risen, as usual, at dawn and interrogated almost forty unbelievers before his breakfast of tiger-bone tea and pork. But now, as sunlight streamed through the stained-glass windows of his opulent chambers, washing the tiled floor with rainbow colours, he was rather afraid he might be bored.

The Magna was a tall, muscular man of some thirty-five years, his beautiful Chinese features as smooth as the sumptuous purple robes which covered him. His hair was long, sleek and coal-black, pulled tautly behind his head.

He got up from his throne and parted his lips into a cruel smile. He had an idea. At last, something to combat the endless ennui!

His rooms were enormous and sumptuously decorated in dark blue and gold leaf. A ceiling of staggering extravagance curved over the whole area like a gilded egg, legions of cool marble columns extending the opulence right down to the floor.

In amongst the muslin drapes, the fountains and exquisitely carved furniture were a series of triptychs, glinting dark and golden in the sunshine. Each showed a tall, sickly-looking man in a variety of pained poses.

In one, he was offering a piece of the Host to a donkey; in another, he was preaching to fish; in a third, a baby was caressing his sad-looking face; in yet another, he was sitting in a nut-tree, a book and a lily clasped in his talon-like hands.

Yong, who knew every detail of the pictures, crossed the black and white tiled floor towards a curtained-off area of the vast room. A subdued mewing was coming from beyond the midnight-blue curtains.

He swept his cloak behind him and put one exquisitely manicured hand on his hip. Beneath his robes, his firmly muscled body was encased in a black skin-tight garment, shimmering like soft chain-mail.

Yong pulled back the curtain and smiled again, his black, almond-shaped eyes wrinkling slightly at their edges.

'So,' he purred, 'you think to outwit me with your little games?'

Before him, stretched out upright on an ivory board was a tiny kitten. Wires cut cruelly into its limbs and its head was pulled back by a series of gold clips. It mewled pitifully as Yong stood before it.

'You still refuse to acknowledge the will of Saint Anthony?' hissed Yong, swirling his cloak impressively.

The kitten cried out pathetically, its bright little eyes wide open in hopeless appeal.

'Then you leave me no choice.'

Yong produced a long, thin rapier from a nearby cupboard and held it next to the kitten's exposed throat.

There was an urgent knocking at the great oak door and De Hooch bustled inside, his fat legs rubbing together grotesquely as he waddled across the room.

'What is it, De Hooch?' said Yong with a heavy sigh. 'I am about to administer absolution – with extreme prejudice.'

'An urgent matter, Magna,' stammered De Hooch.

'Can't it wait?' Yong eyed the kitten with sadistic interest. It opened and closed its mouth in silence.

'It's that woman, my Lord.'

Yong glanced at his second. 'The one you've been keeping an eye on?'

De Hooch nodded furiously, his skull-cap slipping backwards a little. Yong tickled the blade under the kitten's jaw. 'What has she done?'

'I was about to bring her to your attention anyway, Magna. She had forgotten one of the precepts.'

Yong rolled his eyes with mock gravity. 'Oh dear.'

De Hooch held up his stunted hands. 'But now it is, worse, my Lord. She has . . . disappeared.'

Yong swept round, the light from the stained-glass window glittering off his tautly muscled body. 'What?'

De Hooch bowed obsequiously. 'She was not at dawn prayer, my Lord. None of my men can find her.'

Yong's expression softened slightly. 'Well, this is a big seminary, Parva. Why don't you run along and see where she's got to? Remember how much rejoicing there is in Heaven when one sinner returns to the fold. We shouldn't be too harsh on her. After all, one's faith is always being tested.'

De Hooch's face fell, disappointed. 'Of course, Magna.'

He began to back out of the room, keeping his fat little head low.

'Oh, and De Hooch?'

'Yes, Magna?'

'When you do find her, be sure and cut out her tongue. Very, very slowly.'

De Hooch's face split into a horrible smile. 'Yes, my Lord.'

The doors closed behind him.

Yong raised the rapier again and laid it at the kitten's throat. 'Now then, where were we?'

He rammed the weapon through the animal's neck until he heard the blade scrape on the ivory board behind. The kitten shuddered momentarily and then was still.

Yong pulled out the rapier, already bored. 'You are forgiven, my child,' he muttered without enthusiasm.

The Doctor breathed in sharply. The oxygen streaming into his bubble-helmet was cold and invigorating but what had actually, literally, taken his breath away was the sight which met his eyes as he stepped out of the TARDIS. He was rather pleased that his jaded tastes could still be so stimulated.

Beyond the TARDIS, the vast blackness of space stretched all around, spattered with tiny stars. The Doctor looked about, his head swivelling within the helmet.

Below and around him floated a carpet of billions of tiny particles, stretching ahead like a circle of luminous dust. Every so often a larger object interrupted the symmetry.

To be within the rings themselves was like standing on a dusty golden runway encrusted with stones, hazy patches of dark space swirling within it.

'Doctor?' Ran's voice cut in via the communications link to the TARDIS.

The Doctor started. 'I'm here, Ran. Got a bit distracted.'

He stepped off the threshold of the ship and drifted

silently into the rings. Forming a fist, he hissed forward through the shimmering debris.

A short way ahead, a larger, football-sized chunk of rock was spinning in silence.

The Doctor advanced towards it and felt in the pouch of his pressure-suit for a small white instrument. Betrushia's star sparkled off the bubble-helmet as he passed the device to and fro over the rock's surface.

A display lit up and the Doctor peered at it. 'Ran? Some data coming through now.'

The machine beeped and a stream of figures shunted across the screen. The Doctor moved on to another rock of similar size.

'Remarkable,' he muttered, stabbing at the buttons on the compact machine.

Ran's voice crackled in his helmet: 'You said you had a theory, Doctor?'

The Doctor said nothing for a moment, merely nodding to himself as though lost in thought. Then he looked out at the magnificent display before him, his voice a low, grave whisper.

'Your meteorites aren't meteorites at all, Ran. They're the rock fragments which make up Betrushia's ring system. And their orbit is decaying.'

There was a crackling pause, then Ran's voice, quiet and concerned. 'Decaying? You mean, something's making them fall?'

'That's right. The whole ring system is falling apart.'

'But what's causing it?'

The Doctor said nothing. Instead he twisted around, gazing out into the impenetrable blackness of space. Out there, something was waiting.

Parva De Hooch strutted up and down the cold stone corridor, his doll-like hands flexing and unflexing in agitation.

Chaptermen Jones and his acne-scarred acolyte

149

approached, their closely shaven heads glinting in the wintry sunlight which poured into the cloisters.

De Hooch's pale eyebrows shot upwards. 'Well?'

'There's no sign of her, Parva,' mumbled Jones.

'Anywhere,' concluded the other.

De Hooch stamped his feet on the flagstones. 'Cretins! Invertebrates! Do I have to think of everything?'

He dismissed them with a pudgy wave and scowled darkly at the elegant glass roof above his head. He blinked slowly, repeatedly.

De Hooch's reputation rested on this mission. Perhaps even his status in the Chapter. And there was so much more to be achieved . . .

He wasn't about to lose it all because of some runaway sinner. She had to be in the seminary somewhere. He darted off down a left-hand corridor and disappeared into the hard black shadows.

A moment later, the woman emerged from an adjacent alcove, her heart slamming in her ribs. She had to get away. Get out of the seminary. Something was terribly, terribly wrong.

She lifted a hand to her shaven head and winced in pain. It was wrong to disobey, she knew. But an even deeper impulse seemed to be raging inside her head.

It was strange but, try as she might, she could not recall ever leaving the place, nor anything of her life before the Chapter. Of course, the old life was dead and she now devoted herself entirely to Saint Anthony. To honour him and love him through pain and suffering . . .

The pain shot across her temples again and she screwed up her eyes in agony. She had to fight it. Fighting seemed to be the only way out.

The woman leant against the alcove for support and suddenly froze at the sound of footsteps. She pressed herself back into the recess and stayed completely still as a group of shambling penitents wandered past, their wounds freshly scourged. The woman fought back nausea as she saw their pus-corrupted blood pooling on the floor.

150

When they had gone, she stepped out again and was momentarily blinded by the sunlight from above. She glanced up and felt her eyes warming. Looking back, the corridor was invisible for a moment, her retina bleached out. When the spots cleared, Parva De Hooch was standing next to her. His walnut face crinkled into a horrible smile. 'I knew it. I could *smell* you!'

He pulled a vicious-looking knife from under his robes. 'You will forgive me, I'm sure, but orders are orders.'

He motioned with his fat hand. 'On your knees, sinner!'

The woman found herself incapable of disobeying. She bent down, her face dripping with sweat. This was not the way it should be.

De Hooch's tongue flicked out and a dribble of saliva trickled down his robes. He brought the knife closer to her face.

honour saint anthony – suffering – pain – passion – humiliation – the passion of saint anthony – no – honour him – the sacred egg – the sacred salt – mixed they formed spiritual semen – spiritual urine – uphold his name – no – inflict terrible wrath on all unbelievers – hammer of the heretics – I am pledged to bring saint anthony's fire to the heathen hordes – no! no! no! –

De Hooch smiled as he pressed the knife to the woman's chin but was more than a little surprised when she grasped his wrist, twisted it and hurled him over her shoulder.

He hit the wall and slid to the floor, winded.

'How . . . dare you?' he spluttered in fury. 'How . . .'

The woman was off and running. She careered around the corner and disappeared into the corridors.

De Hooch pulled himself up to his full three feet and picked up the knife. His little eyes protruded like mistletoe berries in his fat, angry face. He stamped his feet in frustration and then scuttled off in pursuit.

The woman reached a junction point where five similar stone corridors split off. This deep in the seminary there

151

was little light but she was grateful to be hidden by the shadows. She had committed one of the worst sins imaginable: striking the Parva. At the very least she would be killed.

Her one chance now was to get out. What must it be like to feel the sunshine outside again? Not live this dreadful closeted existence. To walk amongst the forests and rivers?

She pulled up as the same dreadful pain cut through her mind. She had remembered something. Water. Trees. Things from the old life. There *had* been an old life.

Somewhat cheered by this, she pressed on.

A short distance on, down the second of the identical corridors, she came upon a huge metal door. The familiar flame-entwined cross, symbol of the Chapter, had been embossed into it. This was a forbidden area.

Uncaring now, since she knew she was doomed if caught, the woman opened the door.

Beyond it, rising high into the roof, was an enormous spiral staircase. It threaded through a network of dense, oily black machinery, like the workings of a titanic clock.

She closed the door softly behind her and began to climb the stairs which rang hollowly beneath her feet. She looked around nervously, conscious of a deep throbbing of power.

The steps rose ever upwards, twisting through shadowed niches in which incomprehensible nests of machinery whirred and clunked.

Baffled, the woman pressed on. As she reached the top of the spiral staircase, another door loomed into view. The surrounding walls were solid and white. There was no cross on the door, instead, unexpectedly, the legend:

GOGGLES MUST BE WORN

The woman looked around. Several pairs of dark glasses were hanging from a rack close by. She slipped some over her eyes and gingerly opened the door.

It was like being slapped across the face, she thought. Light flooded the area beyond and she stepped back involuntarily. She could see nothing. Nothing but the blaze of furious white light.

The pain in her head stabbed across her goggled eyes.

After a moment, however, she began to make out shapes in the whiteness and realized she was standing in a vast room, its walls lined with blinking panels and controls.

In the centre of the chamber, behind a metal barrier, was an incalculably huge ball of light, its surface crackling with plasmic energy.

Even with the protective goggles, the woman had to cover her eyes. She was on the point of advancing further when a strong arm grabbed her around the throat. She spun round and twisted her head as the pressure increased. A Chapterman was standing behind her, looking rather like a giant bat in his cloak and goggles.

His fingers squeezed into the flesh of her neck and she gasped as she felt her airway being cut off.

She lashed out with her foot and he fell forwards, giving her the leverage she needed to slam him to the ground. He was up again on the instant, punching her viciously in the face and torso. She reeled backwards, wheezing, and cracked him across the nose with her elbow. He cried out as blood spurted from the crushed bone but staggered on and fastened his big hands around the woman's throat. She could see the muscles bulging under his skin-tight bodysuit.

Unhesitatingly, the woman brought up her knee into his groin and pinioned his arms behind his back. Immediately he tried to pull her over his shoulders but she resisted. They tumbled towards the barrier, the painful light flooding their eyes.

The Chapterman punched again and again and the woman toppled to the floor. He smiled cruelly and walked towards her cowering form, fist clenched to deliver a killing blow to her throat.

But she was on her feet and kicked out, catching him under the chin, propelling him over the barrier into the nebulous ball of energy. He screamed shrilly and, with a flare of light, disappeared.

The woman sank down and turned away from the agonizing display. She coughed wretchedly, still no nearer to finding a way out.

The Doctor formed a fist and the propulsion unit in his pressure-suit responded, sending him back towards the TARDIS.

There was much more to be discovered and he needed to analyze the bizarre readings the little white instrument had relayed to him. Something was very odd about those rings.

But for now, he needed to get back to the TARDIS. Time was running out for Betrushia and the sooner he solved the mystery, the sooner he could apply his powers to helping the doomed planet.

'Ran,' he whispered into his helmet, 'I'm on my way back –'

'Doctor!' cut in Ran's voice. 'There's something behind you. I can't – Doctor!'

The Doctor managed to turn his head.

A vast black ship was ploughing through space towards him, its immense prow humming with a radiant red light.

As the Doctor watched, a column of searing flame blasted through a section of the rings, disintegrating thousands of rock fragments.

Ran's hysterical voice blared in the Doctor's ears: 'The Keth! The Keth are come!'

The Doctor looked up, too late, as an asteroid fragment piled into his chest and he tumbled uncontrollably into the void.

12

Return of the Keth

Liso rammed down the brass levers before him and the
copter dived headlong towards the jungle. Bernice wrapped the leather straps around her fists and closed her eyes,
her stomach lurching sickeningly.

The morning air was thick and sticky, great clouds of
steam rising from the wet jungle into the cloud-heavy sky.

When the craft levelled out and they were hovering
some thirty feet above the tree-tops, Bernice glanced over
her shoulder.

The vast black ship, ethereally beautiful in the hazy
sunlight, seemed further away but was clearly advancing
towards them. She tapped Liso on the shoulder.

'I know, I know,' he murmured evenly without looking
back.

Bernice gripped the sides of the copter and peered
down. The dense greenery now seemed reassuringly
closer. A little further and she could have brushed her
hands over the foliage. But what she was actually looking
for seemed rather more elusive.

'We're almost there, I think,' said Liso. 'Can you see
this box of yours?'

'No. I'm sure it's around here . . .' She sat up quickly
and pointed. 'There! There! That's the clearing I'm sure.
I recognize the fallen trees.'

Liso inclined his head. 'I'll put us down.'

The copter swung round and began to circle as Liso
craned his neck to see the clearing.

Bernice shot one last look at the distant black craft before her view was obscured by the enormous trees. The copter descended with extraordinary grace and landed with only a slight jolt in the clearing.

They sat in silence for a moment as the brass blades whirred gently to a stop. Liso tapped the fuel gauge and sighed.

'Well, we did very well, considering. These things weren't designed to travel far. The dug-out is just across there. Where's the box?'

Bernice clambered out and ran across the clearing into the tree shadows. The grass and lianas at her feet had been compressed into a familiar square but of the TARDIS there was no sign.

She turned to Liso, who had come up behind her, and shrugged. 'It's gone.'

Liso looked round the clearing. The jungle seemed sweaty with unease, raucous bird-like squawks erupting from all around. 'You say this "Doctor" can help us?'

Bernice nodded. 'If anyone can find out who's done this to your people, the Doctor can. He's a bit of a specialist in these matters.'

Liso sat down on a fallen trunk, his breeches soaking in the moisture from the bark. He put his heavy head in his claws and a shudder of grief fluttered involuntarily through him.

Bernice sat down beside him and put an arm around his shoulder. To her surprise, he did not resist.

'What is it?' she asked gently. 'Porsim?'

He looked up, his one good eye blurred with tears. 'I suppose so. More than that. I feel . . . I feel as if I've lost something.'

His back bowed, he let his head sink onto his chest and began to weep bitterly.

'If it's family . . .' began Bernice.

'I have no family,' said Liso hoarsely. 'It's not that. I've lost . . . I've lost my certainty. Everything that's kept me going all these years.'

156

He laughed dully. 'It's quite something for me to admit that Grek was right. That this whole conflict, the war against the Cutch, has been pointless. Fighting amongst ourselves when the real enemy was out there all the time.'

Bernice cocked her head to one side thoughtfully. 'But now you know who you should be fighting, what's to stop you getting together? Uniting against them?'

Liso's face filled with a kind of horrified pity. 'Such naïvity. It's not easy forgetting ... well, even if we could work together ...' He tailed off, stroking his empty eye-socket.

'But *we* have. And you were threatening to chuck me off your airship once upon a time.'

'It's more complicated than you think, Bernice. You cannot fight the Keth. They are death. It is finished.'

His head sank back into his claws. Bernice turned away and brushed a lock of glossy black hair from her eyes.

'Blimey,' she said.

The Doctor blinked into consciousness and, for a moment, had no idea where he was. Space was a broad, black panorama around the confines of his helmet. In a rush, he remembered being struck by the asteroid fragment and spinning away from the mysterious ship.

He felt a strange tugging sensation on his skin and realized he was slowly gliding through space, caught in some kind of tractor beam. The vast prow of the black ship, its hull covered in strange, spiky protuberances, loomed into view.

The Doctor tried to look back, to see whether the TARDIS was still there, but he felt woozy and the pull of the beam was too strong. There didn't seem to be anything he could do to break away.

Idly, he wished he still carried the specially adapted, vacuum-resistant propulsion-powered cricket ball which had got him out of that spot with the Urbankans. But the useful toy was nestling in an old coat pocket in some dusty corner of the TARDIS.

A vague humming sound began to pound in his head and, as he was dragged remorselessly towards the strange craft, the Doctor drifted back into unconsciousness.

Ran thumped the TARDIS console in frustration. On the scanner screen, he could see the vast alien ship and the tiny figure of the Doctor. The path which the ship had blasted through the ring system had left a strange, hazy hole.

Ran looked about and threw up his claws in desperation. If only there were some way he could help.

But the roundelled walls revealed nothing and the hum of the TARDIS around him only heightened his sense of isolation.

He glanced down at the twinkling console displays, all now registering an alarming crimson, and then out at his beloved planet, spinning unperturbedly in space.

Ran stood up straight and held his arms at his sides, a vague plan forming in his mind. His face twitched as he wondered how long until the TARDIS's pre-programmed return to Betrushia came about.

He smiled as he thought of Testra, laughing with her beautiful head thrown back, her eyes brimming with tears.

He could do it. For her.

Magna Yong was bathing when De Hooch came thundering into his chambers, his fat little arms spiralling in agitation.

'Magna! Magna!' he cried.

Yong plunged himself into the giraffe's-milk pool and his sleek black hair blossomed on the surface.

De Hooch threw himself down by the side of the enormous circular bath and splashed his hand in the warm milk. 'Magna! My Lord! Hear me!'

Yong's head appeared, milk dripping over his almond-shaped eyelids. 'De Hooch, for a little person, you make an awful lot of noise.'

De Hooch ignored this and smoothed down his

wrinkled robes. Yong stepped from the bath and towelled off the excess milk from his honey-coloured skin. As he pulled on a black robe he noticed the extensive bruising on De Hooch's face. 'Dear me, you have been in the wars. Has the lady eluded you, Parva?'

De Hooch bowed his head, ashamed. 'She is a hell-cat, Magna. I was about to cut out her tongue when she flung me against the wall.'

Yong's black irises dilated. 'The nerve.'

'Indeed, my Lord.' De Hooch clasped his hands behind his back. 'Then she ran off.'

Yong glided across the tiled floor and sat down in his opulent throne. Spread out on the table before him was an assortment of jellied sweetmeats. Children's limbs in jars and pickled organs in dark glass bottles dominated.

Yong chose a shrivelled, etiolated baby's cheek and nibbled quietly at it, his eyes scanning De Hooch amusedly as the dwarf continued.

'In my considered opinion, Magna,' said De Hooch, 'her conditioning is failing.'

Yong stopped eating, his face suddenly set in an expressionless mask. 'That is impossible, De Hooch, as well you know. Our conditioning never fails.'

'Of course not, my Lord,' bleated De Hooch, 'but there is always an exception which proves the rule.'

Yong's eyes glittered like jet. 'Then I shall change the rule. This woman must be made an example of. Find her, Parva. Find her and bring her to me.'

'Yes, my Lord.'

Yong slid a long, thin finger over his mouth. A droplet of giraffe's milk clung to his lips. 'Don't let me down, De Hooch. I should hate to have to make an example of you as well.'

De Hooch's throat constricted. 'No, my Lord. I mean ... yes, yes Magna.'

'Is there anything else?'

De Hooch gathered Yong's fresh robes and bodysuit

159

from a bench and passed them to the Magna. 'Not that I know of, my Lord.'

Yong began to pull the sleek material over his muscled legs. 'Then leave me to dress, Parva. It must be nearly evening. Put out the sun as you go.'

De Hooch's stunted hand felt for a switch and the light which blazed through the stained-glass window was abruptly cut off.

The woman awoke from uneasy dreams as she realized she had been plunged into darkness. Cursing herself for falling asleep, she slipped off her goggles and gazed into the sudden, intense blackness.

Within its shield, the vast ball of plasmic energy seemed to have dimmed to a fraction of its former power. There was a low pulsing sound underscoring the humming and twittering of the machinery.

The woman stood up, feeling her skin bruising under her hessian robes, and moved across the chamber. She shot a look at the banks of circuitry and frowned. They reminded her strongly of something.

She passed a weary hand over her eyes and tried to concentrate. What was going on here? The seminary had always seemed such a simple place. Spartan even. The highest level of technology the Chapter possessed had produced the pewter plates and cutlery in the refectory. Now she had stumbled across a whole forbidden area. None of this tallied with her faith, with her understanding. It was all wrong. Just as it was wrong for her to obey that vile creature De Hooch.

The woman leant against the barrier and felt her shaved head. That was wrong too. She opened her mouth and tried to form words, almost remembering something. It was so tangible she could almost taste it. Pain shot across her temples again and the moment was gone. She stumbled, her face screwed up in agony.

There had to be a way out. Walking quickly around the

160

perimeter of the chamber, past the throbbing banks of circuitry, she emerged next to another large door.

It opened with a squeal and the woman passed through.

Ahead was a metal corridor. Blank. Featureless. Subdued lighting gave it a chilly, clinical glow. She made her way quickly down the passage, her bare feet clapping on the steel-panelled floor. This looked promising. Perhaps even the way out. If she didn't find it soon then the Chaptermen would discover her. And they had quite a few fates worse than death up their sleeves.

Bernice stepped back and looked around rapidly as though smelling the air.

Liso looked up. 'What is it?'

'Listen!'

Liso's snout crinkled worriedly. 'The stone rain? We'll have to get under cover.'

'No. Look!'

Liso's gaze flicked across to her outstretched arm. Something was materializing out of thin air above the square depression in the ground. A light flashed and, with its familiar thump, the TARDIS returned to the jungles of Betrushia.

Bernice almost skipped towards the battered blue box, such was her relief and excitement.

'Is this it?' queried Liso.

'Yes!' She slapped her palm against the door. 'Doctor! Come out wherever you are.'

The doors remained obstinately shut. Bernice frowned. 'Doctor?'

She stepped back as the double doors creaked slowly open. To her great surprise, Ran's bemused and twitching face appeared around the jamb.

'You!' she cried. 'What are you – '

Liso rushed to support his comrade as Ran stumbled from the TARDIS

'Ran? Ran, what is it? What happened?'

161

Bernice had more pressing concerns: 'Where's the Doctor?'

Ran shook his head. 'It's no good. They've taken him. The Keth came and ... took him.' He gazed up at the blurred halo of the rings. 'I was up there, Liso. In space. I saw them.'

Bernice shook him frustratedly. 'Someone took the Doctor? Who?'

Ran closed his eyes. 'The Keth. A great black ship.'

Liso and Bernice exchanged glances. Ran struggled to his feet and rubbed his twitching eyes. 'You must excuse me. I have things to attend to.'

Liso grabbed him by the shoulders. 'Get hold of yourself, man. What are you talking about? We need to know what's going on.'

Ran almost smiled, something of his old humour returning. 'You really want to know, Liso? The Doctor showed me everything. Betrushia is dying. Pulling itself apart.'

'What?' Liso looked appalled. 'I don't believe it.'

'How long?' said Bernice directly.

'Days. Perhaps hours.'

Liso turned away, his broad shoulders sinking. 'Then there's nothing we can do.'

Ran moved across the clearing, his boots slicing through the dewy grass. 'No. But there's something I can do.'

'Where are you ...?'

'I'll be back,' cried Ran, disappearing into the jungle.

Bernice tugged at Liso's arm. 'We must find the Doctor.'

'It's too late, Bernice. The Keth have him. The Keth will have consumed him. And now they will consume my world.'

Bernice's eyes flashed angrily. 'And you're just going to let them?'

'I've told you. We cannot fight – '

'Yes we can! Look, Liso. You told me these ... Keth things were some sort of ... evil ... from your planet's pre-history, right?'

'Yes. They came when ...'

162

'Never mind. Well, I don't know many mythical bogymen who have to do their chain-rattling in spaceships.'

'What do you mean?'

Bernice sat down on the tree trunk. 'I mean that I reckon your Keth are a bit more corporeal than you imagine. And what's corporeal can be hurt.'

Almost as though challenging Bernice's defiance, lightning streaked across the inflamed sky. Corresponding thunder grumbled distantly.

Liso looked appealingly into Bernice's face, his solitary eye blinking thoughtfully.

'You have spirit, Bernice. I admire you.'

'Well, don't give up on me then,' she said, smiling. 'You may have lost your certainty but there's always a cause. And this is a very good one as causes go. What d'you say?'

He grunted, half smiling. ' "For the Greater Glory of the Ismetch. My Country or my Soul".'

'No,' said Bernice, extending her hand. 'For yourself.'

Grek and Imalgahite sat alone in Grek's quarters. There was a long moment of uneasy silence, broken only by the rumbling atmospherics from outside.

'I find this . . . difficult,' confessed Grek.

'Of course. So do I. It's not easy forgetting fifteen years of enmity.'

Grek looked up. 'Have you forgotten?'

Imalgahite smiled and shrugged. 'Do I have any choice?'

The bowl of wax at the side of Grek's bunk suddenly began to shudder across the table.

Imalgahite whirled round, alarmed. The walls themselves were vibrating violently. Planks splintered and burst upwards from the floor as mud began to seep into the dug-out.

'Quake!' barked Grek. 'A big one by the – '

'We've got to get everyone out. Come on!'

Imalgahite grabbed the speecher and managed to

163

bellow an evacuation order before the wires were severed in a flurry of sparks as the far wall bulged and mud surged inside.

He grabbed at Grek's uniform and together they staggered for the entrance, the floor rippling under their feet. Water from the trenches was gushing through the doorway as the floor level heaved, rose and then dropped heavily.

Grek launched himself into the trench and up the ladder, scrambling over the mud onto the surface. Imalgahite was close behind. Both their remaining armies raced from the dug-out as its walls began to collapse.

Out of the corner of his eye, Grek saw Thoss crawling over the ground. The very air itself, already heavy with electricity, seemed to be juddering as though shimmered by heat-haze.

In the midst of the chaos, Thoss threw himself to the ground and pointed up into the darkening sky. 'The Keth!' he screamed. 'The Keth are come!'

Grek clung to the shaking ground as steam belched from the earth. Finally, he managed to raise his head and turned terrified eyes onto the scene above.

Hanging in the sky, so vast that it blocked out half the visible rings, was the great black ship. Clustered in the hollow of its prow like frightened sheep were the three Ismetch dirigibles.

Imalgahite slammed his face into the soil, his claws rammed against his ears, the throb of the great ship's engines almost overpowering him.

The black ship was quite still, its rasping engines stirring the air into agitated eddies.

One by one, the tiny dirigibles began to drift away, as though granted their freedom. Their propellers made a tiny, pathetic sound next to their shepherd's enormity.

Thoss had completely prostrated himself by now, his claws digging into the soil and his mouth opening and closing in silent prayer. Grek felt his heart slam against his ribs and a sheen of cold, glutinous sweat break out over his body. This was it.

'Grek,' called Imalgahite in a terrified whisper. 'It's . . . it's letting them go.'

Grek looked again. The dirigibles had made progress and were heading for the landing plain some distance away.

He flinched and a terrible feeling of dread rose up in his stomach. 'I don't think so,' he said in a whisper.

The rumble of the black ship's engines increased in pitch and a new sound cut into it, chime-like and crystal clear. Then the fabric of the hull seemed to blister and an immense red circle, like the mouth of Hell, opened in the darkness. The hole seemed to shift, turning slowly and efficiently so that it faced the dirigible fleet.

'Oh God,' cried Grek. 'Oh God.'

For an instant the throbbing of the engines cut out and there was a dreadful, heart-stopping silence. Then a tunnel of flame, so intense that it made the watching soldiers clutch their faces in agony, roared from the vast black ship and slammed into the dirigibles.

There was a brief, standstill moment of time, then all three erupted into a colossal bloom of flame, fire burning outwards, ever outwards, deafening the spectators with explosive percussion.

Immediately, fiery debris began to rain down from the sky and the soldiers broke and ran for the still-shaking jungle.

As the earthquake subsided, the black ship glided through the tattered remains of the dirigibles drifting slowly to earth and began to descend.

Grek and Imalgahite stood up together, shaking in terror.

The Keth had returned.

13

Auto-Da-Fé

The Doctor moved his closed eyes slowly under their lids. Left to right. Right to left. Slowly he became aware of a gentle humming somewhere beneath him.

For a moment he imagined he was lying in the TARDIS, the reassuring sound of his beloved ship cocooning him. Still without opening his eyes, he unsealed the bubble-helmet and placed it on his chest.

The sharp metallic tang in the atmosphere and the constant drip-drip of water brought him immediately back to reality. Reluctantly he flicked open his eyes.

He was no longer in space but inside an enormous hangar, its rough steel walls mottled with rust. Functional metal struts rose from the plated floor to a flat, grease-heavy ceiling. Scattered in piles all around him were fragments of the ring system, now little more than a thick carpet of glistening dust.

The Doctor stood up and brushed some of the detritus from his pressure suit. He could make out little in the gloom and walked carefully away from what he took to be the airlock, his feet crunching in the thick layer of asteroid dust.

Sniffing, he paused and pulled out the white instrument from the suit pouch. The display glowed dull red in the near-darkness.

'Analysis not completed,' he read out loud. 'Please wait.'

He put the instrument down and began to clamber out of his pressure-suit. He piled it neatly in one corner of

166

the hangar with the helmet on top, so he knew where to retrieve it in the event of a hasty retreat. Hasty retreats were second nature to him, after all.

Glancing down at his ruined waistcoat and trousers, the Doctor sighed. If he ever got through this alive then a trip to a tailor seemed imperative. He slipped the white device into his trouser pocket.

It took the Doctor some minutes to walk the length of the hangar and when he finally reached the end he was confronted by a bewildering selection of round metal doors. A small flashing panel at the side of each seemed to indicate an opening mechanism. The Doctor pressed his palm to one and it slid quietly upwards.

'Humanoid, then,' he said to himself.

Beyond the door stretched a maze of blank metal corridors. The floor plates were stained and corroded, the grilled ceiling above his head heavy with dust and filth.

'Corridors, corridors . . .' he mused. 'Just like home.'

An insistent bleeping in his pocket made him pause. He pulled the white machine from his trousers and gazed in wonder at the read-out.

'Final analysis of Betrushian ring system reveals . . .' He read the rest to himself and then carefully switched off the machine.

His face set in a rigid frown, he strode off down the corridor.

The woman found herself in an ornately panelled corner of the seminary. Cold stone corridors branched off from a hallway decorated with crimson drapes and hundreds of shadowed niches, each containing white marble representations of Saint Anthony, their anguished or impassioned faces wreathed in cobwebs.

She almost smiled at the similarity between the holy figures; all painfully thin, balding men with deep-set eyes rolled heavenwards and their hands outstretched in curious two or three-fingered gestures. In many, rays of marble sunlight from an unseen Heaven poured through holes in their flesh. Some held miniature bells. One was straddling a marble pig.

The woman's smile vanished as she felt the pain again and a frightening voice admonishing her for her levity. How dare she mock Saint Anthony? How dare... How...

She placed her hand against the panelled wall and fought to keep control. Examining the calloused palms and battered fingers of her hands, she frowned, feeling salty sweat drip unpleasantly into her eyes. Who was she? Why couldn't she simply accept what the voices told her? The will of Saint Anthony was pure and good. Why couldn't she do as she was told? Life would be so much simpler...

No. No. NO!

She screwed up her eyes and dug her nails into her palms. All that was needed was one great effort and the whole thing would give way. She was convinced of that. If she could only remember. Clear the log-jam...

She flinched and dived for cover as a nearby door opened and a Chapterman stepped out. He was splendidly dressed in freshly pressed purple and had on a ceremonial skull-cap trimmed with gold.

A draught of air from the room he had vacated reached her. It had the sickly-sweet quality of a crypt.

When the Chapterman had disappeared from view down one of the long corridors, the woman crossed the hall and slipped quietly into the room.

It seemed to be some kind of viewing point. Small, dark and cramped, it was nevertheless furnished with a wooden bench and a variety of gently rocking candle-holders.

What passed for a window was in fact a highly decorated wooden fenestella, the fluted holes in its structure giving a view of some impenetrable darkness below.

The woman crept across the room, bending almost double in order to do so. She sat down on the bench, crossed her legs and gazed out of the wooden frame. She could make out little or nothing of what was below.

Suddenly, a pinprick of light appeared in the darkness, sailing about like a will-o'-the-wisp. Its sputtering yellow glow betrayed it as a candle. It was instantly joined by another, then another.

Soon she could see Chaptermen scurrying about, lighting tall, tall beeswax candles. They seemed to be in a circular pattern and this was explained when, with a dreadful, tortuous creak, a vast wooden chandelier was hauled towards the roof of the chamber.

As the chilly light spread, the woman realized that she was looking down into the cathedral.

The place was filling rapidly now, dozens of Chaptermen beginning to take their places, kneeling on the uncushioned stone floor and abasing themselves, chanted prayers spilling from their lips.

The cathedral was now ablaze with candle-light. Under other circumstances it could have been a lovely sight, the woman decided, but something unnatural was going on. She could sense it.

The great doors burst open and two lines of penitents stumbled inside, their hopeless faces downcast in abject misery. All wore huge pointed cylinders like dunces' caps, the brims banded with heavy lead and steel. Even in the candle-light, the woman could see the caps cutting into the penitents' foreheads, reopening scarcely healed scars already livid on their sweating skin. Blood dribbled down their faces.

Great thick, tarry ropes were slung over their shoulders and they hauled behind them four enormous metal cages on spoked wheels.

Somewhere, a great gong was struck repeatedly in time to the penitents' advance.

As they trundled inside, clattering over the flagstones, the woman was startled to see the cages packed with people. Mostly they were men and women but here and there were children, some as young as six or seven. All were howling in fear, gripping the bars, their eyes wild with terror.

The woman blinked slowly in her hiding place, the light from the cathedral bathing her face. Somehow these people seemed familiar.

The cages came to a juddering halt and the cathedral fell silent save for the pounding of the gong and the wretched whimpering of the prisoners.

Footsteps.

The woman felt her throat constrict.

Something terrible was about to happen.

'Well, they certainly like to make an entrance.'

Bernice kept her head down as the last echo of the dirigibles' explosion died away on the wind and the rain of fiery debris abated.

Liso was cupping his claw over his good eye and bending apart the branches before him. 'I can see Grek. Some others I know. The rest . . .'

He stepped back, his translucent reptilian eyelid closing. 'The rest seem to be Cutch.'

Bernice shrugged. 'All friends together?'

Liso looked over 'You don't have to humour me. We're fighting the Keth now.'

The great black ship was descending rapidly in a vortex of twisting air, the jungle thrashing about as it was buffeted by the downdraught.

Bernice shook her head and let a thin whistle escape between her teeth.

The colossal craft slammed down onto the tree-tops, steam billowing from its exhaust ports. Surrounding trees buckled and snapped under the pressure of the spiky hull.

Liso jerked his head back and forth in agitation as he watched his comrades and former enemies scatter back towards the dug-out.

The ship finally came to rest and sat like a vast patient spider on the muddied, cratered battlefield.

'Well,' breathed Bernice as silence returned. 'What do we do now?'

Lightning flashed again in the opaque clouds. Liso's eye

swivelled round. 'I don't know. But if your Doctor friend is right, we'd better start thinking. Fast.'

Bernice smiled ruefully. Beneath her feet the ground was trembling.

Ran thrashed at the jungle with his claws, striding unperturbedly through spiky cane plants and dew-heavy ferns. He found the familiar clump of spindly trees, rounded them and pulled up sharply at the shelter.

It was a small brick and metal construction, rounded like a pottery kiln. Moss and glutinous vegetation had crept over its surface, providing excellent natural camouflage.

Ran was grateful for this. The shelter contained the most precious thing in his life. He unbolted the door and stepped inside.

Inside, it was hot and dark, a few low-level gas jets giving fitful illumination. At the centre of the circular room stood a large brass and crystal construction, thick wires plugged into its sides leading to the gas pipes which covered the walls.

Ran approached the machine and bent down reverently, his boots creaking as he sat on his haunches.

The light from inside was warm and comforting. Ran stretched out his claw and placed it against the crystal front. He closed his twitching eyes and smiled.

The Doctor was lost. Although, he told himself, whether or not it was actually possible to be lost in a place you did not know your way around in the first place, he couldn't say.

The featureless metal corridor had given way to another, then yet another, at right angles.

'To my way of thinking,' he muttered, 'this betrays a very dull sort of imagination.'

It had long been a pet hobby-horse of his to berate architects and town planners for their lack of verve. Surely even the most functional of corridors could be given some individuality.

'And it might help me remember where I'm going,' he added aloud.

He stopped suddenly as a low mumbling sound broke the silence. He pressed his ear to the cold metal wall and listened attentively. The noise was so indistinct, he couldn't tell if it was made by voices or machinery.

The Doctor pulled away and bit his lip thoughtfully.

Ahead of him, the corridor continued unbroken. He sighed and walked on, his hands plunged disconsolately into his trouser pockets.

The corridor walls, however, were not entirely uniform. As the Doctor passed, a section of the wall hissed backwards and slid open with a soft click. Someone stepped out of the darkness and, with great care, began to follow him.

The woman tensed as she heard the approaching footsteps ringing through the cathedral. The gong continued to boom out through the echoing stone vaults.

In her heart of hearts, she knew to whom the footsteps belonged. This ceremony could have only one purpose.

The cathedral was packed with Chaptermen shuffling like bees over every inch of the flagstones. Lining the walls, flagellants scourged themselves with knotted ropes, biting their lips until they bled in an effort to stop themselves crying out. The penitents lay in front of the cages, swaying and moaning in unison, the absurd but hideous cylinders pressing down onto their yielding heads.

Inside the cages, the imprisoned wretches had begun to wail.

On the opposite side of the hall, a second pair of huge oak doors shook as bolts were drawn back. The doors were flung open and a man was silhouetted in the doorway, his cloak streaming behind him.

As he stepped into the blaze of the candles, the woman gasped. He was the most beautiful man she had ever seen.

172

Beneath his billowing robes, every detail of his magnificent body was revealed. The fine webbing of his chest and stomach muscles, the firm lines of his calves and thighs. So close-fitting was the man's bodysuit, it was as though a perfect physical specimen had been dipped in tar.

And his face . . .

The woman gazed at the flawless complexion, the jet-black, glossy hair, the large almond-shaped eyes and delicate, full-lipped mouth.

Yet she knew he could only be one man, the Magna, and a wave of cold terror swept through her as he advanced into the cathedral.

The prostrate Chaptermen scuttled away at his approach, clearing a pathway to the steps at the far end of the chamber. Yong swept up the steps and positioned himself on the bare, plain wooden throne. Fifty feet above his head, inset in the ceiling like a great sleeping eye, was a circular wooden panel. A matching panel some hundred feet across occupied most of the cathedral floor.

The woman had seen these features before but had never noticed how exactly they corresponded. But for now she was more concerned with the ceremony in the cathedral.

At a nod from Yong, the massed ranks of Chaptermen rose to their knees, silk robes whispering, and began to chant a strange *dies irae* in a low, humble murmur. The mournful song rang throughout the cathedral, rising above the constant pounding of the gong.

The woman closed her eyes and shivered as a further pang of remembrance stabbed at her.

A few of the supplicants struggled to their feet and, crossing the floor, picked up rows of censers. They processed down the cathedral aisle, swinging the incense-filled spheres back and forth and gurgling incomprehensible intonations. Sickly vapour gushed from the censers and the woman fought back a coughing fit as it filtered through the fenestella into her hiding place.

Yong stood up and his gaze swept over the assembly.

His coffin-black eyes narrowed and he bent down to retrieve a huge wooden cross from behind his throne. The shaft was covered with a filigree of gilded flame.

He leant on it as though it were a walking stick and stretched out his other arm, his elegant fingers splayed wide.

'Hear me!' he bellowed. 'O, fragile and unworthy animals! Though you think yourselves pure and unpolluted, I tell you that in the eyes of Saint Anthony you are naught but the offal of beasts!

'And though your hubris may convince you that you are worthy of His mercy, I tell you that he will show none in the face of your grave and unforgivable sin.'

The ranks of Chaptermen, penitents, flagellents and general suppliants murmured in hysterical dismay.

Yong's expression lightened slightly. 'Yet I tell you now, o pigs of Saint Anthony, that you might yet find absolution in the conversion of heathens, for He looks kindly upon those who spread His gentle creed.'

The assembled groaned with relief. This was a familiar ritual. The woman herself had heard it several times.

Yong descended the steps, the huge cross in one hand clattering on the stonework.

'There are among us today some wretched souls who do not believe as we believe, whose darkness has yet to be illuminated by the one true faith.'

He pointed towards the cages and the inhabitants cowered as his voice echoed around the cathedral. 'These scum. These pustules on the body politic. These poor unfortunates must now know the glory of Saint Anthony!'

He reached the bottom of the steps, laid down the cross and flung his muscular arms wide. 'Bring them to me!'

The Chaptermen scuttled across to the cages and unlocked the heavy padlocks. Terrified and cowed, the wretched people began to spill out into the cathedral, hugging at each other for comfort.

The woman hid her face. She felt sick and scared, almost as though she were down there herself.

The Chaptermen began to prod at the prisoners with spindly spears and herded them up the aisle towards the throne. Yong stepped forward, wreathed in the thick incense which was clinging to every stone of the cathedral.

Chapterman Jones jabbed at a small, skinny child and she stumbled forward, her wide eyes gazing appealingly at Yong. Surprisingly, he smiled.

'Child,' he whispered, 'do you know the extent of your sin?'

The girl's eyes brimmed with tears. 'I . . .'

'Do not think of yourself, wretched creature,' warned Yong. 'Do you not realize how depraved you are?'

The girl looked down at her bruised body in its ragged clothes. 'No,' she mumbled.

Yong's face hardened. 'Then you shall, child. You shall.'

Without warning, he punched her in the face, sending her screaming back into the crowd of prisoners. Yong looked up to the roof, his face filled with insane fervour. 'All! All shall know the wrath of our Patron!'

He nodded towards a Chapterman who vanished behind a curtain into a recessed alcove. There was a queer, oily, grinding sound and almost at once the two great circular panels in the floor and ceiling began to glide open.

Yong stepped back until he was once again before his throne. 'All shall know the sweet and glorious pain of Saint Anthony's Fire!'

The room exploded with crimson light. A vast shimmering column of flame stretched between the two panels like a fork of blood-red lightning trapped forever between heavens and earth.

As the woman shielded her face in awe and terror, she could make out a roaring, boiling energy twisting in spirals within the column.

The assembled fell back in abject terror. Only Yong stood straight and still, his face glowing in the incredible fiery display.

'Do not despair!' he cried. 'For your hour of glory is at

175

hand. This day, your *dies profesti*, you shall join Saint Anthony in eternity!'

The prisoners began to scramble around in absolute panic. Immediately, the Chaptermen herded them towards the column of fire with their spears.

'Rejoice!' yelled Yong. 'Rejoice and be purged!'

The Chaptermen closed in on the prisoners and slowly, inexorably, pushed them towards the roaring shaft of fountaining light.

The small girl whom Yong had struck made a bolt for freedom but Chapterman Jones casually ran her through with his spear. For a moment, she stood stock-still, her mouth gaping in silent agony. Then Jones hoisted her up and tossed her into the fire.

The woman turned from the window, closed her eyes and sobbed.

The child was hurled around inside the column as though in a whirlwind. Her anguished face stared out at her horrified friends for an agonizing minute, then her features began to trickle outwards as though liquefying. In an instant she was gone and only her screams remained, reverberating through the fevered atmosphere of the cathedral.

At once, the Chaptermen began to herd the rest of the prisoners into the flames.

The woman opened her eyes and stood up, cracking her head off the low ceiling. This could not be allowed. It had to be stopped. The Chapter of Saint Anthony had lied to her. Everything she had been taught had been a terrible, vile lie.

Barging out of the little room, she pelted down the corridor. She knew her way around this section of the seminary, even at night. Finding the far door at the opposite end of the cathedral, she hauled it open and ran inside.

'Stop!' she screamed. 'You must stop this slaughter!'

There was an awed silence as she ran up the aisle. The Chaptermen did indeed stop and the column roared in the silence as they gawped at the new arrival's audacity.

'You must stop this!' spat the woman in a hoarse, desperate whisper.

Yong's mouth hung open in amazement. Before he could say anything, the double doors opened and, of all people, the Doctor tumbled inside. He sprawled at the woman's feet. Behind him stood De Hooch, a knife clutched in his sweaty little hands.

'An intruder, Magna. He was brought in with the last of the rock samples. I found him wandering in the lower levels.'

Yong turned surprised and oddly delighted eyes to the Chapterman in the alcove and flapped his arm. The column of fire abruptly cut off.

The Doctor raised exhausted eyes to the woman who stood above him. The shaven head was a bizarre touch, to be sure, and there was a disquieting fever behind her wide eyes but she was still unmistakable.

'Ace!'

The woman's mouth began to tremble and she stumbled to her knees. The dam-burst she had been seeking exploded in her brain and she sobbed: 'Doctor ... Oh God, Doctor ...'

The Doctor put his arm around her and gazed about at the shell-shocked Chaptermen, supplicants and reprieved prisoners. Yong was looking at him interestedly.

The Doctor glanced across at the huge circular panel through which the column of fire had passed.

All it revealed now, through the transparent membrane of the hull, was the blackness of space and the silent green majesty of the planet Betrushia.

Liso and Bernice stood at the edge of the jungle in silence. The great black ship steamed but showed no sign of activity.

Suddenly, from out of the trenches came Thoss, his eyes rolling with fervour. 'Keth! Keth!'

He threw himself down before the enormous craft and

didn't look up, even when the bulkhead slid slowly open and a ramp began to descend into the mud.

Liso stepped back involuntarily as two pink-skinned beasts walked out of the ship, their strange bodies covered in some kind of loose material. Their tiny eyes were fixed in an unnaturally happy state.

One of them stepped forward and looked down at the prostrate form of Thoss. It smiled a beatific smile and swept its purple robes around for effect.

'Hello,' it said.

14

Papal Bull

Yong was finishing the remains of something very unsavoury when a battered and dishevelled Doctor was ushered into his opulent quarters. The Magna stood up, dabbing his mouth with a silk napkin and extending a hand. 'My dear man! Come in! Come in!'

Warily, the Doctor walked across the black and white tiled floor towards Yong's throne. A mild breeze was stirring the muslin drapes.

'Tiger-bone tea?' asked Yong.

The Doctor's eyebrows rose quizzically.

Yong grinned. 'I find it most efficacious after a really good rant.' He poured two cups of steaming black liquid from a large, elaborate china pot.

'Earth tigers?' said the Doctor at last. 'I remember them as an endangered species.'

'They were,' said Yong with what may have been genuine sadness, pressing his manicured fingers to his chest. 'Unfortunately, there are none left at all now. Only the bones.'

He rolled his eyes and took a long drink. The steam rose up until his forehead glistened.

'Where is my friend?' said the Doctor quietly.

Yong put down his cup. 'Ah, yes. The young lady. She's been quite a thorn in my side, I can tell you.'

'I can imagine,' said the Doctor without smiling.

Yong's eyes narrowed. 'She's safe.'

The Doctor plonked himself down in a padded chair

and put up his feet on Yong's desk. His tea remained untouched.

'What I want to know is how she came to be here in the first place. I left her, you see, on a planet not far from here. Massatoris. Perhaps you know it?'

Yong tapped his fingers against his chin. 'Massatoris . . . Massa . . . ah, of course. I remember now. We had a little trouble with the locals. Difficult bunch.'

'Trouble?'

'Yes. They didn't quite see things our way.'

The Doctor rubbed his eyes and the dusty wrinkles on his face concertinaed. 'Why haven't you killed me?'

'Well, we haven't been introduced for a start,' smiled Yong.

There was an icy pause.

'Doctor,' said the Doctor.

Yong slid a finger over his rosebud lips. 'Doctor. I see.'

'I don't,' said the Doctor with sudden anger. 'I don't see what you're doing rampaging around the galaxy in a battlecruiser got up as a cathedral, why you imprisoned my companion, what you did to Massatoris and who the devil you think you are.'

Yong blinked slowly and half smiled. 'Do you want the answers one at a time or all at once?'

The Doctor glared at him.

Yong sat back in his chair and steepled his fingers.

'I am William Hon Yuen Yong, Magna of the Chapter of Saint Anthony.'

'The what of Saint who?'

Yong stood up and strolled across the room, his robes swishing over the glistening second skin of his bodysuit. 'You haven't heard of us? Oh, how distressing.'

He cleared his throat. 'The Chapter of Saint Anthony was formed after the eventual dissolution of the High Catholick Church. As I'm sure you remember, all the faiths of the Earth were merged with the idea of creating planet-wide peace.'

The Doctor looked up. 'What happened?'

180

'It was a disaster. No one could agree on anything. It was then that the Chapter stepped into the breach. Nature abhors a vacuum. People need discipline, the Chapter gave it to them.'

'Really?' said the Doctor sardonically.

Yong put his hands behind his back where they hung, pale and ghostly, like a clump of dripping church candles.

'The Old God tempted Saint Anthony. His faith was tested. The Chapter has extended this brave principle to our missionary cause. We travel throughout the wastes of the galaxy in search of those not yet blessed.'

The Doctor swallowed hard. 'I see. So you root out these . . . heathens and test their faith. How do you test it?'

Yong swung round, artificial sunlight glittering in his black, black eyes. 'How else, Doctor? By completely destroying them.'

Bernice and Liso crept from the edge of the jungle and around the steaming mass of the black ship. They pelted towards the dug-out and Liso pulled Bernice over the lip of the trench, sliding expertly down the ladder. They waded through the filthy trench-water towards Grek's quarters and, as they emerged through the doorway, Grek and Imalgahite whirled round.

'Liso!' cried Grek delightedly. 'I never thought I'd be . . . Well, good to see you.' He clapped a claw on the young officer's shoulder and nodded to Bernice. 'We thought you'd perished in the explosion.'

'We escaped over Porsim,' said Bernice simply. 'But they followed us. I think that little bang was a show of strength.'

She shot a hostile look at Imalgahite. 'Hello again.'

Imalgahite turned away shamefacedly. 'They do look a lot like her, don't they? You have to admit it.'

Bernice held up her hands. 'Don't blame me just because they're humanoid. What are they up to out there anyway?'

181

Imalgahite sighed. 'Just scouting about. They've taken most of our men on board. We managed to get away.'

Grek sat down heavily on the ruins of his bunk. 'I must admit they're not how I imagined the Keth.'

Bernice shook her head. 'They're not the Keth. I'm sure of it. More like your average everyday invasion force.'

Liso looked up. 'I think she's right. They're flesh and blood. We can fight back.'

Imalgahite waddled towards him. 'But you saw what they did to your airships. And your cities? Yes?'

Liso looked down. 'Yes.'

'Then what can we do against firepower like that?'

'Whatever we have to,' said Grek gravely.

Liso looked around concernedly at the devastated room. The earthquake had left it virtually unrecognizable.

'There's more to it than you think, I'm afraid,' he said. 'We saw Ran. He and the Doctor went up there.' He jerked his claw upwards. 'Into space. The Doctor said the whole of Betrushia is pulling itself apart. It could be days. Even hours.'

'What?' breathed Grek. 'You're sure?'

'If the Doctor says so,' said Bernice with a shrug.

Imalgahite gnawed at his talons. 'Then our priority is not to fight these invaders but to get away from here as soon as we can.'

'How?' cried Grek.

Imalgahite trotted to the dug-out entrance and pointed outside. Just visible over the lip of the trench were the spiky protuberances of the black ship.

Much to his surprise, the Doctor had been given the run of the ship. It was certainly impressive, in an unhealthy sort of way, although to an expert eye the stonework of the seminary was clearly artificial. The sun which gave light and heat to the ship and simulated day and night, however, must be an engineering marvel.

But the Doctor's only concern now was Ace and how she had come to be in this fearful place.

182

He found his way to her cell without difficulty and pushed open the door. She was sitting in the corner, her knees pulled up to her chin, eyes closed, ersatz sunlight bathing the side of her face.

'Did you do it for a bet?' asked the Doctor with a small smile.

Ace looked up quizzically.

'The haircut,' said the Doctor. He wandered over and sat down next to her. 'Between you, me and the gatepost, I don't think it really suits you.'

Ace smiled wearily and buried her face in the torn folds of the Doctor's waistcoat. When she looked up, her eyes were wet with tears.

'You look a right state,' she said. 'What's been going on?'

The Doctor detached himself from her. 'Later, Ace. I'm more concerned about you.'

'I'm fine,' she muttered, wiping her eyes with the back of her hand.

The Doctor shook his head. 'No. No, you're not. They must have used some pretty unsavoury methods to be able to brainwash you.'

Ace clenched her fists and closed her eyes. 'I can't . . . I can't seem to . . . There's a barrier. I . . . Oh Christ!'

She thumped the mattress, her eyes flashing with anger.

'All right,' said the Doctor soothingly. 'Let's take it from the beginning.'

He fixed Ace with a penetrating stare. His dark eyes seemed to turn a watery grey, then emerald green, or were they blue? Perhaps bluey-green, like the sea, or . . .

She felt herself go limp and relax back against the wall. 'Take it easy,' murmured the Doctor. 'Take . . . it . . . easy . . .'

Ace felt waves of reassurance pass through her mind and the Doctor's voice calling as though from a long way off.

The Doctor ran his hand through his muddied hair, speaking calmly and clearly: 'Where are you?'

Ace's voice was quiet, almost serene: 'Where you left me.'

'Massatoris?'

'Yes. It's beautiful. I want to stay here a while. Things to think about.'

The Doctor nodded to himself. 'Bernice and myself have left you there. We've said goodbye. What's happening now?'

Ace's face was wreathed in shadow. 'The TARDIS has gone. I'm on my own again. But there are people near. They're very friendly. I like them,' she said simply.

'And do you stay with them?'

'Yes. For a long time. All through the night. Then it's morning and the sun . . . it's reflecting off the lake. I'm going to get water and food with a girl. Can't remember her name. Then – '

She scowled and looked frightened. The Doctor leant forward. 'Then?'

'They've come! Something in the sky. There are men everywhere. The Chaptermen. Killing. Killing so many. Or taking them. For conversion. I can't see . . .'

'You must,' insisted the Doctor. 'Go on. Go on.'

'The black ship is in the sky. Something's coming out of it. Boiling away the lake. The forest's on fire. Oh, God, Doctor. It's fire. Coming out of the ship. Fire!'

Ace leapt to her feet and screamed in the Doctor's face. He snapped his fingers and she crumpled in a heap at his feet. He put an arm around her and made gentle, soothing sounds. 'It's all right now, Ace. Shhh.'

She looked up. 'They took me. Strapped me down. I remember now. I remember!' Her voice shook with relief. 'They've got some kind of machine. They . . . changed me. I tried to resist but . . . I'm one of them. I can't help it!'

The Doctor patted her back. 'Not any more.'

He got to his feet, frowning. 'They must select a few they think will make good converts and cull the rest.'

Ace rubbed her red, swollen eyes. 'But what are we going to do? Where are we?'

'We're moving back to the place Bernice and I came to. Betrushia. It has its own problems.'

Ace nodded absently.

The Doctor made for the cell door. 'I want you to stay here for now. There's just a chance I can persuade the Magna not to visit any further destruction on this planet.'

Much to the Doctor's relief, Ace nodded slowly and sank back onto the bunk. In a few moments she was asleep.

The Doctor smiled as he left. 'Sweet dreams,' he murmured.

Ran made his way through the steaming jungle towards the Ismetch dug-out. In his claws he carried a bulky crystalline box, its rounded edges covered in a long oily cloth.

He looked down warily at the snaking lianas at his feet which might trip him up. This cargo was too precious to drop. The obvious trembling of the ground beneath his boots and the unhealthy electric charge in the atmosphere were inescapable.

The Doctor's prophecy of doom seemed to be coming to pass. Pockets of steam were belching through the jungle floor and the noonday sky was thick and threatening.

Ran stopped abruptly as he noticed something else in the greasy, cloud-heavy sky. For a moment he took it for the rings but whatever it was seemed to shadow their faint halo; a sickly yellow echo of their majesty.

He squinted to make out the shape but it seemed defiantly intangible, a thread on the far horizon.

Ran frowned and walked on towards the edge of the jungle.

The great black scout-ship of Saint Anthony still steamed on the muddy field in front of the Ismetch dug-out. By now, several Chaptermen were busily engaged around it, examining the jungle foliage and making copious notes on long scrolls of parchment.

Two of them, sporting curved translation devices in

185

their ears and both clad in the familiar purple of the Chapter, looked around inquisitively at the sweltering jungle.

'I don't like it,' whispered Miller, a shaven-headed, intense-looking man, a good foot taller than his companion.

'You never do,' drawled Martino, his pale blue eyes flicking absently from the scroll to the sky.

'It's too quiet,' hissed Miller.

'You always say that as well,' added Martino with a smile. 'Even when the most threatening lifeforms are monocellular algae. In case you've forgotten, comrade, we're here to do a job, not to let the local savages put the wind up us.'

Miller swivelled his dark eyes. 'I still don't like it. Who knows what they might be fermenting in their vile little brains? I mean, did you see the ones we took inside?' He shuddered at the memory. 'Those proles on Massatoris were bad enough.'

'Be content, Miller,' said Martino gruffly. 'They will be converted or destroyed as usual.'

'It is the will of Saint Anthony,' chimed Miller automatically.

Both made a curious crossing gesture with their hands.

Miller stalked around the hull of the ship and then looked up. 'When does the Magna's ship land?'

'Soon,' purred Martino with a mixture of excitement and fear.

Miller suddenly stood erect, towering over Martino. He grasped his fellow Chapterman firmly by the elbow. 'Look!'

He pointed towards the horizon where the sky had taken on a strange yellow hue. 'What the hell is that?'

'The Magna has decreed that you are to be afforded every privilege as an honoured guest,' said Parva De Hooch with a sigh.

He and the Doctor were making their way through a

maze of dark stone corridors towards a huge circular metal iris. De Hooch stopped sharply and adjusted his skull-cap. 'Though personally, I would've burned you alive.'

The Doctor gave him a pained smile. 'And this is where you run things, is it?'

De Hooch pressed his hand to a panel at the door's side and the iris opened with a squeal of metal.

'The co-ordination of Saint Anthony's will is enacted here, yes. Events are assessed and their bearing on the crusade are considered by the Magna. He then gives orders to implement various scenarios.'

The Doctor hopped through the entrance. 'Ah yes. The bridge.'

What De Hooch had described was, indeed, the heart of the vessel, a colossal hexagonal room, its walls crammed with navigational consoles. Chaptermen of a dozen different races scurried back and forth, checking, analysing, assessing. A circular viewing screen dominated the far wall.

In the centre of the room, immaculate in his purple gown, stood Yong. He flashed the Doctor a delightful smile.

'So glad you could come,' he purred. 'It's so rare for me to be able to show off my little toys to someone who appreciates them.'

'Yes,' said the Doctor carefully. He spread his arms wide and swung round. 'It is rather nice, Magna. How long have you been on this . . . crusade of yours?'

Yong cast his eyes over a list of figures and rapped out a series of orders to a hovering Chapterman before turning back to the Doctor. 'Oh, about a century, Doctor. My family have been at it for years. According to my grandfather's diaries, Earth was becoming quite an amusing place when they left. All that chaos. They left China when it was taken over by Hong Kong. The crusade began shortly afterwards.'

The Doctor nodded slowly, tracing his fingers over the

complex machinery all around him. 'And do you have an ultimate goal? I mean, most crusades have a purpose. An end.'

Yong smiled, his smooth features glowing in the twinkling lights of the bridge. 'I bring Saint Anthony's Fire to the heathen hordes. It's as simple as that.'

'Yes,' muttered the Doctor under his breath, 'I was rather afraid it might be.'

'I'm under no illusions about your enmity, Doctor,' hissed Yong. 'I'm allowing you to live because, quite frankly, I'm bored. It's been so easy for so long. I'd like to see how far you can get in thwarting me before my inevitable victory.'

The Doctor regarded him steadily. 'Very well.'

He turned to the vast viewing screen which dominated the bridge. 'There's something I want to talk to you about, anyway. This planet you're about to reach has a few teensy-weensy problems of its own and I think, on balance, it might be wiser to move on somewhere else.'

Yong swung round, his cloak swooping over De Hooch's head and completely concealing him. 'Impossible, Doctor. The will of Saint Anthony cannot be changed. Besides, we're coming in to land.'

He glanced down at the strange bulge in his purple robes. 'De Hooch, what are you doing down there?'

Huffily, the dwarf extricated himself from Yong's robes and smiled sheepishly. 'Should I escort the Doctor to his quarters for the remainder of the voyage, Magna?'

'No, no. Let him run loose. It amuses me to have some opposition.'

'But Magna . . .'

'Do it!' spat Yong. De Hooch marched a thoughtful Doctor off the bridge. Yong turned back to the screen. 'Now, time to blow up a few more of those silly ring things.'

He crossed to the navigational consoles. 'In the name of Saint Anthony, let us bring His mercy and terrible wrath to . . .'

He looked down irritably at the nervous navigator. 'Dear me, what is this planet called again?'

'Ace? Ace, wake up.' The Doctor tapped his companion lightly on her cheek.

She blinked rapidly, still frightened. 'Doctor? How long have I . . .?'

'Never mind. Listen, Ace, we've got to get off this ship. It's no use trying to talk to this lot. They're all completely mad. And things are too far advanced on Betrushia for us to get stuck here.'

'What do we do?' Something of Ace's old determination seemed to be leaking back into her exhausted body.

The Doctor sucked his fingers thoughtfully. 'We're coming in to land, according to the Magna. He's giving me enough rope to hang myself but I might knot some sheets together instead, if you get my drift.'

'No.'

'No, well, never mind. The point is, I can't do anything till we're off this ship. And the problem is you, really.'

'Me?'

'Well, you're officially one of them, even if you have resisted their conditioning.' He ran his hand playfully over Ace's scalp. 'I'm sure I can think of something.'

'As soon as you get any brilliant ideas,' said a voice from the doorway, 'do let me know.' De Hooch raised his blaster and smiled alarmingly. 'I'm simply dying to hear them.'

Yong's ship ploughed through the remains of further Betrushian rings, scattering the debris into luminescent clouds as it made planetfall.

Inside, Yong walked grandly around the ship's bridge.

'Report from the scout vessel?' he enquired.

The helmsman pressed a row of buttons and read off the screen: 'Scout-ship reports all major cities destroyed, Magna. They've landed near to some sort of concentration of native life. Awaiting your arrival and further orders.'

'Excellent, excellent. Take us down.'

The mothership slipped through the heavy blanket of Betrushian cloud, untroubled by the sheet lightning crackling through the sky.

Flashing data shone in Yong's eyes as the ship roared over the jungle towards the Ismetch base. The scout-ship, once identified, filled the screen, thousands of navigational calculations scrolling over its image.

On Betrushia, Miller and Martino looked up in undisguised awe as the immense mothership, which dwarfed even their own, flattened the jungle and came to rest in a pall of vapour.

For a time, wreathed in steam, the two ships stood side by side in silence, like watchful black beetles.

Then, with a roar of power, the bulkheads glided open and a swarm of the mothership's Chaptermen spilled out. At their head was Yong, striding out proprietally onto Betrushian soil.

Martino immediately advanced towards him, his head bowed.

'Report, Chapterman Martino,' said Yong, looking at the flattened trees.

'A fertile planet, my Lord. With countless lifeforms, dominated by reptilian humanoids with quite a highly developed culture.'

Yong nodded and gazed about him at the magnificently lush jungle and the glittering rings insinuating themselves like sheaves of shattered golden rainbow through the darkening clouds.

'Get rid of it,' he muttered.

15

Yellow Fever

The fugitives had made their way out of Grek's quarters and were skulking in the trench. It had all but collapsed in on itself, the duck-boards scattered haphazardly about in a slurry of black mud.

Grek managed to climb up the ladder and poked his head over the edge of the trench. He squinted at the bulk of the scout-ship and its even bigger twin.

'They don't seem to be making any attempt to find us,' he said at last.

Bernice stood at the bottom of the ladder. 'Maybe they don't know the strength of the opposition. I mean, they might think we've got an army down here.'

'We *did* have an army down here,' said Liso sadly.

'Look,' said Imalgahite, his claw sinking into the mud wall. 'If we can take that ship and get off this planet then there's a good chance that our people,' he looked about at his former enemies, 'and I do mean all our people, can survive. Or at least enough to ensure we proliferate somewhere else. If we stay here debating then we'll die as surely as Betrushia.'

Bernice nodded. 'He's right. The question is, can we convince those lot that the planet's about to blow?'

Grek clambered back down the ladder. 'And if not, how do we attack?'

Bernice folded her arms and sighed. 'I wish I knew where the Doctor was. And what he's up to.'

Imalgahite seemed suddenly struck by inspiration. 'That old man you mentioned?'

Grek looked round. 'Thoss? What about him?'

'They took him on board, didn't they?'

'Yes. He was amongst the first. Didn't show any resistance.'

Imalgahite rubbed at his snout thoughtfully. 'I wonder whether it isn't time for us to start playing dumb.'

Liso looked at him with his sound eye and smiled.

Martino and Miller watched Yong stride back to the mothership and then let out a collective sigh of relief.

'He seemed quite pleased,' said Miller.

'Hmm,' muttered Martino. 'We'll start by razing the jungle. Miller, establish a couple of teams would you? A nice blaze should do us all good.'

'What if they're hostile?' gulped Miller.

'Well, of course they'll be hostile,' said Martino with a sigh. 'We just go about things in the usual way.'

'And what about you?' muttered Miller, tapping his translator.

Martino frowned. 'I'll supervise things this end. Chapterman Fung and myself have some very complex navigation to work out. Now get about your conflagration duties.'

Reluctantly Miller picked his way through the steaming, flattened foliage towards the scout-ship's bulkheads. From inside, he produced a heavy twin-canistered flame-jet pack which he shrugged over his shoulders. A corrugated pipe led from the canisters and terminated in a shining chrome nozzle.

He nodded to some waiting Chaptermen and they put on their own equipment.

Once they were ready, the strange group of a dozen men formed into a line. 'All right,' said Miller. 'Let's get on with it.'

They trooped off into the jungle.

* * *

192

De Hooch stood in the doorway of the cell, a crazed expression on his fat, round features, like a child's drawing of a face on a balloon. Sweat sprang out on his domed forehead. 'Yong may think he's got the better of you but I won't make the same mistake, Doctor. I think you're far too dangerous to have around. And as for that . . . thing!' He gestured furiously at Ace. 'She's caused me quite enough trouble.'

The Doctor regarded the dwarf coolly. 'You don't agree with the Magna then?'

'Of course not! He's insane.'

'Isn't that rather a dangerous allegation to make?' said the Doctor slyly.

De Hooch grinned. 'It may well be, Doctor. But you won't live long enough to tell any tales. If it's of any interest, Yong's rule of the Chapter of Saint Anthony will shortly be over.'

The Doctor pulled a face. 'Oh, I see. Some sort of palace coup on the cards, is there?'

Ace began to move surreptitiously across the mattress. De Hooch's gleaming eyes were fixed on the Doctor.

'Of course,' the Doctor began to expound, 'you have the classic motive. Years of abuse at the hands of an intellectual inferior who got where he is through outrageous nepotism. It's only right that you should take over.'

De Hooch's prune face broke up into a sickly grin. 'You can't fool me, Doctor. Switching sides is the oldest trick in the book.'

The Doctor pointed to his ruined clothes. 'Well, Parva, it seems I'm a turncoat without a coat to turn.'

De Hooch raised the blaster. 'Rest assured, Doctor, that shortly you will be nothing very much at all.'

Ace leapt across the room, her legs arcing through the air and contacting De Hooch's body at the base of his neck. He squawked and fell backwards against the cell wall. The filigreed cross on the wall fell off and cracked him across the forehead.

Ace grabbed the blaster and tossed it to the Doctor,

who immediately tossed it back to her with a disgusted frown. 'No. You keep it. Let's go.'

'Hang on.' said Ace. She picked up the unconscious De Hooch in both hands and, grunting with effort, stuffed him into the cupboard.

'That was cruel,' said the Doctor.

'Yeah,' smiled Ace, 'but he had it coming. And I enjoyed it.'

They ran from the room and back into the endless sun-drenched corridors.

'What are you going to do?' called Ace breathlessly as they ran. 'Blow up the ship? That artificial sun of theirs should make quite a bang.'

'No, no, no,' cried the Doctor, glancing at the rows of doors. 'We need the ships intact if we're to get any of the Betrushians off alive.' He pulled up sharply. 'Listen.'

'What?'

'Did you hear . . .'

They were both silenced by a low groaning from a nearby cell. The Doctor dashed across the corridor and slammed his shoulder to the door. It resisted. Ace blew it off its hinges with one blast from De Hooch's gun.

Inside, almost invisible in the gloom, lay Thoss, curled up in a foetal ball.

'Keth . . . Keth . . .' he muttered.

'No, Doctor, Doctor,' said the Doctor lifting up the old reptile's head. 'You haven't told me everything have you, Thoss?'

The old man's blue eyes flickered. 'It's too late, Doctor.'

The Doctor hauled him to his feet. 'It's never too late. Come on. We're getting out of here.'

Miller's team had penetrated well into the sweltering jungle when he held up his hand and halted. Spindly trees, their rain-heavy leaves curving overhead to form a natural green ceiling, rustled in the wind.

'This'll do,' muttered Miller and began to charge up his flame-jet.

Once, he reflected, this sort of work would have given him great pleasure. As a youth, and a member of the Chapter's Initiate League, he had been amongst the first to torch the old city of Urrozdinee following its government's suicidal refusal of the rule of Saint Anthony.

He could never forget the thrill the blaze had given him, nor the sight of the once-proud buildings silhouetted against a fiery red sky as the conflagration took hold.

Perhaps he was just getting old but it just didn't have the same appeal anymore. And, besides, burning trees was so *passé*.

He sniffed and pressed two black buttons on the side of the nozzle. A tongue of fire leapt out with a whoosh and incinerated a nearby cycad. The flame-jet was ruthlessly efficient. The tree crumbled to sooty black ash almost at once and fell in on itself.

Miller turned and began a systematic torching of the surrounding foliage, his comrades doing likewise, all looking rather bored. Flame began to erupt in a wide circle as the Chaptermen fanned out.

It was only during a lull in the proceedings that Miller became aware of a rumbling, cracking sound deep beneath his feet.

Again he held up his hand for silence and looked around curiously. The ground was trembling. The air itself seemed to break into shuddering waves as the jungle thrashed and swayed.

Miller was about to order his men back to the ship when a torrent of mud burst from the ground, spitting steam into the atmosphere. Great clods of earth tore through the jungle canopy.

Something was wrong with this place. Clearly. Miller had known it all along.

He began to hobble backwards over the shifting ground, stumbling over thick tree roots and vines, but his attention was soon caught by something else making its way out of the new crater.

It was thick and glutinous, like a river of vomit, pulsing

out of the ground and then partially solidifying like pillow lava. In an instant it liquefied again and rolled over the freshly burnt foliage towards them.

Miller felt cold sweat break out under his purple robes and a horrible looseness around his sphincters.

'Get out! Run! Run!' he bellowed hoarsely.

His men needed no encouragement as the tide of yellow paste slurped across the soil.

Miller pointed his flame-jet at the thing and pressed down hard on the nozzle buttons. Fire blasted out of the device and roared into the oncoming substance. It was immediately absorbed, as though swallowed, and the yellow tide powered remorselessly on. Glittering mucus shone over its surface.

Miller turned on his heel and ran.

Almost at once, the ground shook even more violently and he was thrown headlong into the jungle, landing at the base of a huge tree and cracking his head off the bole. He sat up, retching, and held his temples as the world spun sickeningly around him. His vision cleared slightly. Trees. Green. Ferns. Wet. Mud.

And all at once it was on him, slavering over his undefended flesh, burning through each layer of tissue, twisting, sucking, insinuating itself into Miller's body.

He tried to scream but the glutinous mass was already half-way down his throat. His eyes bulged, expanded, popped but then he felt no more as the yellow paste swallowed him completely.

It seemed to pause for a moment, its slippery surface writhing around as though contemplating its next move. In the darkening sky, the rings of Betrushia were beginning one of their final displays.

Beneath them, bowling over the horizon like a hurricane, the yellow thread continued to grow.

In an instant, the slobbering mass containing the remains of Chapterman Miller had vanished.

Ran's claw curled around the trunk of the tree as he gazed

at the sight before him. The two great black ships took up the entire battlefield and much of the jungle perimeter.

He glanced across at the familiar dug-out and then back to the ships. If the Doctor was dead then the only chance of getting his precious cargo to safety was in the mysterious alien vessels.

He looked at them gingerly, a slight twitch agitating his eyes. The ships were massive and ugly, steam pouring off their bristly black hulls. Several of the alien mammals in purple were milling about before them, fiddling with some kind of apparatus on their backs.

Ran stepped back involuntarily as flame shot out of one of the machines and incinerated a clump of trees.

Imperceptibly at first, the ground began to shudder once more and lightning seared the rapidly darkening sky. A creeping yellow haze, like an infection, was bleeding through the clouds. By now, Ran had decided this was something to do with Betrushia's terminal decline.

He looked down towards the ships, lit up by the fire in the jungle. There had to be a way of getting inside.

He frowned. Something strange was going on just in front of the ships' ramps.

Bernice felt very foolish as she walked across the mud towards the alien ships, head bowed and arms spread wide.

With her were Grek, Liso and Imalgahite, all with similarly obsequious expressions as though overpowered with guilt. When they were close enough to be noticed but, they hoped, too far away to be incinerated they threw themselves down in the mud and began to moan.

'Keth! Keth!' cried Grek. 'They have come at last.'

'The Masters! We obey you, masters!' joined in Liso with gusto.

Bernice winked at him and set up a terrible wailing. 'Mercy!' she called ridiculously. 'Mercy, O masters of Betrushia!'

197

Chapterman Jones eyed them wearily. 'Oh, Saint Anthony. More of the locals.' He swung round. 'Martino!'

The smaller man emerged from behind the bulkheads. 'Yes, Jones?'

'Get these lot inside, would you? The Magna will want to know if they're suitable for conversion.'

Martino advanced towards the party of unlikely pilgrims and prodded Grek in the side with his boot. 'Up! Come on!'

He gestured with his hands and then, threateningly, with the nozzle of his flame-jet. 'Inside! Understand? Get in!' He waved his hands in the direction of the ship and the pilgrims dutifully got to their feet.

Grek, Liso and Imalgahite disappeared inside through the bulkheads but Martino laid a hand on Bernice's arm as she made to pass.

'You. You're not one of them. What're you doing here?'

Bernice's mind raced. She had been amongst the Ismetch and the Cutch so long she had almost forgotten how different she was.

'I serve you, master,' she stammered, licking her lips nervously. 'True, I am not of their race. They . . . er found me in the jungle and raised me as one of their own.'

A story spilled from her lips with just enough conviction. She must have read something similar somewhere.

'All right,' said Martino at last. Sighing, Bernice slipped past him into the ship and the custody of the Chapter.

Martino turned away. In the darkness, he failed to see the other bulkhead open and the Doctor, Ace and Thoss slip out into the night.

Yong had returned to his quarters and was reclining on his bed when the eyes of a stuffed gorilla at his side began to flash. Wearily, he stretched out a long digit and pressed the gorilla's shiny nose.

'Yes?'

A crackly, static-filled voice came through from the

bridge: 'Chapterman Jones reports some more heathens have been taken aboard, Magna.'

'Really?' drawled Yong with a yawn. He frowned, conscious for the first time of the ship's trembling. 'What is that dreadful motion?'

'Seems to be some sort of earth tremor, my Lord.'

Yong fell back against his silk pillows. 'Oh. I hope you haven't landed us anywhere nasty.' He examined his fingernails thoughtfully. 'Still, it doesn't matter. Soon this place will be nothing but dust.'

'It is the will of Saint Anthony,' intoned the voice.

'Mmm,' said Yong. 'Where is Parva De Hooch?'

'Here,' said a little voice.

Yong turned his head and switched off the communicator with a jab at the gorilla's nose. He couldn't suppress a giggle at the second's dishevelled appearance.

'De Hooch,' he said, biting his lip, 'she hasn't got the better of you again?'

The dwarf caressed his bruised face with a pudgy hand. 'She was not alone. That Doctor, whom you have allowed to run riot, aided her escape.'

Yong's eyes narrowed. 'Do I detect a note of rebuke, Parva?'

De Hooch's face darkened as he struggled to keep his emotions under control. His scowl magically transformed into a concerned frown.

'My only fear is for you, my Lord. And how this treacherous Doctor might upset our . . . your plans.'

'I've told you, De Hooch, it pleases me to have some competition now and again. Remember the old days when we actually had to struggle to do our work? All those bleeding-heart liberals with their arcane views. They were troublesome, yes. But don't you miss the cut and thrust?'

De Hooch shrugged. 'I suppose so.'

'There you are, then. Let this Doctor do as he pleases. Allow him to think he's got the upper hand. It'll be all the more satisfying when we triumph.' He licked the ends of his elegant fingers excitedly. 'Saint Anthony will not be cheated, De Hooch.'

'Of course not, Magna.'

'Now,' said Yong, sitting up and plumping his pillows, 'can I trust you to attend to the little matter of some newly arrived locals?'

De Hooch looked hurt. 'Yes, Magna.'

'You have let me down recently.'

De Hooch bowed low. 'Then I humbly beg forgiveness, my Lord. I seek only the true path of righteousness.'

Yong smiled sweetly. 'Good for you.'

He sank back onto his bed and rang for some tea. 'The new arrivals probably aren't suitable for anything but culling, but you never know. I shall leave it to your . . . discretion.'

'Thank you, my Lord.'

De Hooch gave a final bow and tottered unsteadily from the room. As he slammed the doors shut his face crumpled into a furious sneer. He would show that irreligious cretin how the Chapter should be run. But not yet. Not quite yet.

He walked away down the corridor towards the interrogation rooms. The heathens were probably the usual trash. Either terrified sun-worshippers or cocky beggars who thought their own primitive beliefs far too precious to be sacrificed to the just and awful wrath of Saint Anthony.

He poked gingerly at the swollen skin of his face. Once this was over and he was Magna, he would make the Doctor and the woman endure all the torments of hell for this humiliation.

De Hooch rounded the corner and unlocked the small steel door of the interrogation room.

Inside, in the dim light were three reptilian creatures. De Hooch smiled his usual smile and was about to deliver his familiar rant when the blaster was wrenched from his hand by an unseen person. He whirled round and realized he had fallen for the second oldest trick in the book.

Bernice stepped out from her hiding place behind the

door and trained the blaster on De Hooch's diminutive form.

'We're stealing your ship,' she said simply. 'Now, if you'd be so kind, take me to your leader.'

De Hooch let out a huge sigh. This really wasn't his day.

The Doctor, Ace and Thoss scurried across the shaking battlefield towards the dug-out. It was night by now and the rings blazed gloriously, joined by diagonal flashes of lightning.

'How long have we got?' shouted Ace above the din.

The Doctor shook his head, supporting Thoss with one hand and hurrying up Ace with the other. 'Hard to tell. The sooner we work all this out, the better.'

Ace jumped over a large crater. 'Work what out? The Chapter want to wipe out this planet and it's going to wipe itself out anyway. Can't we just help the good guys get out of here and then ... er ... get out of here?'

'Bernice said something similar,' cried the Doctor as they reached the Number Seven ladder-hole and climbed down.

Ace nodded. 'I'm beginning to think she speaks more and more sense, that girl.'

'I'm not here for the good of my health, Ace. Nor even to get rid of those over-zealous friends of yours.' He helped Thoss down the ladder.

'So what's the problem, then?'

'I'll explain. First we need to get into the Temple.'

Thoss was already staggering down the corridor. 'This way,' he called over his shoulder.

They made their way through the gloom, the surrounding gas jets faltering as though they too had given up all hope.

'Doctor,' said Ace as they reached the Temple entrance. 'The Chapter and all that. They're not what worries you, are they?'

'Far from it.'

The Doctor pushed open the door and all three began to clatter down the steps towards the shrine. 'They're simply an annoyance. Confusing the real issue.'

'Which is?' asked Ace.

The Doctor hopped off the last step. Thoss looked down at the base of the shrine, gasping for breath.

The Doctor stuffed his hands in his pockets. 'Betrushian legend – '

Thoss looked up. The Doctor corrected himself: 'Betrushian religion; faith; what you will, states that this planet was devastated an eternity ago by something called the Keth. And that the original inhabitants, who looked a lot like me and you, Ace, were wiped out.

'The legend also states that when the earth turns over in its sleep and the rain turns to stone . . .'

Ace nodded her understanding of recent events.

'Then the Keth will return,' continued the Doctor. 'Our mistake was to think the Chapter of Saint Anthony were our missing bogymen.'

Ace frowned. 'Then who, or what, is?'

The Doctor approached Thoss. 'Well, Thoss? Isn't it about time you told us the whole truth?'

Thoss turned away. 'I don't . . . I don't know . . .'

The Doctor stood up. 'Well, maybe I can help. How's this for starters?'

He pulled the handful of stones from his pocket. 'These meteorites aren't meteorites.'

Ace looked up. 'They're from the rings, you said.'

'Yes and no.' said the Doctor gravely. 'They're from up there but they're not real.'

'Not real?'

'They're constructs. There's a mechanism inside each one.'

He hurled the stones at Thoss's feet. 'Your entire ring system is artificial!'

202

16

Slayed in Flame

Martino rubbed his small, pale button of a nose as acrid smoke wafted into his face.

He watched the jungle blaze with great satisfaction. Fire licked at the diamond-patterned bark of a hundred different trees, sending seed-pods exploding outwards as the flames roared through them. The two black ships were wreathed in heavy, sooty vapour.

Despite his professional pride in the destruction, however, Martino felt uneasy. Miller should have returned by now. The constant trembling of the ground set his teeth on edge. In a few moments he would confide in Chapterman Jones and begin an analysis of this strange planet.

For now, though, he kept his fingers pressed down on the nozzle of his flame-thrower and watched the fire lash out like an enflamed red tongue into the jungle.

A small, dazed-looking mammal, something between a bear and a monkey, dropped from a burning tree, chittering in pain as its skin was singed.

Martino smiled at it, cooing gently, and stroked its face with the nozzle of his flame-jet. Then he blasted the fur from its body.

Just for fun, he sprayed the air with fire in a wide arc, like a child with a water-pistol. He dropped his arm suddenly as something in the night sky caught his eyes. The flame-jet fell from his hand.

Under the rings, bowling through the jungle like a glutinous whirlwind, something was approaching. It had no form he could recognize, just a massive concretion of hovering ooze, sparkling in the starlight, trailing a comet-tail of dreary, swirling dust.

Dimly, Martino could see it rippling through the burning jungle, flaming debris sucked up its dark core.

He began to walk backwards towards the ship. The Magna had to be told. It seemed Miller's fears about this planet were justified after all.

'Down here,' said Thoss in a sepulchral whisper.

The hole beneath the shrine in which the Doctor had hidden yawned open, Thoss's old claw gripping at the hefty flagstone.

The Doctor stepped through. 'Do you have any torches?'

Ace and Thoss followed onto the first of the stone steps. 'There's no need,' said Thoss cryptically. 'This place lights itself.'

Intrigued, the Doctor pressed on, feeling his way downwards in the pitch black, his hands sliding unpleasantly over the slick, moss-covered walls.

After a time, he felt a change in the texture. Ace called from behind him, 'Doctor, it's getting lighter.'

The Doctor looked back. He could now see Thoss and Ace, albeit dimly, and the walls had taken on a dull metallic sheen. In addition, they were quite warm.

'It's reacting to our presence,' muttered the Doctor, looking round. The light was gradually increasing, revealing the metal walls of some kind of shaft. The Doctor ran up to them and felt the surface.

'Intriguing.'

'Has it been bored?' said Ace.

The Doctor didn't look round. 'Well, haven't we all at some time?'

Ace tutted. The Doctor smiled.

'No, it seems to have been ... grown. As though the metal were exuded by something.'

Ace stepped from the stairwell. 'Something like this, Doctor?'

The Doctor whirled round.

The steps had led them into a small chamber. At the centre, bathed now in an orange light, was a many-sided metal object, like a huge irregular die.

'What is it?' said Ace with a gasp. 'Doesn't fit in with the rest of the decor, does it?'

'Quite,' said the Doctor. 'Thoss? Care to enlighten us?'

Thoss strode up to the polygon and ran his claw over the metallic surface. 'There are many such things all over Betrushia. Relics of the Time Before. No one knows what their function was. I discovered this one below my Temple some time ago.'

The Doctor looked at him quizzically, his face half-hidden in the shadows. 'No one *knows* their secret or no one *knew*?'

Thoss inclined his head. 'One day it opened up. It ... began to tell me things.'

The Doctor nodded. 'Things you couldn't explain, or tie in with your faith's traditional view of things?'

'You may mock me, Doctor,' said the old man sadly, his rheumy blue eyes watering. 'But the Faith has been my only support for most of my life. It isn't easy to admit you're wrong.'

He pressed one panel of the polygon and a concealed door shushed open, revealing darkness beyond. Thoss extended a claw in a gesture of invitation. 'I could not listen to the things it said. Perhaps you are made of sterner stuff?'

'I don't doubt it,' said Ace.

The Doctor advanced. Ace grabbed his elbow. 'It could be a trap.'

He shook his head. 'I don't think so. Do you want to stay outside and ... er ... watch my back?'

'I'd rather go in with you. But I suppose I should stay out here, yeah.'

205

The Doctor patted her arm. 'Tactics, Ace, tactics. Obviously that military training didn't go to waste.'

She smiled ruefully.

The Doctor put out his hands and pulled himself across the threshold into the polygon. The door slid shut behind him, seamlessly resealing the panel.

Ace sat down on the cold metal floor and examined the blaster in her hand. It was an ugly, inefficient little weapon of a type for which she might once have had a certain fondness. Now it felt cold and alien in her hand.

Thoss stood some distance away, looking blankly into space.

Ace cleared her throat. 'Read any good books lately?'

'Yes,' said Thoss without a trace of irony. 'But it didn't have a happy ending.'

Bernice prodded De Hooch in the back. As the strange party advanced through the corridors, she was forced to admit it was the oddest spaceship she had ever seen. Fluted columns and high vaulted ceilings were everywhere, enraptured statues in niches, stone-flagged floors and, virtually everywhere, the reassuring flood of sunshine. If the air had not been so stuffy, Bernice might almost have believed the illusion.

'Why do you do all this?' she asked as De Hooch led the way.

'All what?' spat the dwarf.

Bernice gestured with her free hand. 'All this. It's pretty impressive. What's it for?'

'I don't have to explain myself to you, or your reptile associates.'

Bernice pushed the blaster into the folds of fat around De Hooch's neck. 'Those are my friends you're insulting. And I'm the one with the gun, so start explaining.'

De Hooch reluctantly gave them a potted history of the Chapter's exploits and dubious motivation.

'But you're not the Keth?' queried Grek.

De Hooch frowned. 'The what?'

Liso waved Grek into silence, his solitary eye fixed on De Hooch's diminutive form. 'Never mind. Why did you come here?'

'I've told you. To convert you heathens to the true faith through the trial of fire and pain.'

Imalgahite's face darkened. 'And for that you destroy our entire civilization?'

'Life's a bitch,' said the dwarf with a grisly smile.

Imalgahite lunged for him but Bernice held him back. 'No. Come on. Let's get on. There isn't time.'

'There never is, my dear,' said Yong as he stepped into the corridor from his quarters.

Half a dozen Chaptermen appeared behind the little group, bringing their blasters to bear. The Betrushians sagged with disappointment.

De Hooch struggled out of Bernice's grip. Yong glared down his nose at the scuttling little man.

'Really, Parva. You're beginning to make a habit of this.'

Miller's men had fled through the jungle at the first sight of the terrifying yellow ooze. Two of them reached the perimeter of the jungle and scrambled over the heat-compressed mud towards the black ships.

Gasping, they slid down against the hull, chests heaving with the effort.

Martino emerged from around the bulkhead. 'Where is Chapterman Miller? What's happened?'

The two men shook their heads breathlessly, their eyes rolling in fear. Martino slapped them about the face but they remained hysterical.

He looked about uneasily in the humid darkness. The light from the distant fires seemed scarcely to penetrate this far. But if orders had been followed properly then the whole jungle should, by now, be aflame.

'Come on. Get inside. I'll question you later.'

They moved towards the ship. Sheet lightning like an upturned crucible suddenly illuminated the black sky.

Martino shuddered involuntarily and looked back. The dark, dark mass of the jungle was swaying violently. He felt the mud beneath his feet begin to vibrate.

He flapped his arms at the two men. 'Go on! Run! Get inside!'

The ground was rippling violently, spitting mud and vegetation into the air. From out of the tortured sky, a hail of meteorites began to thunder to the ground, smashing against the hulls of the two black ships.

Throwing up his arms in terror, Martino fell a short way from the ramp and felt mud slap into his eyes. With a staggering roar, the ground opened up all around him, a great, cavernous fissure running right across the battlefield.

'Help me!' he screeched, reaching out his hands.

The Chaptermen lunged for him but the ground rolled again and all three toppled dangerously close to the chasm. Steam gushed from the ground and a tumultuous cracking of moving earth filled the air.

Martino clung to the soil with both hands as his legs flopped into the fissure. He could feel the slippery mud sliding between his fingers.

All at once, he was aware of a different sensation as something began to trickle from the ground. He glanced behind him and squealed in panic as the yellow ooze ejected from the fissure.

This close he could make out the fine detail of its sparkling, mucous surface and all the strange and oddly familiar shapes twisting and writhing in its undulating form.

It began to gurgle around his heels.

'Help me!' he screamed, but the Chaptermen fell back in terror. Martino scrabbled for the cross around his neck and thrust it at the oncoming yellow tide.

'Back! Back!' he managed to gasp. 'You are an abomination in the eyes of Saint Anthony!'

The yellow ooze gushed over his calves, sliding, swirling, twisting.

'I cast you out, demon!' shrieked Martino. 'In the name of my patron I – '

The ooze drew back as though considering Martino's words and then rained down upon him. He yelled and yelled until the air in his lungs was exhausted and his body was sucked into the foul creature's innards.

In a moment, he was gone and the yellow ooze had vanished back into the earth.

Counting their blessings, the Chaptermen took to their heels and scrambled into the mothership.

Bernice pulled at the straps digging into her wrists. Sweat sprang out uncomfortably under her arms and her aching hands.

She found herself lying flat on a slab in a small, cold room. Next to her were two things; a bulky, sinister-looking machine, its surface crammed with switches, and the even more sinister-looking Parva De Hooch who was shuffling up and down over the floor.

'Where . . .' she began weakly.

'Where are you?' returned De Hooch. 'You're in the conditioning block.'

Bernice tried to move her head but it was clamped tightly to the slab. 'Where . . . are the others?'

De Hooch's face crinkled into a frown. 'Others? Oh, those creatures. Well, they weren't suitable for processing so I've ordered them to be destroyed.'

Bernice's eyes widened. 'Destroyed?'

'Yes. It's the kindest way. I mean, they're not like you and I, are they?' He shuddered. 'All those scales.'

'Look,' said Bernice hoarsely. 'I'm not at all clear about this.'

De Hooch walked up to the slab and laid a fat hand on Bernice's burning forehead. 'After the conditioning has done its work you will obey Saint Anthony without question and all things will become clear.'

Bernice pulled again at the straps. 'But what about the Doctor . . .?'

209

De Hooch stood up straight. 'The Doctor? You know him?'

'Of course. We travelled here together,' said Bernice. 'Why?'

'The Doctor has caused me much humiliation. He will pay dearly for it. And the woman too.'

'What woman?'

De Hooch sneered. 'Some trash we picked up on Massatoris. She has flouted the will of Saint Anthony. She has incurred the wrath of the Chapter. And she stuffed me in a cupboard.'

'Look, never mind your personal vendettas,' sighed Bernice. 'There's a lot you don't know. This planet hasn't got much time left. It's going to blow.'

'Going to *blow*?' chuckled De Hooch. 'What's that supposed to mean?'

'I mean we've got a couple of days if we're lucky. There's some kind of instability . . .'

'You'll have to do better than that.' He traced a stunted finger over her eyes and mouth.

Bernice shuddered. 'It's true. Whatever your plans for this planet, they'll mean nothing. You've got to get out of here.'

De Hooch cocked his head. 'And that would suit you and your Doctor friend very well, wouldn't it? No, no. This planet will succumb completely to the will of Saint Anthony. And when we've finished with it, it will rest comfortably in absolution: a burning cinder in space. And your Doctor and his friend will be there to enjoy the show, one way or another.'

'Where is he then?' asked Bernice. 'The Doctor? Where is he?'

De Hooch frowned. 'He has . . . temporarily eluded me.'

Bernice managed to smile but it hurt, the band across her head pressing into her flesh.

If the Doctor was on the loose then there was still a fighting chance.

210

In the power room, the acne-scarred Chapterman pulled the goggles over his eyes and advanced towards the banks of consoles which hummed with power. The shields around the artificial sun glowed in the half-dark as he fed information into the machinery. When the order from the Magna came through, he would be ready.

The complex instrumentation which channelled the sun's power through the ship had been the invention of the Magna's father and was kept running through the diligence and loyalty of many Chaptermen. It gave light and heat to the entire seminary as well as raw power to the greatest of the Chapter's gifts: Saint Anthony's Fire itself.

Magna Yong, in a work of quite astonishing ingenuity, had devised a method of focusing the sun's power into the colossal weapon now at his disposal. It could be used purely for the purging of unbelievers or as a gigantic weapon, penetrating the ship's hull and blasting out into space. Such was its strength, it had been known to destroy whole moons. The destruction of a paltry ring system was very small fry.

For Acne-Scars, though, the greatest pleasure came in the *autos-da-fé*. It was sweet indeed to see the heathens' pathetic faces twisted into silent screams in that great crimson column.

A tiny light winked on the panel before him. The Chapterman made a final adjustment to his goggles and pulled down two sets of steel levers.

The sun began to burn.

In the great hall of the cathedral, Yong was once again seated on the throne, the giant cross in his hands. He rubbed an eyelid wearily. It wasn't his eyelid, of course, but someone else's which he kept in a little wooden box to poke in moments of stress.

It was nice to have the Doctor around, putting up the semblance of fight. Yong had meant what he said about missing the glory days of his crusade. Days when he had

211

to hack his way through the heathens with a broadsword. Perhaps Saint Anthony might have other tasks ahead for him. Time would tell.

He motioned to Chapterman Jones and the massive ritual began again. Pot-bellied supplicants, their skin lathered in sweat, began to haul the cages inside. At a word from Yong, the chanting and the pounding of the gong began to echo throughout the incense-filled vault.

Yong eyed the usual crop of gibbering fools who filled the cages: a very few of the survivors of Massatoris mingled with the remains of the Cutch and Ismetch garrisons.

In the first cage, manacled together, were Grek, Liso and Imalgahite, united as never before.

Yong stood up. 'Hear me! O, fragile and unworthy animals!'

'Wait!' bellowed Grek. 'Listen to us. It's vital!'

Chapterman Jones, all eyes and foam-flecked mouth, dashed up to the cage and cracked his whip against Grek's claw. The Ismetch leader darted back, clutching his seared flesh.

'Listen to him!' continued Imalgahite defiantly. 'Whoever you are. This planet is dying. If you don't believe us look – '

'Silence!' roared Yong.

'Look outside. Use your eyes!' yelled Imalgahite.

Yong did not take kindly to being stopped in mid-flow. 'You cannot hope to save yourselves with this babble.'

'For God's sake,' cried Liso, his eye flashing in fury, 'no matter what you do to us, Betrushia is dying. And unless you get out of here you'll go up with it!'

Yong ignored him and clicked his fingers. Jones stole to the recessed alcove and the familiar oily grinding of machinery began to build. The panels in the ceiling and floor began to slide open.

'All shall know the sweet and glorious pain of Saint Anthony's Fire!' cried Yong.

The vast column of fire belched from the ceiling to the floor, fiery shapes twisting in its terrible mass. The chanting and the beating of the gong reached a deafening climax.

Jones unlocked the cages and the Betrushians were forced unwillingly out at spear-point.

Jones lashed at Grek with his whip. The Ismetch leader growled at his persecutor but the Chapterman merely nudged him towards the roaring, boiling fire.

Bored, Yong sighed and moved swiftly towards the double doors, his cloak fluttering behind him.

'Goodbye,' he yawned. 'So nice to have met you.'

He swept from the room. Grek, Liso and Imalgahite exchanged glances as they were herded forwards.

Inside the polygon, the Doctor was scarcely aware of the latest pounding earth tremor as it shook the Ismetch dugout.

The structure was comfortably padded and, in its darkness, oddly reassuring, like a warm cinema on a wet day. Two chairs had been bolted into its centre. Beneath these was a smooth black console, a red light blinking slowly on its surface.

The Doctor sniffed the stale air. How long had this remained untouched, he wondered.

With some trepidation, he sat down in the chair. At once, a strange, electric current ran up and down his spine, the light on the console snapped off and three low chimes sounded in the silence.

One panel of the polygon began to glow and the Doctor's face was bathed in a miasma of shifting colours. Out of this an image began to resolve itself.

The Doctor settled back in the seat, tense with expectation.

The image on the wall cleared and the face of a humanoid woman stared out. She was mammalian but with a shrewish face and bright yellow eyes.

'This is Neerid,' she said. 'You cannot know me. This spool has been recorded as a warning to any who may

213

come after us, that you may not repeat our folly. Please listen to everything I have to say.'

17

Time Before

As the last of the captive Massatorans were thrust into the flames, the floor of the cathedral lurched and shook as a fresh earthquake rolled under the mothership.

Grek seized his chance, darting through the miserable supplicants who milled around him. He lunged for a Chapterman and pulled the whip from his side. Looking around hurriedly, he called to his men to make a break for it.

The Chapterman scrambled for his blaster but Grek was too quick, lashing out with the whip and pulling the man to the floor. In an instant the unfamiliar weapon was in Grek's claw and he was loosing off bolts of energy around the hall.

'Careful with that thing!' cried Liso delightedly, running for the great double doors. Grek brought down two Chaptermen and roared with exhilaration.

Imalgahite was already at the doors, pushing the Betrushian troops through. 'Come on! Let's go!' He ploughed his fist into a Chapterman's throat and pulled the blaster off him. The unfamiliar weapon felt strange in his claw.

As the Chapterman struggled to his feet with a murderous expression on his face, Imalgahite accidentally blew half the man's face off with one bolt from the blaster. He grinned and turned towards the shuddering column of fire, jerking about and picking off the few remaining zealots.

Grek and Imalgahite were through the doors now, panting with exhilaration. Grek was peering about for Jones but his tormentor had left the cathedral shortly after the Magna.

'All right, Liso, let's find a way out,' he said at last.

'No, sir,' said Liso. 'With respect, that's the last thing we want. This ship is our only chance. We have to take it over, not run away from it.'

'It won't take them long to realize we're on the loose,' said Imalgahite.

Grek rubbed his jaw. 'The little one mentioned a bridge – command deck. If we can find that and take it . . .'

Liso's eyes flashed with excitement. 'Yes sir!'

Grek clapped him on the shoulder as they jogged up the stone corridor. He indicated the blaster with a smile. 'If we'd had a few of these, what wouldn't we have done to your lot, eh, Imalgahite?'

The Cutch leader smiled grimly. 'Well, my friends. It's time we took on the real enemy.'

De Hooch looked down at the floor as the earth tremor took hold. Panic flashed momentarily across his ugly little face. Bernice, recumbent on the slab and wriggling with her restraints, smiled tightly.

'You see? What did I tell you? This planet is shaking itself apart.'

De Hooch scowled at her. 'It cannot be. Saint Anthony would not lead us into barren pastures.'

The door opened with a crackling hiss and Yong stood there. 'Quite right, Parva. This planet will provide ample resources for all our needs.'

His gaze flicked down to Bernice's prone form. 'You haven't introduced me to your friend.'

De Hooch shifted uncomfortably. 'She's a crony of the Doctor's. Seems to have some sort of scientific training. I thought she might well be of use.'

Yong considered this with a slow nod of the head. 'Have you begun the conditioning?'

'Not yet. I thought it wiser to glean as much as possible before her . . . independence is taken from her.'

216

'Good, good. This is more like it, De Hooch. You have pleased me.'

De Hooch smiled, his tiny eyes flashing with resentment. He bowed stiffly.

'Are you in charge here?' said Bernice sharply.

Yong smiled. 'I have that honour.'

'Well, maybe you'll listen to me, then. This planet is unstable. That's why we're having all these earthquakes. The Doctor says the planet is destroying itself.'

Yong yawned and patted his mouth with the back of his hand. 'Well, he would, wouldn't he? I'm quite well aware of the Doctor's plans to sabotage my crusade. I suppose I should have killed him straight away, but I'm terribly sentimental, you know.'

Bernice sighed exasperatedly, attempting to hide her struggle against the straps. 'Look, let me out of here. I've no quarrel with you. What the Doctor says is true. It'll do none of us any good to stay put.'

Yong smiled pityingly. 'Don't fret, child. Soon all your troubles will melt like lemon drops. You will have but one priority: the service of Saint Anthony.'

A small grille inset in the wall beeped. Yong went up to it and pressed the side.

'Yes?' said the Magna.

'Bridge, my Lord. There's . . . I think you should come up here. I . . . There's something you must see.'

Yong frowned. 'Very well. I'm on my way.'

He patted De Hooch on the head. 'You extract as much as you can from her, Parva, then begin the conditioning. Let us hope you do a better job than on the last one.'

As the Magna left, De Hooch readjusted his disturbed skull-cap and spat on the floor.

'You don't like him, do you?' said Bernice. She almost cried out with joy as she felt her left wrist beginning to slide from its restraint.

'Shut up,' hissed De Hooch. He approached the table, the floor still trembling beneath his feet. 'Now, tell me, what was the Doctor's purpose in coming here? How long

217

has he known of our crusade? And what are his plans to disrupt it?'

'Well . . .' Bernice pulled her hand free but kept it hidden by her side. 'Maybe I'll tell you later. I'm a little tired now.'

De Hooch marched up to the table, his face twisting into a snarl. 'Impudent filth! You will answer my questions now! D'you hear me!'

Bernice turned her head away. De Hooch grabbed her hair and twisted her head round to face him. In one rapid movement, she grabbed his fat neck with her free hand and slammed his face onto the cold steel of the table. His nose made a satisfying crack as it broke and he slid to the floor.

Bernice sat up and pulled her other hand free. She rubbed her wrists, swung her legs off the table and reached down for De Hooch's blaster.

The bulk of the conditioning machine lined the whole of one wall. Cocking an eyebrow, Bernice pumped a dozen shots into it until it exploded in a flurry of sparks and soot, components shooting out and ricocheting off the walls.

She nodded to herself, satisfied, and stepped out into the corridor. All the time she had lain on the table, the image of Porsim in flames had dominated her thoughts. Setting the blaster to maximum force, Bernice set out for a little retribution.

The polygon was vibrating gently, the recessed instrumentation which packed its innards humming with long-dormant power as though it were relieved to be finally giving up its secrets.

The vibration of the now-continuous earth tremors blended with the shuddering of the black console at the Doctors feet.

Colours flashed over his still features. He could feel the chair cocooning him, willing him to become part of the information the polygon was relaying.

The Doctor's hands clenched into fists as the spool of data spilled out its story.

As images scrolled over the wall, he began to slowly shake his head.

Yong swept onto the bridge and was immediately surrounded by fawning Chaptermen, their hands full of densely printed scrolls. Yong waved them away.

'Why was I summoned?' he snapped.

One of the helmsmen tapped the screen in front of him. 'There's something out there, my Lord.'

The great, round central screen darkened and began to fill with pixellated images. Information scrolled up and down the screen.

'We can't make out anything definite, Magna, but it's heading this way.'

Yong rolled his eyes. 'What is?'

The helmsman pressed a button at his side and the screen cleared to reveal the view in front of the ship. The night sky was illuminated by the blazing jungle and the top corner by a hint of the rings. But Yong's attention was arrested by something quite different.

Dominating the horizon, its dimensions swollen to colossal size, was the twisting, yellow ooze. It was tearing through the jungle, funnelling the flaming trees into its core, seemingly digesting the fire as it went. It stood out against the night sky like a vast yellow flame.

Yong's jaw literally dropped open. 'What ... is ... that?'

The helmsman shrugged helplessly.

'Magnify,' croaked Yong.

The image expanded until it filled the screen: a livid, boiling mass of putrescent yellow.

For the first time in his life, Yong could think of nothing to say. He sank down into his chair and waved his hand towards the Chaptermen. The image vanished and the bridge fell into a kind of blank silence.

Eventually, Yong looked down at the scrolls piled on

219

his chair and glanced across the bridge. 'Progress report,' he whispered.

A nervous Chapterman Jones hovered at his side. 'We've had no word from Miller or Martino, my Lord. I despatched them on conflagration duty some time ago.'

'Then where are they?'

Jones's face crumpled disconsolately. 'I cannot say, Magna. Perhaps that . . . thing . . .'

Yong's face filled with a disquieting radiance. 'Never mind that, Jones. Never mind that. I will not be distracted from my goal. Saint Anthony will not be cheated of his prize. Where is Parva De Hooch?'

Jones shifted his weight. 'No one has seen him either.'

Yong seemed not to be listening. 'Well . . . you carry on, Jones.'

'Yes, Magna.' Jones shot Yong a quizzical look and exited from the bridge, the iris clanking closed behind him.

Yong stood up. 'Screen,' he ordered.

The helmsman switched on the main screen and the room was once again bathed in the sickly light of the twister as it rampaged through the jungle. Yong gazed at it in awe.

Ace examined her face in the polished surface of the blaster. It made her features balloon comically but she looked passable enough.

The shaven head she could get used to, she decided, and the bruises would heal. Most importantly, the eyes which glared back at her were her own eyes, with her own thoughts behind them.

Something felt different, though. Something inside her. Right now she should be burning with justifiable rage, with an unquenchable desire for revenge. After all, the Chapter of Saint Anthony had put her through hell. And as for what they had done to the innocents on Massatoris . . .

Ace pinched the bridge of her nose and closed her

220

eyes wearily. The blaster felt even stranger in her hands, clammy and cold, where once any weapon would have felt like an extension of her arm. Ace did want the Chapter to suffer but her own feelings felt somehow muted.

She rubbed her muscles, still taut and fit under the uncomfortable loose hessian of her robes, but she felt no need for her combat suit, nor any nostalgia for the paraphernalia which had got her through more conflicts than she cared to remember. Was she changing? And was it the trauma of her conditioning or something more profound? The something, perhaps, which had led her to seek temporary release from her travels in the TARDIS in the first place?

She sighed and pushed her thoughts to one side. The most important priority was still to get off this planet in one piece.

Ace glanced over at Thoss. She had assumed he was sleeping but he seemed to be staring into space, his eyes narrowed to slits. His snout, which sagged with age, was fixed expressionlessly.

Standing up, she walked towards the steps and cocked her head but could hear nothing above them except the constant trembling on the earth. Turning back into the room, she bit her lip anxiously.

'Come on, Doctor,' she urged. 'I don't fancy being underground when the next big one hits.'

She smiled at Thoss but he didn't react. Pulling a face, Ace crossed to the polygon and ran her hand over its smooth surface. It was surprisingly warm.

She jumped as, with a hiss of machinery, the door opened and the Doctor stepped out into the pale light.

'Got what you wanted?' said Ace brightly.

The Doctor's face was ashen. He looked at her briefly and then bolted for the stairs.

'Come on!' he cried.

Ace looked puzzled. 'What . . .?'

'Come *on*!'

221

He clattered up the steps, scrabbling at the slimy moss with his hands, Ace close behind.

Thoss stayed where he was. He turned his aching old body towards the polygon and struggled to his feet. Then he put out his claw and waited for the hidden door to open once again.

Yong was still staring at the screen when Jones sidled up to him.

'Magna . . .'

Yong could not pull his eyes away from the yellow luminescence. 'What is it?'

'Grave news, my Lord.'

Yong closed his coal-black eyes. 'Well?'

Jones cleared his throat. 'The planetary survey is complete, Magna. Although Betrushia is rich in minerals and could be exploited by us, there is a dangerous instability in its core.'

The ship trembled as though in confirmation.

'How long?' said Yong.

'A day. Perhaps two.'

Yong stood up, punching the arm of the chair in fury. 'No! No, it cannot be! Saint Anthony would never have led us here only to deny us our victory. And if anyone's going to destroy this planet, it'll be me!'

As Yong's voice echoed around the room, a second voice cut in.

'Wrong, Yong.'

Yong spun round to see De Hooch standing by him, a blaster in his stubby hand.

'De Hooch? What's hap – '

Yong cut himself off as he took in De Hooch's battered appearance, missing skull-cap and bloodied, spongy nose.

'What has always happened, Yong,' spat De Hooch with as much venom as his shattered nose would allow. 'I have been made the scapegoat for your incompetence.'

He slid the back of his hand over his bloodied face and pointed the blaster at Yong's forehead.

222

'My dear Parva,' said Yong coolly, 'you can't be serious. Is this . . . is this mutiny?'

'It is. And not before time.'

Yong glared down at the dwarf. A low rumble of fury began to rise in his breast, trembling through his face and suffusing it with rage. 'How . . . *dare* you challenge me? How *dare* you?'

De Hooch cocked his head. 'I have the gun. Hasn't that always been our way? The strong punishing the weak for their sins. Well, you are steeped in sin, Yong, and your time has run out. I shall be Magna now.'

Yong laughed harshly. '*You*? You, De Hooch? Don't be ridiculous. I only promoted you through some misguided sense of pity. Magna? You? You ridiculous little freak. I am Magna! I! I! For all time!'

He flourished his cloak around him, his magnificent torso glinting mustard-yellow in the lurid light of the viewing screen.

De Hooch gave a horrible little chuckle. 'Have you quite finished?' He pointed the blaster defiantly at Yong's head. The Magna looked about desperately. Nobody seemed inclined to move.

'My hour has come,' intoned De Hooch in a dream-like voice. 'The burden of command passes to wiser shoulders.'

'How right you are,' said Bernice as she stepped onto the bridge, levelling her own weapon at the dwarf.

'Oh, not again,' said De Hooch, crushed.

Yong whirled round as Grek, Liso, Imalgahite and the remains of the Betrushian forces filed onto the bridge, brandishing their purloined blasters.

Bernice walked carefully into the centre of the room, keeping her gun levelled. She looked down at the anxious helmsman. 'Give me a front view from the ship,' she snapped.

The helmsman's hands flicked on the screen.

Betrushia's last dawn was beginning. The jungle was thrashing from side to side as the ground rumbled and shook beneath it. The sky was thick and yellow. Bernice

gave it a cursory glance and then sat down on the edge
of the console. 'Right boys. For once, I'm going to talk
and you're going to listen.'

Ace found herself in the all-too familiar position of running after the Doctor, demanding answers and getting
none.

They hared back through the shuddering tunnels and
the Doctor had one foot on the rung of the ladder before
Ace got him to stop.

'Hang on! Doctor!'

'What? What?' His eyes flickered feverishly from side
to side.

'Would you mind telling me what happened inside the
furry dice?'

'No time. It's too important.'

He clambered up the ladder. She looked worriedly at
the shaking walls. The bare boards were cracking, releasing torrents of mud into the tunnels. 'What's too
important?'

'Come *on*, Ace. We've got to get back to their ship. It
might be our only chance. I need to know anything you
can tell me about the layout.'

They scrambled to the blasted surface. Ace felt her feet
submerge in the thick black mud of the battlefield. 'What,
the seminary?' she howled above the din.

The Doctor waved his hand. 'No, no. The real ship.
Especially the artificial sun. In detail. Detail is important.'

Ace shrugged as they set off towards the trembling
jungle perimeter. Lightning streaked across the sickly sky.

Ace was half-way through an account of her journey to
the power room when she noticed something.

'Doctor,' she said quietly.

Rather to her surprise, perhaps because of the tone of
her voice, he stopped and looked.

The yellow ooze seemed to be coalescing, fragments
of cloud tumbling together into a tremendous, boiling
whirlwind.

224

The Doctor's face turned as pale as his ruined suit.

Ran slipped quietly through the darkened corridors of the mothership. He saw scarcely anyone on his journey save for the occasional scurrying Chapterman racing through the shadows.

The bulky crystalline box in his hands was making his muscles ache but he had to plough on, had to make things safe.

He turned a corner and pressed himself flat against a wall. Ahead was a metal door with some sort of symbol embossed on it.

Ran took a deep breath and marched towards the door, the box banging against his side.

The Doctor and Ace were running at full pelt towards the mothership. Freezing rain from the rolling, shuddering sky lashed savagely at them. The great sickly whirlwind was dominating the whole sky as though the horizons were coming loose.

Ace grabbed at the Doctor's shirt and whirled him round. 'What is that thing?' she screeched above the gale.

'I'll explain, I promise. We need to get to the ship.'

They staggered on through the cratered mud. The Doctor reached the bulkheads of the mothership and paused, gazing in undisguised horror at the sky.

They both jumped as Bernice's voice cut in, broadcast from unseen speakers. 'Hey, you two! Come on in. We're on the bridge. The cavalry has taken over!'

Ace smiled delightedly. The Doctor merely nodded as though the capture of the ship simplified matters slightly.

He grabbed Ace's hand, which she found strangely reassuring, and pelted inside.

The ship was already rocking like a vessel at sea, its great stone interior groaning violently. Statues of Saint Anthony toppled to the tiled floor, shattering into pieces. The Doctor seemed to know just where to go and they zigzagged through endless corridors towards the bridge.

Finally they stopped in front of the metal iris and the Doctor put out his hand to press the panel at the side. Ace touched his shoulder lightly and he looked round.

It occurred to Ace that, beneath the mud which covered him, beneath even his strange grey eyes, the Doctor had never looked so grave.

'Doctor,' she said at last. 'Our priority is still to get off this planet before it explodes, right?'

The Doctor looked into her face and sighed, 'Oh no, Ace. There's far more at stake than that.'

18

Revenge of the Chaptermen

Ran placed the box carefully between two banks of instrumentation. Heat seeped from the massive artificial sun, imbuing the whole room with radiant warmth.

He smiled, his eyes twitching behind their protective goggles, and pushed the cloth-covered box out of sight. Warmth was good. Warmth was exactly what the box needed.

Satisfied that his precious cargo was safe, Ran straightened up and began to think about what he should do next.

Whatever had taken place in his absence, his priority was to ensure that the ship left the doomed Betrushia behind as soon as possible. He looked around the power room with interest.

'Doctor!' cried Bernice with relief. 'Do you know, I'm actually pleased to see you.'

The two dishevelled travellers passed through the metal iris onto the bridge. The Doctor squeezed Bernice's arm and smiled. 'Mutual,' he said, stepping past her towards Grek.

Ace came through and Bernice gasped. 'Christ, what happened to you?'

Ace smiled ruefully and gave her friend a hug. ' "Just gimme that ol' time religion",' she said.

Bernice frowned. 'What?'

Ace shook her head. 'Nothing. Just glad to be back.'

The Doctor was looking around the bridge with agitated

eyes. Yong was back in his chair. De Hooch and the remaining Chaptermen had been disarmed and pushed into the corner. Grek, Liso and Imalgahite flanked Yong, not quite sure what to do next.

'Welcome, Doctor,' breathed Grek with relief. 'I'm glad to see you again.'

Yong sneered. 'Really, Doctor, how you can give the time of day to these primitives . . .'

'Shut up!' snarled the Doctor. 'I don't have time for your pathetic games.'

He glanced down at the humming consoles. 'Grek, what's the situation? As regards Betrushia?'

Grek shrugged helplessly.

Yong rested his head on one hand, enjoying his enemy's discomfort. 'I believe your miserable world has about twenty-four hours. What a shame.' He smiled and examined his fingernails.

The Doctor ignored him and seated himself at the navigational console, his fingers racing over the rows of buttons and monitor panels.

Grek peered over his shoulder. 'Are you going to get us away from here?'

'Not yet,' said the Doctor through gritted teeth. 'There's some business that needs to be sorted.'

Ace crossed towards him, holding the blaster awkwardly in her hand. 'You did promise me an explanation.'

The Doctor didn't look up as data filled the screens before him.

'It's growing,' he whispered.

'What is?' said Bernice.

The Doctor spun round in his chair. 'All right. Everyone listen to me.' He rubbed his chin, collecting his thoughts, and then stood up.

Pointing to Grek and his men he said, 'You Betrushians have been labouring under the assumption that your . . . mythical nemesis, the Keth, have returned. It was only natural that we should all mistake these interlopers – ' he

228

cast a venomous look at Yong who smiled back sweetly, – 'for them.'

'You also know,' continued the Doctor, 'that your planet is dying. In fact, as Magna Yong tells us, it has about one day of life left to it. Perhaps less.'

The Betrushian soldiers began to murmur anxiously. Bernice looked pityingly towards them.

The Doctor held up his hands for quiet. 'Well, this may seem difficult to accept, I know, but all these events are interrelated. I know because I've seen this planet's past.'

Liso leant towards the Doctor and blinked his solitary eye. 'What do you mean?'

The Doctor sighed. 'You were right. The Keth have returned. In fact, they – or rather it – never really went away.'

There was more frightened muttering from the Betrushian soldiers. The Doctor raised his voice. 'I'll be brief. Time, as they say, is of the essence.'

Ace looked around the bridge. Everyone was hanging on the Doctor's words. Even Yong seemed mildly interested.

'A very long time ago, in the Time Before, as Betrushian religion has it, this planet was inhabited by a mammalian species. It's clear from what I've seen of their technology that they were highly advanced. But, like many intelligent species, they got a little above themselves.

'They invented, devised... grew... an evolutionary catalyst. An organism, a regulator if you like, which would assess various lifeforms' fitness for survival. If the lifeform didn't come up to scratch, threatened the eco-system or was pursuing an evolutionary blind-alley then the regulator's function was to annihilate it.'

'Sounds like an eminently laudable scheme, Doctor,' chimed in Yong. 'I just know you're going to tell us something awful happened.'

The Doctor's face was grave. 'It did. The regulator found all life unsuitable and began to consume all life on this planet. I think this is where the Keth legend comes from.' He glanced over at Grek. 'A race memory of this all-powerful force.'

He leant wearily against the navigational console. 'The original Betrushians recognized their folly but it was far too late. The only thing they could do was to stop the thing from spreading anywhere else. In the time they had left they constructed what amounts to an engineering miracle.'

He paused. Imalgahite frowned. 'Well?'

'They built a necklace of orbiting satellites around the planet, each one containing a mechanism which somehow restrains the regulator's behaviour. Probably some sort of inhibitor aligned to its original chemical structure. These satellites kept the thing on Betrushia but only at the expense of their entire civilization. It sated itself on them but could never escape from this planet because of the power of the satellites.'

'So ... what happened to these satellites?' queried Liso.

'Oh, they're still there,' said the Doctor. 'Over the millennia they accrued dust and other natural asteroid fragments until they – '

'The rings!' shrieked Bernice. 'Of course! The ring system.'

'Exactly,' said the Doctor. 'Their influence has kept the organism dormant for millions of years. It's become part of the planet itself, unable to escape its earthly prison, allowing the Ismetch and the Cutch, or rather their ancestors, to evolve in place of the original inhabitants.'

'And the meteorites?' said Grek. 'The earthquakes?'

'Well, all was fine until our friends here,' he gestured at Yong, 'came crusading. As soon as they began blasting their way through the rings, the imprisoning mechanism started to fail. A chain reaction which began gradually bought the organism back to life. I think that it's been part of the planet's structure for so long that it's caused the instability which will destroy Betrushia in a very few hours.'

He chose this moment to activate the main viewing

screen. There was an audible gasp as everyone took in the shivering yellow sky and the matrix at its centre.

'Really,' yawned Yong, 'do you expect me to believe that?'

'I do,' hissed the Doctor. 'You and your cack-handed maniacs have not only doomed this planet, but, if we don't prevent this thing from leaving Betrushia, all life in the galaxy as well!'

Thoss staggered through the shuddering dug-out, gazing appealingly into corners as though expecting to see people he knew. It was strange for the place to be unoccupied after the long, long years of war.

He made his way through the creaking tunnels towards the Number Seven ladder-hole and hauled his weary old body to the surface.

Outside, the air was thick and oppressive. He could scarcely see the perimeter of the jungle for the yellow, smoke-like excrescence hovering in the atmosphere.

He might once have sunk to his knees in the presence of the Keth but now he knew the full truth. The polygon had given up all its secrets to him at last and it had been worse than he could ever have imagined.

He had sat in the padded chair, weeping uncontrollably as the story unfolded before his exhausted eyes. After all this time, his precious Faith was based on nothing but a disastrous scientific experiment.

Thoss turned away angrily from the livid sky. This was not how it was meant to be. Had he laboured long years in training in the Temple to have this as his ultimate reward? Yet personal aggrandizement was anathema to the first principles of the Faith. Perhaps, after all, this was the ultimate test. Thoss could no longer tell anything for sure. It was all so mixed up, so strange . . .

He stared upwards until his neck ached. The sky was swirling round and round, a miasma of cannibalized matter pouring into its impossibly dark heart. Fire bloomed in the jungle but this too was absorbed into the yellow whirlwind as though it were able to make use of everything and draw strength from it.

Thoss looked down at his bare, clawed feet and the mud which covered them. The ground was shaking violently and great fissures had opened up in the surface. Steam billowed out in enormous hot fonts.

He eyed the two vast black ships warily. Perhaps these were the Keth and the polygon had lied. Would they forgive his faithlessness? What if they were new Gods who had overthrown the power of the Keth in some unimaginable struggle of the titans? What was there left to him but his faith?

He gathered up his robes and stumbled towards the mothership, the ground oscillating beneath him.

The Doctor got up from the bridge console. The huge round screen now showed a three-dimensional image of Betrushia and the rings which surrounded it, tiny winking points of light studding their immensity.

'Those are the satellites still functioning?' asked Liso.

The Doctor nodded. 'Yes. They're our last hope.'

He dashed across the room towards Grek. 'Has the other ship surrendered?'

'Yes. It seems that just a threat to the Magna was enough. And it only has a skeleton crew. I've got most of my men over there now.'

'Where have you put Yong and the others?'

Grek smiled. 'Your friend, Ace, suggested a place.'

William Hon Yuen Yong did not take kindly to sharing a cage with anyone but was gratified that, dutiful to the last, the Chaptermen at least gave him a little space in the cramped prison. The cages stood where they had been abandoned in the cathedral, all three full to bursting with the captured zealots.

De Hooch was nursing his broken nose in fury. 'Look where your incompetence has got us, Yong. Prisoners of those heathen reptiles!'

Yong passed a hand over his smooth, composed features. 'Do keep your voice down, De Hooch. I can't hear myself think.'

The dwarf scowled at him and picked a bloodied fragment of bone from his nostril. 'Think? You? I should have overthrown you years ago. Then we wouldn't be in this mess.'

Yong glared at him. 'May I remind you De Hooch, that you have not succeeded in overthrowing me. You had a gun at my head when the animals took over the bridge but that was all. My loyal acolytes would have disarmed and executed you.'

De Hooch laughed. 'You really believe that? You're even more insane than – '

'Oh shut up! Both of you!'

Yong and De Hooch turned in surprise to Chapterman Jones who was glaring at them from the side of the cage. Not long before, Jones would have faced instant death for such impudence. The weary strain behind his large, bloodshot eyes showed that he was beyond such fear now.

'Face facts,' he continued. 'We're in a hole. And the first thing you do when you're in a hole is stop digging!'

He frowned at his superiors. 'We have to get off this planet before it blows up, yes? Now, if we have to help this Doctor with his scheme in order to do it, then so be it. What we should be thinking about is how to regain control once we're back in space.'

Yong looked coolly at the Chapterman and then smiled. 'Bravo, Jones, bravo.' He flicked a glance at De Hooch and sneered. 'I think I know who my new Parva will be.'

De Hooch beat his fists against the bars in frustration.

The double doors swung open and the Doctor came into the room accompanied by Grek and Imalgahite. He peered through the bars at the purple silk mass of the captives.

'Yong, you're coming out.'

The Magna stood up and brushed himself down. 'You've

233

seen the error of your ways at last, Doctor, I suppose. And realized the futility of fighting the will of Saint Anthony.'

'Something like that,' said the Doctor.

Imalgahite carefully unlocked the cage and pulled Yong out. At once, he relocked the prison.

Grek prodded Yong in the back with the blaster. 'All right. Get moving.'

'Where am I moving?'

The Doctor turned at the double doors. 'To your power room, Magna. You're going to help me do a little spot of re-engineering.'

'Is it possible?' said Liso, rubbing his empty socket. 'Do we have time?'

Ace shrugged. 'I don't know. See what the Doctor thinks.'

Bernice looked around the empty bridge. 'It makes sense. Even to try. Two whole ships at our disposal.'

The metal iris scraped open and the Doctor's party walked in at a brisk pace. The Doctor immediately checked the progress of the organism outside. He frowned worriedly.

'Right,' he said, turning to his little audience. 'This is what we're going to do. The undamaged "rings" can still keep the organism on Betrushia, but only if they're boosted by another power source. The Magna and myself are going to rechannel the power from both ships' artificial suns into the satellites.'

'Are we now?' said Yong sardonically.

Ace jabbed the blaster into the small of his back. 'Yes you bloody well are.'

'And then what?' asked Bernice.

'It sounds desperate, I know, but all we can do is to keep the organism trapped on Betrushia until the planet destroys itself. Not even this thing could survive the explosion.'

The Doctor began to move back towards the doors.

Bernice laid a hand on his arm. 'Doctor, we want to try something.'

'Mm? What?' The Doctor's attention was already elsewhere. 'Try what?'

'Liso wants to take the second ship and try and pick up anyone still left around. I mean, the more Betrushians we get out of here the better, wouldn't you say?'

The Doctor shook his head sadly. 'That's not possible, I'm afraid. It's a very nice idea, but we'll need both ships' suns to keep the thing trapped. We don't have time.'

Liso rubbed his crest in agitation. 'Please, Doctor, let me try. It's vitally important.'

The Doctor shook his head. Bernice tried again: 'If you can get this ship into orbit and start the process, we can soon join you. Isn't that feasible?'

The Doctor's face darkened. 'It's too dangerous, Bernice. Don't you understand? If that organism gets off Betrushia, who knows when it will end? It could go on forever!'

'A chance, Doctor,' said Liso quietly. 'Just give me a chance.'

The Doctor sighed. 'Very well.' He rubbed his heavily lined forehead. 'Once this ship is in orbit I'll give you two hours. Then you must be in position.'

He indicated that Grek should take Yong out into the corridor. 'The other ship has its own navigator, apparently, so you should be all right flying it.'

Bernice smiled at the Doctor. 'Thanks.'

'It's a very brave thing to try, Bernice. I admire you for it.' He managed to return her smile. 'Just get back in time.' He turned rapidly. 'Ace!'

Ace looked up. 'Yeah?'

'Come on, woman. You're needed.'

She grinned delightedly and followed the Doctor from the bridge.

Liso's eye was watery. He smiled at Bernice, his tiny teeth glinting in the winking lights from the console. 'Where shall we start?'

* * *

Betrushia was burning. The conflagration in the jungle had been superseded by the seismic disruptions ripping through the planet's structure. The ground seemed to be in a state of constant motion, rippling like water. Whole acres of trees vanished into the liquefying ground. Lightning crashed through the vile, vomit-hued sky.

With a final echoing roar, the Ismetch dug-out collapsed in on itself. Mud swept through the network of tunnels filling Grek's quarters, the conference room, even the tiny cell in which the Doctor had first been imprisoned. Black, liquefied soil gushed through the soaked planking, running deep, deep down into the lowest levels. The ancient Temple walls crumbled, slamming into the shrine which toppled forwards, its jewels cascading from the shattered stone. Mud gushed through the secret hatchway, drowning the polygon forever.

Above all this, spinning through the shimmering air, the organism grew stronger. Everything in sight was absorbed into its fearful matrix, creating a vortex of raw, yellow ooze. Gradually it edged its way towards the great black bulk of the Chapter's ships.

The Doctor slipped a pair of goggles over his face and flung open the door to the power room. Similarly equipped, Grek and Yong advanced inside, the Magna at the point of Grek's blaster. The glare from the artificial sun was almost unbearable.

The Doctor's gaze ranged around the humming machinery as he began to step down the power of the sun by degrees.

'This is it? The source of your power?' yelled Grek above the throb of machinery.

Yong nodded. 'We bring Saint Anthony's Fire to the heathen hordes.'

'Yes, yes,' muttered the Doctor. 'Well, now you're going to help me bring it somewhere else.'

He turned to Grek. 'Do we have a link to the other ship yet?'

'Yes. We did as you instructed.' Grek's tongue slithered over his recessed blue eyes. 'Here.'

He passed the Doctor a bulky cylinder. The Doctor tapped it and a rush of static came through.

'Bernice? Liso? Are you there?'

Bernice's voice came through faintly: 'Just about to set off, Doctor. The helmsman has full instructions.'

The Doctor nodded to himself. "Good. Good. Now, when I'm finished here I'll relay the refinements needed for your ship's sun, all right? You have to be on-line at precisely the right moment.'

'I understand,' said Bernice. 'Good luck.'

The Doctor switched off the communicator and turned to Yong. 'Now then, Magna, I'll be watching you very carefully. Roll up your sleeves. It's high time you got those pretty hands dirty.'

Silently, reluctantly, Yong knelt down and began to unscrew the panelling of the device.

The sunlight flared off his goggles and neither Grek nor the Doctor saw the surreptitious glance he shot at Ran's mysterious box, nestled between two banks of machinery.

Thoss had grown used to extraordinary things, but the interior of the mothership was something else entirely.

The stone corridors reminded him of his Temple, even though the deity to which they had been erected was completely alien to him. A short time after entering the ship, he found himself in the great musty hall of the cathedral.

It was truly overwhelming. The throne at the top of the stone steps. The twin circular panels through which Saint Anthony's Fire was channelled. The three huge cages with –

'You there!' came a tinny voice.

Thoss peered into the cage. A very small mammal was glaring at him from inside, its beady little eyes blazing in fury.

237

'Free us from this cage,' bellowed De Hooch. 'We are your masters.'

Thoss frowned confusedly. 'You are the ones whose coming was foretold?' he stammered unthinkingly.

'Er ... yes. Yes!' boomed De Hooch. 'We have come to judge you! Now, set us free!'

Thoss shambled towards the cage and began to wrestle with the lock.

'Hurry! Hurry, old man,' insisted De Hooch.

All at once the lock sprang open and the Chaptermen piled out in a flurry of purple robes. Gleefully, De Hooch scuttled to the floor like a spider freed from a bottle.

'Come on!' he cried to the Chaptermen. In a bellowing rush, the vengeful prisoners ran out of the cathedral, knocking the unthinking Thoss to the floor. He curled up into a ball and began to weep.

Ace stood in the gently humming console room of the TARDIS, anxiously chewing her nails. When the Doctor had said she was needed, manning the TARDIS ready for his return was not what she'd expected. Why he couldn't just rematerialize on board the mothership she didn't know, unless he was afraid it might fall into the wrong hands. She had noticed how protective he had become about the TARDIS lately, as though he felt he'd been taking his old ship for granted. Perhaps it was something of an honour for the Doctor to have placed her in charge. A measure of his trust.

Ace sighed wistfully. She had organized the evacuation of the unwilling supplicants and penitents into the TARDIS interior where, the Doctor assured her, he would find time to deprogram them all. Ace flinched at the memory of her own release from the embrace of Saint Anthony and silently wished for her fellow sufferers to have an easier time.

In truth, Ace was somewhat relieved. The calming grace of the ship's interior was like heaven after recent events. She operated the scanner and looked out worriedly at the

238

boiling mass of Betrushia outside. Fire was everywhere, blown into billowing clouds by the dying planet.

'Come on, Doctor,' she urged for the second time that day. 'Get a move on.'

Almost without thinking, she bent down and depressed the door lever. Outside, the ground was in a state of flux. Burning trees toppled to earth all around.

On the threshold of the TARDIS, Ace found her breath coming in short, panicky bursts, hoping that the Doctor would be able to get back across the dying jungle. She was turning back into the ship when she saw it.

Towering hundreds of feet above the jungle was an immense, monstrous creature, its volatile hide formed from the suppurating flesh of the millions of organisms it had consumed. It was a dreadful, colossal thing, mucus sliding over the composite remains of Betrushians, animals, even the jungle itself.

Ace gasped, gripped her stomach in shock and stumbled back into the TARDIS. The creature screamed in triumph.

19

Sun Stroke

The Doctor rubbed his exhausted eyes with oily fingers and then slammed the panel back into place. 'That's it.'

The artificial sun was throbbing gently on its night-time setting, a vast dull-orange ball.

The Doctor turned to Yong who, still covered by Grek's blaster, was rising and folding his arms. 'Thank you for your help. I couldn't have done it without you.'

Yong smiled, his goggles sparkling like the eyes of a fly. 'I would've attempted sabotage if possible, Doctor. I hope your scheme fails.'

An angry Grek jabbed at him with his blaster. 'Don't you understand, you idiot? This is more important than your stupid crusade.'

The Doctor put a hand on Grek's shoulder. 'It's no use trying to reason with him, Grek. He's too far gone.'

He glanced at the sun. With the light so diminished it was possible to see the network of conductors and pathways extending through the transparent floor, which channelled the orb's power throughout the seminary and ship.

'Take him back to the bridge,' said the Doctor. 'I don't want him on the loose until all this is over.'

'What do we do next?' asked Grek, relieved to have someone else making the decisions for once.

'I'll feed the instructions through to the second ship. Then the difficult bit really starts.'

Grek marched the smirking Yong out of the power room.

The Doctor began to punch a series of commands into the banks of controlling machinery which would automatically realign the scout-ship's sun. Now all that was needed was for their twin power sources to combine and be channelled through Betrushia's rings.

The Doctor still did not notice the cloth-covered box jammed tightly below his eye-level. He was too busy crossing his fingers.

'That's it. It's coming through.' Bernice nodded in satisfaction as the altered program was beamed through from the mothership, chattering across the screens of the scout-ship's bridge.

Liso was standing over the nervous helmsman in the otherwise empty room. 'All right. Take us up.'

The helmsman, a slender, youthful Chinese called Libon, one of the only survivors of Miller and Martino's aptly named skeleton crew, spread his delicate hands over the controls and the ship began to rise from the shaking jungle.

Bernice's stomach lurched. She made a mental note to stay put somewhere for a while once all this was over. If it ever could be over. As the ship soared into the yellow sky, she felt only a slight rocking sensation and turned to Liso. 'Where do we start looking?'

He stroked his empty socket nervously. 'There were a few villages, or the remains of them, scattered about in the jungle. That's all we've really got time to look for. Oh, and one big town. It's called Jurrula. Up in the hills.'

Bernice nodded and crossed to Libon. 'You've keyed in the course for planetary orbit?'

Libon nodded. Bereft of his Magna and the Chapter, he was no more than a frightened boy.

'Very well, then,' said Liso. 'Take us just above the trees. We need to get to those settlements as soon as possible.'

Bernice smiled. It was remarkable how easily he had adapted to the strange new technology. The Chapter's ship was a quantum leap on from the Betrushian dirigibles yet Liso took command as though he had been flying them all his life. He looked oddly fitting, she thought, leaning over the navigation console, his black uniform still fairly pristine.

The round viewing screen flickered into life, showing a vista of burning jungle and violently shaking earth, plumes of smoke curling high into the clouds. Lava was belching from freshly opened fissures.

Bernice clung grimly to her chair as the ship vibrated. She glanced across at Liso but, apart from the feverish swivelling of his eye, his expression was unreadable. It couldn't be easy seeing the world you loved tearing itself apart.

She shook herself from her reverie. They were there to save life, to give Betrushia a fighting chance.

The ship banked over the flaming tree-tops, its massive bulk flattening the blackening foliage.

'There! There!' cried Liso, pointing urgently at the screen.

From their viewpoint, the village was no more than a clearing with a few shambolic huts. Betrushians young and old were milling about in terror, scattering into the jungle, unable to comprehend what was happening to their land. An old woman, her knobbly spine sticking out of the back of her rough garment, looked up in terror.

'Take us down,' Liso barked at Libon, his eye glittering triumphantly.

Bernice got out of her chair and headed for the door. 'Well,' she said, 'if we don't scare them to death, I think we might be in business.'

Grek felt the stone-flagged floor shake as the mothership took off and was grateful that Imalgahite was on the bridge, delivering the Doctor's navigational instructions to the press-ganged helmsmen.

It would be a relief for Grek to get Yong back behind bars. He expected the wily mammal to try some trick every time they rounded a corner but, so far, he had merely walked ahead with his hands in the air.

Grek felt pleased that his initial misgivings about these – he shuddered at his own words – *beasts* had proven so inaccurate. Well, the Doctor and his friends anyway. They had been brave, loyal and unselfish. It was odd to think that the future of his people now lay in the hands of that funny little mammal.

What future, though? Where could they go? The whole of Betrushian civilization wiped out in a matter of days.

Grek sighed philosophically. Despite the anguish he felt about his world's imminent demise, his sense of self-preservation was paramount. He was glad the mothership had left the nightmarish jungle far behind.

Yong remained silent as they walked, his cloak swishing behind him.

The bulky communicator at Grek's side gave a little beep and Grek fumbled to remove it from his belt. Yong dutifully halted, a wry smile playing on his lips.

'Grek?' came Imalgahite's voice from the communicator. 'Can you come to the bridge?'

Grek put the instrument to his snout. 'Are we in orbit yet?'

'Yes, yes,' said Imalgahite impatiently. 'There's something else. Come to the bridge.'

Grek shrugged. 'On my way.' He put the communicator back in his belt.

Yong pointed down a right-hand corridor. 'It's this way.'

Grek pushed him in the back. 'I know.'

The Doctor pressed his handkerchief to his face and raced across the heaving earth towards the TARDIS. Smoke stung his eyes and he was almost consumed by steam and lava as huge gashes opened up in the ground. He dashed through the burning jungle towards the clearing, hoping that Ace was all right and the pathway to his ship unobstructed.

There was a great, mournful roar, as though the planet

243

were giving out its death-rattle. It was only as the Doctor approached the TARDIS through a hail of fire that he saw the creature.

It was dominating the sky above the jungle, its hide constantly shifting, shifting, shifting, in restless motion. It had a face, then nothing but a blur of components, then another face, fashioned from who knew what hellish source. Electricity arced over every terrible fragment of blood and bone.

The Doctor let himself into the TARDIS and Ace ran round from the other side of the console.

'What is it?' she cried. 'That thing?'

'It's changing,' he said, feverishly setting the co-ordinates. 'Re-inventing itself.'

He flicked a switch and the time rotor began its slow rise and fall. The Doctor glanced at Ace. 'Remember its original function was to seek perfection in all lifeforms. Perhaps it finds its own design imperfect and can't rest until it's restructured itself.'

Ace grimaced. 'Out of all that . . . gunk?'

The Doctor shrugged. 'That's its essence. A matrix of all the matter it's ever absorbed.'

Ace looked down at the console worriedly. 'Doctor? Is . . . is everything going to be all right?'

The Doctor looked at his watch. 'Well, if Bernice and Liso have finished their rescue attempt, both ships are in orbit, the re-engineering of the artificial suns works out and I can co-ordinate the power, then yes, everything will be fine.'

Ace frowned. 'There's a lot that could go wrong.'

'Yes,' said the Doctor, with something like his usual humour, 'but that's half the fun.'

As the TARDIS finally faded away from Betrushia, the creature suddenly doubled in size as it sucked in the mass of the flaming jungle. Fire roared through its veins, became part of its being, shot across the contours of its glistening flesh.

It gazed at the dying world through a thousand pairs of

eyes and roared with power; triumphantly, appallingly alive. *Alive*!

In the scout-ship's hold, Bernice pressed her hand against the door panel and the bulkhead slammed shut. She turned to the frightened group of Betrushians milling about in the corridor and tried to placate them. Most fell back against the rough metal walls, clinging to each other in fear. Children hung around their mother's skinny reptilian ankles and sobbed.

Resisting the urge to speak to them in a very loud and slow voice, Bernice took out her communicator and called up Liso.

'I think they need to see a friendly face,' she said. 'And you're the nearest thing to it. I'll take over on the bridge if you want to come down.'

'On my way,' came Liso's voice.

Bernice looked around. They hadn't done too badly. The two neighbouring villages and the town Liso had mentioned had yielded about a hundred and fifty Betrushians. Mostly women and children but that was probably for the best in survival terms. Most of the men had probably been drafted into the Ismetch-Cutch war. They could never have foreseen it would all end like this.

Bernice left the Betrushians in the hold and headed through the blank metal corridors towards the bridge. Their two hours were almost up.

As she reached the bridge, giving Liso a warm smile as they passed each other, she saw the viewing screen showing a receding image of the dying planet. Libon calmly took them into orbit and their prearranged position in the Doctor's bold plan.

For the sake of them all, she prayed it would work.

Grek marched Yong through the metal iris onto the bridge of the mothership and then froze as he felt the cold muzzle of two blasters at his scrawny throat.

Imalgahite was standing helplessly at the navigation

console. Jones and the other freed Chaptermen were at their posts. Sitting in Yong's chair, looking out at the swirling globe of Betrushia below, was De Hooch. He swung round in the chair and smiled.

'Welcome back,' he said in a quiet, dangerous whisper.

Yong scowled at him. Grek's blaster was wrenched from his claw and he was pushed over to join Imalgahite.

'I'm sorry,' said the Cutch leader. 'They came out of nowhere. I don't know how they escaped.'

Yong strode towards De Hooch. 'You're sitting in my chair, De Hooch,' he hissed.

'*Magna* De Hooch to you,' said the dwarf, licking his lips with relish.

Yong smiled. 'A bloodless coup? Really, that's not our style at all.'

De Hooch frowned. 'Things will be different now. Zeal will be tempered with pragmatism. This scheme of the Doctor's, for example, is clearly very sensible. We can't allow this creature to spread from Betrushia. It would destroy everything. Including us.'

Yong's eyes lit up with messianic fervour. 'Oh, you are so blind, De Hooch. Don't you see? Saint Anthony led us here for a purpose!'

'And what was that?'

'A meeting with our destiny! That creature *is* Saint Anthony: Saint Anthony personified. Grief, pain, suffering, misery, judgement, all in a physical form. It is exactly what I've been searching for all these years. The crusade is at an end. We must submit to it! Glory in the devastation it brings!'

Grek looked at the raving Yong and swallowed. 'You're completely insane.'

'Am I?' Yong seemed to consider this and then smiled, saliva dribbling over his beautiful lips. 'You know, I think you may be right.'

De Hooch turned away in disgust. 'Once we have finished here you will be executed for treason. A new order will begin.'

He swung round in the chair, swamped by its size, his little legs dangling over the side. 'You,' he addressed Grek. 'The power from our ships is to be redirected through these . . . these rings of yours, yes?'

Grek's scalp contracted in the familiar Betrushian affirmation. 'Yes.'

'And how is this to be achieved?'

Grek looked around. 'The Doctor will co-ordinate the operation. Your second ship should be coming into position about now.'

De Hooch nodded slowly. 'And where is the Doctor?'

On cue, the bridge filled with a cacophonous wailing and the TARDIS materialized out of thin air right next to De Hooch's chair. The Chaptermen stepped back in shock.

Yong seized his chance, punched his guard in the face, grabbed his blaster and ran out of the room.

'After him!' squealed De Hooch, jumping madly up and down on his chair. 'But I want him alive!'

Three Chaptermen tore from the bridge in pursuit.

The TARDIS doors opened and the Doctor and Ace stepped out. The Doctor smiled as he saw Grek and Imalgahite but his face fell as he looked around the bridge.

'The *status quo* has been restored, Doctor,' said De Hooch. 'Or something like it. As predicted, I am now in command.'

'But I have to stop this creature . . .'

De Hooch held up a pudgy hand. 'I appreciate that. I have a little more sense than my illustrious predecessor. We will co-operate with you. For now. Begin your work.'

Ace was disarmed and nudged over to join Grek and Imalgahite. The Doctor moved towards the console. He leant over and pressed a button.

'Bernice? Bernice, Liso, can you hear me?'

There was silence. The Doctor frowned. Ace shot him an anxious look.

'Ber –'

'Doctor? Yes. Sorry. Couldn't find the right switch.'

The Doctor sighed in relief. 'Are you ready to begin?'
'I think so.'

A few corridors down from the bridge, Yong stood panting against a wall, strands of his sleek black hair tumbling into his eyes.

The Doctor's conversation boomed from hidden speakers in the stone passageway.

'Remember,' came the Doctor's voice, 'it's crucial that the two suns' power be aligned simultaneously. Have the modifications gone through?'

'The helmsman says yes,' came Liso's voice.

'Very well,' said the Doctor. 'Let's begin.'

Yong smiled as he listened to the crackly conversation and fondled the muzzle of his blaster. Then he slipped away into the shadows.

The Betrushian sky was pitch black save for the brilliant sheets of lightning which crashed from horizon to horizon.

The colossal, amorphous creature now stood hundreds of feet high, absorbing every inch of the burning jungle which surrounded it.

It had begun to form a kind of structure, translucent bones tumbling together in a twisted rib-cage, the line of an immense jaw visible in the sickly yellow blob of its head. Eyes rolled about, jerking out of half-formed sockets as though unable to fix themselves down.

Spreading wide its web-like arms it bellowed and began to filter the very elements from the burning air. In its search for perfection, it broke down everything to its constituent molecules; analysing and calculating, splitting genes and reforming them into complex new patterns.

With a tremendous surge of energy, the creature expanded again, taking on a vast rectangular shape like a bolt of sagging, rotten cloth. Light shimmered across its mucus-drenched surface.

Huge legs thundered into the rolling soil as it metamorphosed yet again. All its restraints were weakening. It would soon be free to fulfil its purpose.

Vertebrae sprang out of the gelatinous pulp and it roared upwards into the clouds, trebling in size.

'Where's Yong?' said Ace with sudden concern.

De Hooch looked acidly at her. 'The former Magna has run away. True to form.'

Ace frowned. 'And what have you done about it?'

De Hooch waved a hand airily. 'Oh, he will shortly be recaptured. Then I shall revenge myself upon him.'

The Doctor straightened up at the navigational console, his strange grey eyes unblinking. 'He's a dangerous man. I suggest you put as many of your people on his trail as possible. He created the power source we're using, remember? He could do a lot of damage if he gets to the right places.'

De Hooch digested this. 'Jones, go after him.'

'No!' barked Ace. 'I want to go.'

De Hooch glared at her. 'You? I ought to have you shot here and now for the humiliation I have endured from *you*.'

The Doctor looked De Hooch hard in the eyes. 'You have to admit she's tenacious, though. And she wants revenge. If anyone can find Yong, it's Ace.'

De Hooch looked across at her. 'Very well. You will go with Jones. All non-essential personnel will search for former Magna Yong. Go!'

The Doctor pressed Ace's arm as she got up. 'It's very important that you find him.'

Ace, Jones and half a dozen Chaptermen hared from the bridge. The metal iris scraped shut behind them.

'Now, Doctor,' said De Hooch. 'Return to your duties.'

The Doctor bent down. His mud-caked clothes glowed blueishly. 'Bernice? Start boosting the power.'

'Got you. Beginning . . . now.'

'Check.'

The Doctor glanced at the helmsman. 'Betrushia?'

The Chapterman shrugged. 'An hour. No more.'

The Doctor nodded. 'All right. Where are the directional controls?'

The helmsman frowned. 'What?'

'The directional controls for this "fire" of yours.'

De Hooch swallowed nervously. 'They're in the cathedral, Doctor. It's a security measure in case of hijack or accident.'

'So Yong could be heading there too?'

De Hooch squirmed in his seat. 'It's possible.'

The Doctor rubbed his eyes warily. 'Too many variables.' He banged his fist on the console in frustration. 'Far too many.'

'Doctor?' It was Bernice.

'Yes?'

'Power rising steadily. No problems.'

'Good. I'll let you know when we reach optimum mark.'

De Hooch smiled horribly. 'Saint Anthony be with you, Doctor.'

Thoss awoke from unpleasant, fire-filled dreams. The cold stone of the cathedral floor had chilled him to the bone and he was shivering as he clambered unsteadily to his feet.

This place was so strange. Who were the mammals he had released from the cage? The Keth? Or were the Keth imaginary? He could no longer remember. The Faith was all he had. And that was gone.

The great double doors burst open and smacked off the cathedral walls. Yong scrambled inside, holstering his blaster. Behind him, two of the three Chaptermen who had originally pursued him were hard on his heels.

Cloak billowing, Yong clattered across the flagstones and collided with Thoss.

The old Ismetch sank to his knees. 'Forgive me, master,' he mumbled. 'I have sinned.'

'Who are *you*?' sneered Yong. 'Get your dirty claws off me.'

250

He pushed Thoss to the floor and ran up the steps to the throne. Diving behind it, he pulled out the great gilded cross and clutched it to his breast.

'Why have you come? To torment me? To test us all?' pleaded Thoss.

Yong skidded towards the concealed machinery and glanced up at the circular panel in the ceiling.

'What are you talking about, you old fool? Now get out of my way, I have work to do.'

Thoss prostrated himself at Yong's feet and pulled at the former Magna's ankles. Yong pressed his blaster onto the old man's crest. 'Get off me or I'll blow your head off.'

Thoss bowed, his old body sinking pathetically. 'If that is your will. The will of the Keth.'

Yong shrugged and pumped bolt after bolt into Thoss's skull. The old man's kneeling corpse stood upright for a moment then slumped to the floor.

Yong tutted at the blood which pooled around his feet. 'Messy,' he drawled.

A blaster-bolt crackled over his head. He responded in kind as the two pursuing Chaptermen crashed into the room, concealing themselves at once.

Yong scooped up the great cross and ran towards the directional controls.

A Chapterman appeared directly in his path and blasted at him. Yong raised the huge cross and it took the full impact, the gilded flames melting and dripping down the front of his gown.

Yong cursed and cast the cross aside. It clattered to the floor next to Thoss's body.

He would never get to the machinery now. His only hope to sabotage the Doctor's work was to return to the power room itself.

He dived for cover as the second Chapterman appeared from behind the throne.

'I'm disappointed in you,' cried Yong. 'So fickle. After all I've done for you, you take orders from a midget!'

He peered around the corner of a pillar. He could clearly see both men and the path back to the double doors was clear. Rapidly he zigzagged across the cathedral and slammed the doors shut behind him.

The two Chaptermen set off in angry pursuit, jumping over the blood of Thoss as they careered for the doors.

Ace, Jones and a single Chapterman ran down the corridors of the seminary, having split off from the other three.

'This is getting us nowhere,' panted Jones. 'He could be anywhere.'

'He's a nutter,' said Ace, 'and a single-minded nutter at that. He won't have just run away. He'll be heading for the power room.'

Jones nodded quickly. 'This way then.'

They scurried off.

Yong pelted up the winding black spiral stairs to the power room, his eyes afire with determination and a manic smile fixed to his face.

He pulled on a pair of goggles and banged open the door. Before him, the artificial sun glowed with power, its intensity increasing as the Doctor's plan unfolded. He noticed the dead body of the acne-scarred Chapterman, propped up by the guard-rail of the gently throbbing sun, but did not bother to wonder why he had died. Or who might have killed him.

Instead, he pulled the bulky communicator from the Chapterman's belt and switched it on.

'You are ingenious, Doctor,' he shouted into it. 'But I did promise sabotage if the opportunity arose.'

The Doctor's voice crackled through. 'Yong? Is that – Where are you?'

'He's in the power room. Must be,' came Grek's voice.

Yong grinned, sweat dripping off the end of his nose. 'Your scaly friend is correct. I'm in the power room. And I'm about to undo all that work we laboured so hard on.'

The Doctor's voice was feverish with anxiety. 'Yong!

Think what you're doing. That creature down there is death personified. All your work will count for nothing. Your chapter, all life, all *life* will be annihilated. Think, man! Think!'

Yong smiled, his goggles shining glassily in the light from the sun. 'No! NO! That creature is Saint Anthony! He has shown me the way. This is his will, that all things shall be consumed.' He stroked the machinery lovingly. 'It's a rather amusing irony, isn't it? I have seen the light!'

He gazed at the throbbing ball of energy and cackled manically. 'I have seen the light!'

'Doctor? What's going on?' It was Bernice, cutting in from the second orbiting ship.

Yong laughed again but stopped suddenly as he noticed the cloth-covered bundle. He frowned and reached out to touch it, but was distracted by Bernice's voice.

'Doctor, shall I start the countdown?'

'Yes!'

Yong raised the blaster and trained it on the mechanism. 'Too late! You're too late, Doctor!'

20

St Anthony's Fire

Yong started as the door to the power room burst open and Ace and Jones, both wearing goggles, toppled inside. The remaining Chaptermen stayed outside, unable to tolerate the growing intensity of the sun.

Ace smiled. 'Good choice, Jones.' She levelled her blaster at Yong. 'Put the gun down, Magna,' she ordered.

Yong turned, his cruel features flaring bone white in the glare. 'You again, my dear? You were so promisingly brutal when we picked you up on Massatoris. What a shame you didn't live up to my expectations.'

He raised the blaster and pointed it at the humming machinery.

'Stop right there or I swear I'll shoot,' bellowed Ace.

Yong's face was impassive. 'Do as you please. I really don't mind. I shall destroy this machine and release the endless, undying wrath of Saint Anthony on you all. It doesn't matter that I shall perish.' He glanced down. 'You might satisfy my curiosity, however, and buy yourselves a little time.'

Ace frowned over her goggles. 'How?'

Yong kicked at the cloth-covered box jammed between the machines. 'Pull that out and show me what's inside. I can't bear the suspense.'

Warily, Ace edged past Jones towards the machinery. She began to move the box out with her toe.

'No tricks now,' purred Yong.

'Would I?'

'Of course. That's why I like you.'

Ace bent down, keeping her gun carefully trained on Yong, and whipped the cloth off Ran's box.

Yong cocked an eyebrow. 'How fascinating. Now, open the –'

Ran appeared out of nowhere, shielded by the glow of the sun, and blew off one of Yong's shoulders with his stolen blaster.

The Magna was hurled backwards, his gun clattering to the floor.

Ace dived for it, rolled, and brought both weapons to bear on her nemesis.

Howling with pain, Yong clutched at the hole where his collar-bone had been and stumbled towards the door. Jones slammed his foot down on the edge of Yong's cloak and he fell heavily against the machinery, his bloodied arm connecting against the metal with a wet slap.

As he crumpled to the floor, his goggles cracked and fell off. For a long, long moment he stared, unprotected, into the naked, furious light of the artificial sun.

Yong grabbed at his eyes and screamed and screamed, clawing at his face to try and shut out the preternaturally intense light. Thrusting his arm over his eyes, he staggered blindly from the room.

'Leave him,' said Ace. 'We've got work to do.'

She pulled out a communicator. 'Doctor, we're back in charge. Power seems to be building nicely.'

'Well done, Ace. Now get back to the bridge. There's a lot still to do.'

Ran walked calmly towards the machinery and picked up his precious box.

'Ace,' said Ace holding up a hand in greeting. 'What *is* in there?'

Ran smiled and strode past her into the reassuring darkness of the spiral stairwell.

The Doctor turned from the console to De Hooch and

breathed out with a sigh. 'We're on course again, er . . . Magna.'

'Excellent, Doctor.' The dwarf leant back in his chair. 'How long before optimum power is achieved?'

The Doctor pressed a button. 'Bernice?'

'I should say about twenty minutes, Doctor.'

The Doctor looked over. 'There you are, twenty minutes and we can boost the power of the rings.'

De Hooch wriggled with excitement. 'And Betrushia destroys itself and this nasty organism with it, Saint Anthony's in his Heaven and all's right with the world.'

'Then what?' said the Doctor.

'What do you mean?'

'What happens to us?'

De Hooch smiled an executioner's smile. 'Oh Doctor, let's not spoil the surprise.'

The Doctor turned back to the navigation console. 'Anyway, it's not as easy as you think. I have to get the power differential just right. Too little and the thing will escape, too much and the rings will be destroyed. Either way, it's risky.'

De Hooch assumed an expression of mock sincerity. 'Anything I can do to help?'

The Doctor could think of a lot of things, most of them involving long walks off short piers.

On the identical bridge of the scout-ship, Bernice listened in grim silence to the Doctor's conversation. She turned to Liso. 'Seems like the holy relics are back in charge.'

Liso's eyelid drooped tiredly. 'Just what we didn't need.' He glanced down at the console. 'Fifteen minutes. Check.'

Bernice nodded. 'What do we do now? We've got a hold full of refugees. Do we turn ourselves in and get killed?'

'Hardly,' muttered Liso. 'We've been through too much to give in now.'

'There must be something,' sighed Bernice.

She turned to Libon, the lone Chapterman who had

piloted the ship. He had been sitting disconsolately in the corner since they had achieved orbit, seemingly unaware of everything, like a lost child. Bernice crossed to him and put a reassuring hand on his shoulder.

'What's your name?'

Libon's eyes were wide and innocent under his brutally cropped black hair. 'Libon,' he said quietly. 'Libon Fung. Ch . . . Chapterman of Saint Anthony.'

'Well, Libon,' said Bernice softly, 'don't you worry about a thing. All you have to do is show me exactly how this ship of yours works.'

Libon looked up at her in bewilderment.

'Ten minutes,' said the Doctor.

De Hooch glanced interestedly at the monitors. 'Is everything proceeding according to plan?'

'Whose plan? Mine or yours?'

De Hooch smiled, exposing rotten, peg-like teeth. 'What a card you are, Doctor.'

'You know, you suit being Magna. You sound more and more like Yong all the time.'

The smile faded from the dwarf's wet lips.

The Doctor crossed to Grek and Imalgahite who were sitting on the floor at the far side of the bridge.

'What're we going to do, Doctor?' said Grek. 'Even if we destroy this thing, what hope is there for our people?'

'To have come this far . . .' sighed Imalgahite, throwing up his claws in desperation.

The Doctor crouched down on his haunches, a strange, faraway look coming into his eyes. 'I'll think of something.'

He patted Grek on the shoulder and glanced at the console. 'Eight minutes,' he said to no one in particular.

The two great ships of Saint Anthony hung in the inky blackness of space. Far below, through the glittering halo of the damaged rings, Betrushia entered her final hour.

Beneath the poisoned clouds, the creature had grown immense. It straddled the remains of the jungle now, miles

257

across, a vast web of shifting matter, seething and expanding as ever more material was dredged into its core.

A million clawed tentacles burst from out of its flesh, a hybrid of incinerated jungle and Betrushian blood.

At once, the structure was rethought and altered again, the carpet of flesh exploding outwards towards the lightning-streaked sky.

It seemed aware that this world was no place for it. It was a dying place. But the creature was alive, constantly, urgently, vibrantly alive. Soon the bonds which tied it to Betrushia would be gone forever.

As though in celebration, the organism split into a thousand components and instantly reassembled, a monstrous triple head erupting from its suppurating skin.

Jones and Ace came onto the bridge. De Hooch looked them over.

'Well?'

'Magna . . . er . . . former Magna Yong was forced out of the power room.'

De Hooch looked behind Jones. 'Where is he?'

The Doctor looked up. 'He could still do some harm.'

Ace smiled cruelly. 'I think he's blind, Doctor. He looked into the artificial sun without protection.'

De Hooch shook his head violently. 'That doesn't matter. His family designed this ship. He knows it like . . .' He struggled out of the chair. 'Leave this to me.'

He took the two blasters from Ace and Jones. 'I've been waiting a long time for this.'

'Wait!' called the Doctor. 'If Yong's trying to damage the directional equipment he'll be heading for the cathedral.'

'I know that!' spat De Hooch, turning to go.

'No, listen, De Hooch. I need you to operate the machinery for me. Do what you like with Yong but make sure you follow my instructions first – otherwise it'll all be for nothing.'

He tossed a communicator across the room and the

dwarf caught it in his stunted, sausage-fingered hand. Then, with a scowl which betrayed his resentment, De Hooch waddled from the bridge.

'Jones, you're in command,' he muttered as he slipped through the iris.

The Doctor watched him go and then turned back to the console.

'Four minutes. Ready, Bernice?'

'When you are, Doctor.'

De Hooch ran as fast as he could towards the cathedral. He had not felt this excited since he was small. Well, since he was a boy anyway. Not since the day he had killed his parents, in fact.

He remembered it all very clearly. A high, bright summer's day in the New Dutch Republic.

De Hooch's early childhood had been idyllic, filled with stories about the Old Country from his indulgent grandfather. Stories of how the seas had claimed Holland, and the Dutch had become the wanderers of Europe. How his family had eventually settled in the land which had sprung up out of the Atlantic following the seismic shifts. All these tales made him achingly nostalgic for a time he had never even known.

After his grandfather's death, however, his parents had abandoned him to the welfare agencies; unable to cope, they said, with such a violent, nasty child. Unable to cope with his genius, more like, thought De Hooch.

He had never forgiven them for their cruelty, and made it his business to track them down and kill them once he joined the Chapter. In his mind's eye he could still see their expressions of frozen horror as he shuffled into the house, the laser-rifle in his sweaty little hands.

And the Chapter, he reflected with a warm glow, ah, yes, the Chapter.

The vacuum in his life had to be filled somehow and, like many in those dark days, he had sought refuge in the new religion. It soon became clear that not just anyone

259

could join, however, and it was only after long months trawling the dirtiest spaceports in the galaxy that he had been successful. After chartering a shuttle to Titan, the ship had been unexpectedly attacked by one of the Chapter's raiding ships. De Hooch's willingness to slaughter his fellow passengers had endeared him to the Chapter and before long he had been initiated and introduced to the Magna.

Yong was everything he had been searching for. Physically magnificent, overpoweringly beautiful and incalculably evil. Before too many years, De Hooch had become second only to the Magna himself, consulted at almost every level on the Chapter's crusade against the heathens.

But with growing power had come growing resentment. De Hooch began to realize just how arrogant was his superior and how dismissive of his Parva's considerable talents. The feeling had grown more and more poisonous, festering inside the dwarf like pus in the boil which De Hooch's head so much resembled.

This current debacle had concentrated De Hooch's wish to overthrow Yong and, at last, become Magna himself.

Now his once-respected, now hated leader was tottering to an appointment with destiny.

De Hooch threw open the cathedral doors and stepped inside. His boots clopped on the chilly flagstones. Thoss lay where Yong had shot him, congealed blood pooling stickily around him.

De Hooch looked around. There was no sign of Yong. If he intended to sabotage the directional equipment he was too late. De Hooch would be waiting for him.

He crossed to the concealed machinery in the alcove and drew back the heavy brocade curtain. The shimmering steel lines of the directional console shone up at him.

De Hooch switched on the communicator. 'Very well, Doctor. I'm here.'

The Doctor's relieved sigh crackled back: 'Good. Now, tell me what you see in front of you.'

The dwarf looked down at the instrumentation. 'Let me

see. Six . . . no, seven levers. Some sort of panel on the left.'

The Doctor's voice whispered in conjunction with Jones's in the background.

'All right,' said the Doctor. 'I'll read you the directional co-ordinates. Key them into the panel, then pull down all the levers in sequence. Got that? All the levers in sequence.'

'Yes, yes,' muttered De Hooch. 'Go ahead.'

The Doctor slowly went through the co-ordinates needed to direct the beam of Saint Anthony's Fire into the rings. De Hooch's fat fingers carefully punched in the digits. 'I've done it,' he squealed.

Slowly he began to wrench down the steel levers. The console glowed with power. His hand was poised on the seventh and final lever when he tensed at the sound of erratic footsteps in the corridor outside.

'De Hooch?' came the Doctor's voice. 'Have you finished?'

'Plenty of time, Doctor. Plenty of time. I have some business to attend to.'

The Doctor spluttered through the communicator. 'Pull the lever! Pull the – '

De Hooch switched off the communicator and, almost in a trance, crept from the alcove and carefully ascended the steps to Yong's throne.

The former Magna fell through the doors into the cathedral. His cloak was ripped and blood was pouring from the gory hole at the top of his arm. He staggered across the room.

'All finished!' he screeched. 'All finished! Saint Anthony will not be cheated!'

He slipped in Thoss's blood and stumbled to the floor, cracking his knees on the flagstones. De Hooch laughed harshly.

Yong's head shot upwards, his hands finding the partially melted cross he had abandoned on the floor. His

261

eyes had misted over completely, like the white marble eyes of Saint Anthony's statue.

'Who's there?'

De Hooch nestled into the throne. 'Why, Yong, don't you know me?'

Yong peered blindly into space. 'De Hooch? Is that you? Oh, my friend. Join me! It's not too late. Saint Anthony will forgive you. We must stop the Doctor's plotting!'

De Hooch took out both his blasters. 'No, no, no, Yong. It ends here. I am Magna now. And you are history.'

He squeezed the triggers. Twin bolts of energy roared across the cathedral and hit Yong in his wounded shoulder. Blood and bone splattered across the floor. Yong collapsed into his cloak like a dying lily, screaming in pain.

The Doctor glared at the viewing screen. 'The idiot! He's jeopardizing everything for his own vendetta.'

'What can we do?' said Imalgahite.

The Doctor looked down at the console. 'Three minutes, Bernice. Are you at optimum power?'

'Almost. On your mark.'

The Doctor turned to Imalgahite. 'I don't know what we can do. If that final lever isn't pulled then the directional controls will overshoot.'

'Well, I know where the place is,' said Imalgahite evenly. 'I'll pull the thing down for him.'

'Two minutes fifty,' read off Bernice from the scoutship.

The Doctor shook his head at the Cutch leader. 'It's too dangerous. The combined power will be astronomical. Anyone in the cathedral would be incinerated.'

Imalgahite looked down, crestfallen.

'Two minutes, thirty,' crackled Bernice.

Imalgahite looked around quickly. 'Grek? Where's Grek?'

They all turned towards the metal iris which was sliding shut.

* * *
262
.

Grek felt a crippling stitch surge through his exhausted body as he ran down the sun-drenched corridors towards the cathedral. He was sure he could remember the way. The cages of the *auto-da-fe* had trundled through these passages and past the bridge.

He paused briefly, struggling to catch his breath, and made a turn to the left. The great double doors of the cathedral loomed at the end of the next corridor.

'We'll just have to hope he gets there in time and manages to save himself,' said the Doctor sadly. 'We can't start again now. The timing is crucial.'

His hand paused over the 'execute' control.

'Four.'

Ace closed her eyes.

'Three.'

Imalgahite turned away.

'Two.'

The Doctor bit his lip.

'One.'

The Doctor jabbed his finger onto the button. 'Now, Bernice! Execute!'

The bridge shook with power. The Doctor glanced at the monitor. 'Come on, Grek. Come *on.*'

He looked out at Betrushia. All they needed was a miracle.

Yong dragged himself to his feet using the great gilded cross like a walking stick. His shoulder was now nothing more than a bloodied hole and his beautiful face was deathly pale and contorted with pain. Sweat soaked his long black hair.

His lips trembled as he spoke. 'I submit ... Magna ... De Hooch.'

De Hooch sat up in his chair. This was unexpected. 'What?'

'Magna De Hooch. You have bested me. I am unfit to

263

lead the Chapter. You are the ... inheritor ... of Saint Anthony's Fire ...'

De Hooch got up out of the chair, his blasters raised suspiciously.

'Come to me,' called Yong. 'I am nothing but a blind fool now. But for the sake of our old association, let me pass on my birthright to you, o brave Magna.'

De Hooch dashed down the steps towards the ailing Yong.

The former Magna pulled himself to his full height with the cross. 'See, the flames of Saint Anthony emblazon this symbol of his power. I hand it to you, my wise and worthy successor.'

In spite of himself, De Hooch felt humbled, moved beyond measure by Yong's words. Of course, it was only natural that he, De Hooch, should lead the Chapter but he had expected to have to force the crown from Yong. A humbled and defeated Magna left a far sweeter taste in his mouth. The dwarf knelt down before the blind man.

Yong put out a shaking, blood-stained hand and felt for De Hooch's skull-cap. He raised the cross high above his head.

'O, mighty Saint Anthony,' he cried, 'I humbly pass the burden of your wrath to a wiser head.'

De Hooch held out his fat hands to receive the cross. Yong's blank eyes rolled insanely and, with a giggling screech, be brought the cross smashing down onto De Hooch's skull.

The dwarf's head cracked open like a rotten egg, spurting blood and pasty cerebral fluid down his startled little face.

Yong cackled maniacally. Pulling blindly at the dwarf's corpse, he dragged his way across the room. De Hooch's head leaving a slug-trail of fluid on the flagstones.

He was half-way towards the alcove containing the humming directional machinery when he felt the floor vibrating beneath him. He dropped De Hooch and scrambled over the floor, feeling the outline of the great recessed panel just as it shot open, releasing the vast, dazzling column of Saint Anthony's Fire into space.

The pure crimson flames roared down from the ceiling, incinerating the flesh from Yong's body. As he died, a final oath slipped from between his perfect lips:

'Bugger.'

On the bridge, the Doctor put his hand to his mouth in despair. 'It's no good. The fire's been released but it's going nowhere. Just dissipating into space.'

Ace looked around the room at the terrified Chaptermen, all frozen into impotence. 'I'm going to do it,' she cried suddenly.

The Doctor whirled round. 'What?'

Ace stood upright and wiped her brow. 'I'm going down there. Somebody's got to.'

The Doctor shook his head desperately. 'You'll be killed. I told you.'

'But if I don't go, that thing will escape!'

'It's out of the question!' roared the Doctor, his eyes flashing.

In a quiet corner of her mind, Ace found his concern inordinately touching.

'It's all right,' said a voice. 'I made it.'

The Doctor flicked a switch. 'Grek? Grek, is that you?'

The cathedral fountained with red light as the gargantuan column of fire spat from the artificial sun through the vaulted ceiling and out into space.

Crouched in the alcove, his skin steaming, Grek held De Hooch's communicator in his claw. 'The last lever, Doctor? The seventh?'

'Yes,' came the Doctor's voice, scarcely audible above the tumult.

Grek's other claw slammed down the final lever and the console roared with power.

'It's done. It's done . . .' gasped Grek as he stumbled from the alcove, his uniform bursting into flame.

'Grek! Grek!' crackled the Doctor's voice.

The communicator fell from Grek's claw and was incinerated as the enormous column of energy began to expand across the cathedral floor.

Grek crumpled and fell, his blue eyes turning in awe towards the staggering majesty of Saint Anthony's Fire.

' "For the Greater Glory!" ' he bellowed one last time.

The twin beams of energy poured from the two black ships and melded together. A great streak of crimson fire raced across space and struck the Betrushian rings at a tangent. They blazed as though furiously alive, each fragment of dust and the mechanism within boosted by the incredible burst of energy. A blazing halo encircled the dying planet.

Below, the organism felt the new power and the restraint return. It strained against it like a lion against its chains, reaching far, far into the atmosphere in an effort to be free. It formed a legion of mouths simply to articulate its roar of protest.

It raced across the burning landscape, spreading wide over the planet's surface.

Still the rings forced it down. It screeched in fury, every fibre of its cannibalized-being raging against submission. Energy flooded through the rings, crushing the organism until it lay like a vast, mucoid blanket over Betrushia's surface. With one, long, final groan of despair, it vanished below the heaving surface.

The Doctor turned sadly from the console.

After a moment, a tiny winking light brought him back. He banged the navigation console triumphantly. 'That's it! It's holding!'

He peered anxiously into the monitor. 'The rings' power has been boosted to maximum.'

Imalgahite looked up. 'And Grek?'

The Doctor shook his head.

'We'd better get out of here,' said Ace.

266

'Sir,' said a Chapterman, addressing Jones. 'Both Magna Yong and . . . er Magna De Hooch's life traces have been extinguished.'

Jones cocked his head to one side. 'What?'

The Doctor sighed heavily and rubbed the back of his neck. 'Well, well. The hour and the man, eh? You know it's traditional to begin a new period of office by pardoning prisoners?'

Jones looked at the Doctor, a disquieting fervour in his eyes. 'Maybe in the degenerate places you come from, Doctor. But I shall begin my reign as Magna by making you suffer.'

'You can't!' cried Ace. 'After all he's done . . .'

'Exactly,' hissed Jones. 'After all he's done to the Chapter of Saint Anthony he deserves to die.'

He shot out of his chair and raised his blaster. 'I am Magna now.'

'In that case,' said a voice from behind him, 'you won't mind surrendering your vessel.'

Jones swung round. A reptile with a box in one claw was pointing a pistol at his head.

The Doctor smiled with relief. 'Very well then, I suggest we leave orbit before Betrushia explodes.'

Ran pressed the pistol behind Jones's ear. 'You. Do as he says.'

The Doctor fussed over the controls. 'We'll return to Bernice's ship in the TARDIS. I'll leave you to your own fate.'

Ace leapt up, suddenly finding a little of that missing thirst for vengeance. 'You can't just let them get away with it!' she cried. 'After all I've been through. After all everyone's been through!'

The Doctor held up his hands. 'Please, Ace. There's been enough killing. The rings have been boosted to maximum capacity now. I'll put that sun of theirs out of action. That'll be an end to their crusade.'

Ace was not to be placated. 'What kind of justice is that?'

She stalked furiously into the TARDIS.

The Doctor's hands dashed over the controls. 'I've put the artificial sun into irreversible decline.' He turned to Jones. 'You'll have to put in somewhere soon if you're not to freeze to death. I'm giving you a chance. It's far more than you deserve.'

He ushered Imalgahite into the TARDIS.

Ran pulled Jones with him, the pistol clamped behind the new Magna's ear, and then pushed him across the room as he ducked into the TARDIS, the precious box in the other claw.

As the TARDIS dematerialized, Jones slammed his fist onto the deck in fury.

Imalgahite gazed around the white-walled console room in surprise. Ran, who was used to it by now, merely stood by the console, cradling his box in his arms.

The Doctor set the co-ordinates for the scout-ship, casting occasional worried looks at Ace who was leaning against a roundel.

'They'll pay for it one day, Ace.'

'Bollocks.'

The Doctor flicked a switch and the time rotor rose and fell once.

'Short hop,' he said. 'Gentlemen?'

The Betrushians trooped out of the TARDIS onto what at first appeared to be the same bridge. Only the presence of Bernice, Liso and Libon showed differently.

The newcomers were enthusiastically welcomed.

'Did it work?' asked Bernice.

'I think so,' said the Doctor. 'We'll soon see.' He pointed to the young navigator. 'Who's he?'

Bernice grinned. 'That's Libon. He's been a great help. In more ways than one.'

Libon smiled shyly.

'All right, Libon,' said the Doctor. 'Get us out of here.'

Libon punched in a course and the ship raced away

268

from the dying planet. Stars burred as they rocketed through space.

The Doctor gazed into the screen until he decreed they had reached a safe distance. 'Very well. That'll do.'

Liso was by his side. 'Where's Grek?'

'I'm afraid he didn't make it.'

Liso heaved a heavy sigh, remembering the Grek he had once loved and respected, cursing his own foolish behaviour.

'He saved us all,' said the Doctor gently. 'He was a brave man.'

Liso's eyes fired with pride. 'Yes he was. And a great soldier.'

He put his claws behind his back and turned stiffly towards the round viewing screen. Ran and Imalgahite joined him. The blue disc of Betrushia was scarcely visible in the great black expanse of space.

Bernice sidled up to Ace. 'What's the matter?'

Ace ran a hand over her shaved head. 'After all those bastards did. He just let them go.'

Bernice rolled her eyes theatrically. 'Ah. Yes. I've been meaning to talk to you about that.'

Ace looked up. 'What?'

Bernice pointed to young Libon. 'Our navigator turned out to be a very nice bloke. Just a bit misguided. You know the type. Easily led. Anyway, Liso and I were worried about the Chapter regaining control of your ship so we had a little chat with Libon . . .'

Ace frowned, then smiled. 'Tell me more.'

Jones threw himself down into the Magna's chair and looked around at his depleted and disillusioned Chapter. He sighed wearily.

'Very well. Get us out of orbit. I'll put this one down to experience.'

The navigator nodded enthusiastically. 'Yes, Magna. It is the will of Saint Anthony!'

269

He punched in a course. The console bleeped angrily. He tried again and frowned.

'My Lord . . .'

Jones got up. 'What is it?'

'The controls, my Lord. They're not responding.'

'What?'

The navigator bit his lip and punched in the course a third time. 'They appear to have been overriden. By an outside force.'

Jones looked wildly about. 'But that can only be done by . . .'

'By another of our vessels,' concluded the navigator.

Jones wiped the sweat from his brow. 'Well, override the override, you idiot! There's not much time!'

The navigator scrambled under the console. Chapter-men scurried to his aid.

Jones glared at the screen. 'Get us out of here!'

The navigator looked hopelessly at his leader. 'My Lord . . .' He tailed off.

Jones pushed his fist into his mouth, his eyes bulging in naked terror.

The organism felt it first. A deep, deep rumbling in the earth, greater than all the earthquakes Betrushia had suffered.

Oceanic plates rose up and slammed together, hurling billions of tons of lava and ash into the atmosphere. The oceans evaporated into a nebula of dust, enveloping the ancient evil which struggled and thrashed in its attempt to make sense of its new environment. It was still meta-morphosing when the planet's core burst asunder and consumed it completely.

White fire flared across the expanding mass and Betru-shia shattered, rolling in a vast cloud of superheated gas; slamming into the atmosphere; expanding outwards, ever outwards in a blossoming cloud of fire and light; annihilat-ing the planet, the brilliant halo of its throbbing rings and the great black mothership of Saint Anthony which vaporized one point four seconds after the planet exploded.

Epilogue

The TARDIS stood at a vaguely crooked angle on the grassy hillside. The sun was shining gloriously in a pale, cornflower-blue sky.

Standing up to his ankles in cool water, the Doctor decided that he really did like Massatoris an awful lot.

Bernice called to him from the lakeside. He waved and splashed out of the water.

Bernice looked him up and down. 'You look awful.'

The Doctor examined his destroyed waistcoat and trousers. His Gladstone collar hung limply from one stud. 'Hmm. I think it's time we were going. I need a bath. And we have a few loose ends to drop off.'

He glanced over towards the TARDIS, inside which Libon and a whole gaggle of recovering converts were awaiting transportation to a new life elsewhere.

Bernice and the Doctor walked together over the brow of the hill towards the familiar village. It was blackened and ruined, of course, and none of the original inhabitants of Massatoris were present. But now the little planet had a new group of colonists.

The Betrushians whom Bernice and Liso had rescued were wandering through the wreckage of the village, discussing repairs and ideas for their new planet. In the middle of the square, sitting on a long bench, were Ran and Imalgahite.

The Doctor approached them. 'We have to go.'

Imalgahite smiled and touched the Doctor's chest with

272

his claw. 'I don't know how to thank you. You've given us a chance of survival.'

The Doctor frowned. 'There aren't many of you. But it's fitting that you should come here. Another world they ruined. Perhaps you can make something of it.'

He shielded his eyes and looked over towards the remains of the burnt forest where the bulk of the black ship stood.

Bernice and Liso stood apart from the little group. The one-eyed Ismetch took Bernice's hand in his claw. 'Quite an adventure, eh beast?'

She smiled. 'More like an ordeal.' She closed her hand over his claw. 'Goodbye Liso – and good luck.'

He smiled, the fresh, real, glorious sunlight glinting off his eye.

Bernice returned to the Doctor. He was peering into Ran's box, which was finally open. Bernice looked inside. Nestled on a bed of oily cloth were three leathery brown eggs.

'Yours?' said Bernice in surprise.

Ran looked down proudly. 'I was too stubborn to admit it. My children. They're a gift from someone very special. Now they have a chance too.'

The Doctor smiled. 'To the future,' he said. 'And do keep them warm.'

They turned away and walked back towards the TARDIS.

'Did you ever remember why you wanted to come here?' said the Doctor.

Bernice laughed. 'I did. It was when I was in the airship with Liso. I was worried for Ace for a while but now I think I know what it all means.'

'How so?'

'Well, I remembered that the eleventh colony disappeared and that another race, an alien race, was found to be living here some time later. Everyone assumed they were an invasion force. I had visions of the Betrushians attacking Massatoris. Now . . .'

273

'So perhaps they'll make it after all,' smiled the Doctor.

Bernice paused at the TARDIS threshold. 'Where's Ace? She doesn't want to –'

'No, no,' said the Doctor. 'Here she comes.'

Ace ran up the hillside, beaming and a little out of breath.

'Come along then,' said the Doctor briskly. He put the key in the lock and turned to Ace. 'Am I forgiven?'

Ace smiled. 'For what?'

'Letting the Chapter off the hook?'

Ace cocked her head. 'Of course.'

The Doctor nodded happily and went inside. Ace took Bernice's arm and winked at her.

'They'll pay for it one day,' she said.

They stepped inside and the doors closed behind them. A few moments later, with a strangulated, grating whine, the TARDIS melted away into the air.

Already published:

TIMEWYRM: GENESYS
John Peel

The Doctor and Ace are drawn to Ancient Mesopotamia in search of an evil sentience that has tumbled from the stars – the dreaded Timewyrm of ancient Gallifreyan legend.

ISBN 0 426 20355 0

TIMEWYRM: EXODUS
Terrance Dicks

Pursuit of the Timewyrm brings the Doctor and Ace to the Festival of Britain. But the London they find is strangely subdued, and patrolling the streets are the uniformed thugs of the Britischer Freikorps.

ISBN 0 426 20357 7

TIMEWYRM: APOCALYPSE
Nigel Robinson

Kirith seems an ideal planet – a world of peace and plenty, ruled by the kindly hand of the Great Matriarch. But it's here that the end of the universe – of everything – will be precipitated. Only the Doctor can stop the tragedy.

ISBN 0 426 20359 3

TIMEWYRM: REVELATION
Paul Cornell

Ace has died of oxygen starvation on the moon, having thought the place to be Norfolk. 'I do believe that's unique,' says the afterlife's receptionist.

ISBN 0 426 20360 7

CAT'S CRADLE: TIME'S CRUCIBLE
Marc Platt

The TARDIS is invaded by an alien presence and is then destroyed. The Doctor disappears. Ace, lost and alone, finds herself in a bizarre city where nothing is to be trusted – even time itself.

ISBN 0 426 20365 8

CAT'S CRADLE: WARHEAD
Andrew Cartmel

The place is Earth. The time is the near future – all too near. As environmental destruction reaches the point of no return, multinational corporations scheme to buy immortality in a poisoned world. If Earth is to survive, somebody has to stop them.

ISBN 0 426 20367 4

CAT'S CRADLE: WITCH MARK
Andrew Hunt

A small village in Wales is visited by creatures of myth. Nearby, a coach crashes on the M40, killing all its passengers. Police can find no record of their existence. The Doctor and Ace arrive, searching for a cure for the TARDIS, and uncover a gateway to another world.

ISBN 0 426 20368 2

NIGHTSHADE
Mark Gatiss

When the Doctor brings Ace to the village of Crook Marsham in 1968, he seems unwilling to recognize that something sinister is going on. But the villagers are being killed, one by one, and everyone's past is coming back to haunt them – including the Doctor's.

ISBN 0 426 20376 3

LOVE AND WAR
Paul Cornell

Heaven: a planet rich in history where the Doctor comes to meet a new friend, and betray an old one; a place where people come to die, but where the dead don't always rest in peace. On Heaven, the Doctor finally loses Ace, but finds archaeologist Bernice Summerfield, a new companion whose destiny is inextricably linked with his.

ISBN 0 426 20385 2

TRANSIT
Ben Aaronovitch

It's the ultimate mass transit system, binding the planets of the solar system together. But something is living in the network, chewing its way to the very heart of the system and leaving a trail of death and mutation behind. Once again, the Doctor is all that stands between humanity and its own mistakes.

ISBN 0 426 20384 4

THE HIGHEST SCIENCE
Gareth Roberts
The Highest Science – a technology so dangerous it destroyed its creators. Many people have searched for it, but now Sheldukher, the most wanted criminal in the galaxy, believes he has found it. The Doctor and Bernice must battle to stop him on a planet where chance and coincidence have become far too powerful.

ISBN 0 426 20377 1

THE PIT
Neil Penswick
One of the Seven Planets is a nameless giant, quarantined against all intruders. But when the TARDIS materializes, it becomes clear that the planet is far from empty – and the Doctor begins to realize that the planet hides a terrible secret from the Time Lords' past.

ISBN 0 426 20378 X

DECEIT
Peter Darvill-Evans
Ace – three years older, wiser and tougher – is back. She is part of a group of Irregular Auxiliaries on an expedition to the planet Aracadia. They think they are hunting Daleks, but the Doctor knows better. He knows that the paradise planet hides a being far more powerful than the Daleks – and much more dangerous.

ISBN 0 426 20362 3

LUCIFER RISING
Jim Mortimore & Andy Lane
Reunited, the Doctor, Ace and Bernice travel to Lucifer, the site of a scientific expedition that they know will shortly cease to exist. Discovering why involves them in sabotage, murder and the resurrection of eons-old alien powers. Are there Angels on Lucifer? And what does it all have to do with Ace?

ISBN 0 426 20338 7

WHITE DARKNESS
David McIntee
The TARDIS crew, hoping for a rest, come to Haiti in 1915. But they find that the island is far from peaceful: revolution is brewing in the city; the dead are walking from the cemeteries; and, far underground, the ancient rulers of the galaxy are stirring in their sleep.

ISBN 0 426 20395 X

SHADOWMIND
Christopher Bulis

On the colony world of Arden, something dangerous is growing stronger. Something that steals minds and memories. Something that can reach out to another planet, Tairgire, where the newest exhibit in the sculpture park is a blue box surmounted by a flashing light.

ISBN 0 426 20394 1

BIRTHRIGHT
Nigel Robinson

Stranded in Edwardian London with a dying TARDIS, Bernice investigates a series of grisly murders. In the far future, Ace leads a group of guerrillas against their insect-like, alien oppressors. Why has the Doctor left them, just when they need him most?

ISBN 0 426 20393 3

ICEBERG
David Banks

In 2006, an ecological disaster threatens the Earth; only the FLIPback team, working in an Antarctic base, can avert the catastrophe. But hidden beneath the ice, sinister forces have gathered to sabotage humanity's last hope. The Cybermen have returned and the Doctor must face them alone.

ISBN 0 426 20392 5

BLOOD HEAT
Jim Mortimore

The TARDIS is attacked by an alien force; Bernice is flung into the Vortex; and the Doctor and Ace crash-land on Earth. There they find dinosaurs roaming the derelict London streets, and Brigadier Lethbridge-Stewart leading the remnants of UNIT in a desperate fight against the Silurians who have taken over and changed his world.

ISBN 0 426 20399 2

THE DIMENSION RIDERS
Daniel Blythe

A holiday in Oxford is cut short when the Doctor is summoned to Space Station Q4, where ghostly soldiers from the future watch from the shadows among the dead. Soon, the Doctor is trapped in the past, Ace is accused of treason and Bernice is uncovering deceit among the college cloisters.

ISBN 0 426 20397 6

THE LEFT-HANDED HUMMINGBIRD
Kate Orman
Someone has been playing with time. The Doctor Ace and Bernice must travel to the Aztec Empire in 1487, to London in the Swinging Sixties and to the sinking of the *Titanic* as they attempt to rectify the temporal faults – and survive the attacks of the living god Huitzilin.

ISBN 0 426 20404 2

CONUNDRUM
Steve Lyons
A killer is stalking the streets of the village of Arandale. The victims are found each day, drained of blood. Someone has interfered with the Doctor's past again, and he's landed in a place he knows he once destroyed, from which it seems there can be no escape.

ISBN 0 426 20408 5

NO FUTURE
Paul Cornell
At last the Doctor comes face-to-face with the enemy who has been threatening him, leading him on a chase that has brought the TARDIS to London in 1976. There he finds that reality has been subtly changed and the country he once knew is rapidly descending into anarchy as an alien invasion force prepares to land . . .

ISBN 0 426 20409 3

TRAGEDY DAY
Gareth Roberts
When the TARDIS crew arrive on Olleril, they soon realise that all is not well. Assassins arrive to carry out a killing that may endanger the entire universe. A being known as the Supreme One tests horrific weapons. And a secret order of monks observes the growing chaos.

ISBN 0 426 20410 7

LEGACY
Gary Russell
The Doctor returns to Peladon, on the trail of a master criminal. Ace pursues intergalactic mercenaries who have stolen the galaxy's most evil artifact while Bernice strikes up a dangerous friendship with a Martian Ice Lord. The players are making the final moves in a devious and lethal plan – but for once it isn't the Doctor's.

ISBN 0 426 20412 3

THEATRE OF WAR
Justin Richards
Menaxus is a barren world on the front line of an interstellar war, home to a ruined theatre which hides sinister secrets. When the TARDIS crew land on the planet, they find themselves trapped in a deadly reenactment of an ancient theatrical tragedy.
ISBN 0 426 20414 X

ALL-CONSUMING FIRE
Andy Lane
The secret library of St John the Beheaded has been robbed. The thief has taken forbidden books which tell of gateways to other worlds. Only one team can be trusted to solve the crime: Sherlock Holmes, Doctor Watson – and a mysterious stranger who claims he travels in time and space.
ISBN 0 426 20415 8

BLOOD HARVEST
Terrance Dicks
While the Doctor and Ace are selling illegal booze in a town full of murderous gangsters, Bernice has been abandoned on a vampire-infested planet outside normal space. This story sets in motion events which are continued in *Goth Opera*, the first in a new series of Missing Adventures.
ISBN 0 426 20417 4

STRANGE ENGLAND
Simon Messingham
In the idyllic gardens of a Victorian country house, the TARDIS crew discover a young girl whose body has been possessed by a beautiful but lethal insect. And they find that the rural paradise is turning into a world of nightmare ruled by the sinister Quack.
ISBN 0 426 20419 0

FIRST FRONTIER
David A. McIntee
When Bernice asks to see the dawn of the space age, the Doctor takes the TARDIS to Cold War America, which is facing a threat far more deadly than Communist Russia. The militaristic Tzun Confederacy have made Earth their next target for conquest – and the aliens have already landed.
ISBN 0 426 20421 2